The TREE of LOST SECRETS

A Novel

LYNNE KENNEDY

Historical Mysteries Solved by Modern Technology

Time Exposure: Civil War photography meets digital photography to solve a series of murders in two centuries. Winner of the B.R.A.G. Medallion Honoree Award for independent books of high standards.

The Triangle Murders was the winner of the Rocky Mountain Fiction Writers Mystery Category, 2011, and was awarded the B.R.A.G. Medallion Honoree Award.

Deadly Provenance has also been awarded a B.R.A.G. Medallion and was a finalist for the San Diego Book Awards. With the release of *Deadly Provenance*, Lynne has launched a "hunt for a missing Van Gogh," the painting which features prominently in the book. "Still Life: Vase with Oleanders" has, in actuality, been missing since WWII.

Her fourth book, *Pure Lies*, won the 2014 "Best Published Mystery, Sisters in Crime" award by the San Diego Book Awards, and was a finalist in Amazon's *Breakthrough Novel* Award.

Time Lapse, her fifth mystery, was awarded a B.R.A.G. Medallion award in 2016.

Lynne's sixth novel, *Hart of Madness*, premiered in August of 2018 to all 5-star reviews. It has garnered discussion about New York City's *Hart Island* in light of publicity during the pandemic.

She blogs regularly and has many loyal readers and fans. Visit her website at www.lynnekennedymysteries.com

For my dear friend, Gordon. Thanks for believing.

A part of us remains wherever we have been.

. . . Chinese Fortune Cookie

Chapter 1

Helen

Brattleboro, Vermont, September 2018

Sunlight shimmered through the branches of the ancient sugar maples as a gentle breeze tossed the leaves that carpeted the ground. A glittery whirl of yellow, rust, and Irish Setter red, the dying leaves were a sign of her own fragility and the bleakness of a wintry future.

Helen stepped out of the Mercedes, its sporty carriage covered with a thick layer of brown dust. She had the sense to wear short flat-heeled boots and couldn't care less whether they were ruined.

Her throat felt dry and she swallowed whatever saliva she could summon, then took a few tentative steps, letting the car door close. The house was up a slight incline, beyond a weather-beaten fence whose gate hung crookedly between two posts. She started up the gravel path to her past . . . and her future. For now, she chided herself, think only her *present*.

She passed a newly painted sign when she turned off the road announcing Ainsley Hill Farm and wondered if her aunt had it refinished for her sake. To make her feel like she was coming home. She was. Ordinarily this would be a happy occasion she looked forward to. A holiday, of sorts.

But life had taken a few wrong turns and she was back home to rest, to de-stress, her agent insisted, and to begin work on her next novel. Her twenty-second mystery. Perhaps her last. Unbidden, her hand touched her head and a shudder ran through her. Peach fuzz. Her once thick and shining mane was only now growing in.

She turned to see her aunt descending the front porch steps and heading toward her. Her father's sister had gained weight but carried it well on her tall frame.

Helen hurried to meet the older woman, who leaned heavily on a cane as she came forward.

"Helen, my dear, you look wonderful."

Helen laughed. "You were never a good liar, Marie. But I love you anyway."

Helen pulled Marie into a satisfying, long embrace. Separating, the two women stared at each other across the years and liked what they saw. Both smiled and nodded, turned, and walked slowly to the old house, no words needed.

The porch creaked and the screen door had a tear in it. The house needed a new coat of paint. Several clapboards were broken and there was a thin crack in the front room window. Helen straightened her shoulders and realized, at that moment, she would be responsible for future care and maintenance of the old homestead. Marie, at eighty-seven, was no longer able to be its caretaker.

Well, she told herself. That might be just what you need.

"Your room is ready, Helen. As always. Waiting for you."

"Waiting for me? Come on, Marie. I haven't been back in, what, ten years?"

"Exactly. It's been waiting. Patiently." Marie pushed open the front door and Helen followed her in.

The front hall seemed claustrophobic. Low, thick heavy-beamed ceilings. Honey-colored, wide pine paneling on the floor. A steep wooden staircase on the left, its treads scraped and beaten with over two hundred-fifty years of hard use. The first few steps into the house was like traveling back in history.

Helen moved through the doorway to her left into the living room, or parlor, and felt grateful the sun was out, providing natural warm light into the room. Otherwise, it would be quite dismal. Unlike her condo in the City, with skylights and high ceilings and white and chrome furnishings reflecting an intensity of light so radiant you needed sunglasses.

She sighed, wondering if this was a mistake. Could she live here again at this time in her life? Then her eye caught something outside the window and she stepped closer, gazed out the rippled glass. In front of the house stood her old friend. A glorious, ancient sugar maple. Two people could stand shoulder to shoulder on one side of the tree and never be spotted on the other. How wide was it? How old was it? Helen wasn't sure, but it was here when the house was built in the mid-18th century.

"What are you looking at?" Marie asked.

"The old maple."

Marie smiled. "That old beauty has seen a lot in its days. Kind of like me."

Helen laughed. "If only it could talk."

"In some ways . . . it does."

Helen raised an eyebrow.

"Shall we get you settled then?" Marie said. "Since my leg has been a bit ornery of late, I've moved down to the bedroom behind the kitchen."

"I'm sorry," Helen said.

"No, no, it's fine. Love it, in fact. It's the warmest room in the house . . . next to the stove, you see. I want you to take the big room upstairs. The master."

Helen's chin came up. Her mother and father's room when she was growing up.

"All right. But before I get my bags, why don't we have a cup of tea?"

After dinner, Helen unpacked and ambled out to the front porch. The evening air felt warm and thick, like a cozy flannel blanket. Birds sang, squirrels squabbled, and the buzz of insects transported her back to her youth. She sank into an old rocker, painted white many times over through the years. It squeaked with pleasure as if remembering its occupant.

In the distance she heard a dog bark. A bark that sounded familiar like the golden retrievers she had over the years. God, she missed them, missed them all. Speaking of God, what the hell was he thinking when he gave dogs such a short life span?

The bark sounded closer now and more insistent. Helen stood and looked around. She stepped down from the porch. There, at the gate by the drive a golden retriever stood and stared at her, tail wagging. A ripple of something akin to joy ran through her. Silly, it's just a neighbor's dog. Helen walked slowly to the animal.

"Hey, puppy. Are you lost? I bet you're just looking for a handout, hmm?"

The dog sat and gave a soft woof.

Helen moved closer, hand out. "What's up, honey?"

The dog bounded up and raced full tilt at her, buried its nose in her knees.

Helen stooped over, afraid to kneel for fear of not being able to get up. "What's up, honey? Are you trying to tell me something?"

The dog sat back and stared up at her.

"Ahh, you're an old girl, aren't you? Look at that gray around your nose. Old, right. Like me." Helen smiled. The dog gave a short happy bark.

"Where's your collar? No tags? Maybe Aunt Marie knows who you are. In fact, I bet she feeds you and that's why you're here." She straightened and walked to the house. "Let's see what she has to say."

The dog followed her to the porch. Marie stepped outside. "Now, who is that?"

"Oh. You don't know?"

"I've never seen her."

"Uh oh." Helen turned to the dog. "Well, we're going to have to find your owners, aren't we?"

"She's not from around here," Marie said. "I know all the folks and their animals for a few square miles and she's not one." She paused. "Sweet, though, isn't she?"

Helen looked at the dog. "Tomorrow, honey, we'll check out your family. Somehow."

"Honey?" Marie said.

"Fits her coloring and personality, don't you think? I'll call her that for now."

Marie smirked. "For now, right."

"What?"

"Don't get too attached, dear. You're not good with loss." Marie turned and went back into the house.

Not good with loss, Helen mused. She's right about that.

Honey turned and ambled off the porch to the bench in the grass under the ancient maple.

"You love that tree too, don't you?" Helen followed her and sat down on the bench. The golden curled herself up at Helen's feet and let out a deep sigh.

"I hope that's a sigh of contentment." She breathed out her own sigh as she leaned her back against the gnarly bark. Within a few minutes, Helen dozed off, exhausted from life's vicissitude. Country girl to city girl. Copy editor to famous author. Married to widow. Healthy to sick. Years ahead of her, now years behind her. And back to the beginning. Country girl.

Honey barked. Helen jolted awake.

The dog jumped up and barked again.

"What?" Helen said. She stood, turned around expecting to find someone walking toward her. Honey seemed focused on the tree. She moved closer to it, sniffing, circling the trunk. A second time. Suddenly she leaped up and put her front paws on the tree trunk stretching as far as she could.

"Is it a squirrel?"

Helen knew right away this was something different. She had lots of experience with dogs chasing squirrels up trees.

"What is it?"

Helen moved closer to the tree and followed the line of Honey's paws. That's when she saw them. Letters carved in the bark. SM-AR, with a heart etched around them. The letters were crude, carved with a knife or chisel, and coated with moss. Old. The letters were old. Who were SM and AR? No one in her family that she could remember. How long ago were these etched?

"It's all right, Honey. Just two lovers who carved their initials in our tree."

Honey looked at her and sniffed the tree again.

"There's a mystery here, to solve, then, isn't there? Maybe it would make a good book? I mean, maybe those lovers lived here when the house was new, when it was an Inn during the Revolutionary War. Hey, right." She stared up at the thinly leafed branches towering seventy feet above her.

Suddenly tired from the fuss, Helen turned and sank down on the bench again. The movement made her dizzy and she squeezed her eyes closed, willing her mind to return to neutral.

Honey jumped up and started barking once more. In a split second, the dog was attempting to climb the tree again.

"Oh, come on."

But the dog would not quit until Helen joined her once again.

"It's just a squirrel . . . it's . . ." Helen's voice dropped an octave. She pushed Honey off the tree and moved closer for another look. She squinted, took a few steps back to improve her vantage point. Then she ran her hands over the initials, or where she believed the initials were carved. She kept looking and feeling the bark.

"What the hell?" Helen walked the circumference of the tree and even stood on the bench so she could get higher and closer. "This is crazy. I must be crazy. It's the light."

The daylight was fading, but the sun cast its last watery glow on the tree. "It has to be the light," she murmured, unsure.

Helen stared at the spot where she knew the initials to be. But now all she saw, all her fingers touched . . . was the craggy bark of an old sugar maple.

The carvings were gone.

Chapter 2

H elen rolled over and gazed at the clock. 3:10 a.m. Progress. Usually by now she'd have awoken three times. She pulled the soft comforter around her shoulders and smiled down at the mass of reddish-gold fur on the floor by her bed. Honey looked up at her as if to say, "You're not really getting up now, are you?"

Try as she would, Helen knew she would not sleep any more this morning.

"Sorry, sweetie." She threw her covers off and sat up. Honey moved out of the way and watched.

Helen sat for a moment gathering energy. A sound alarmed her. What's that? She listened in the stillness of her bedroom. Upstairs, someone was upstairs. In the attic. At three in the morning? Marie?

She stood and grabbed her robe, then quietly made her way to the hallway. She padded down the carpeted corridor to a door at the far end. One that was never opened that Helen could remember. A small thud upstairs made up her mind. Helen opened the door and peered up into a dimly lit staircase.

What if it's not Marie? God. Maybe she should call the police. She waited, listening again. That's when she heard it. Crying. Someone was crying upstairs.

Helen started up the steep, treacherous steps, praying she didn't get a splinter in her bare feet. They creaked. The crying stopped.

"Marie? Aunt Marie?"

"Oh. Helen, I'm sorry. I didn't mean to wake you."

"You didn't, actually. I don't sleep very well. I was up and heard . . ."

Marie didn't say anything.

"Why are you up here now?"

"I was looking for something."

"At three in the morning? Must be important," Helen said.

Marie looked at her across the dust and cobwebs, trunks and boxes, the faint light from a low wattage bulb hanging above barely illuminating the space.

Helen leaned over and touched a suitcase then rubbed her fingers together to wipe off the dust. "Why were you crying, Marie?" she said softly.

Marie inhaled a deep breath. "Why don't you go downstairs and start some tea? I'll be down presently."

Helen stared at her a moment. She turned and did as her aunt wished.

The old house was never silent. Creaks, groans, the scuttling of mice made a haunted backdrop. Air whistled through the spaces that were never airtight; the rustling of leaves could be heard outside as nocturnal creatures foraged about. The scent of ancient ephemera, musty as old books, permeated the air. The ghosts of long-dead mortals, and the remains of their historic relics were ever a grim presence.

Helen remembered loving this old house when she was a young girl. She wanted to recapture that happiness she had here. Was it possible?

She set the kettle on the stove and prepared two cups of tea. Her hands shook, prescient of what was to come. She had never witnessed her aunt crying, nor seen her look so bereft, disheveled, as she had in the attic. A worm of worry crawled up her back. Honey whined from her makeshift bed of blankets in the corner. Helen leaned over to rub her silky fur.

Marie came into the kitchen, reasonably put together, hair combed and eyes dry. She smiled at Helen and sank down in the nearest chair. "I'm sorry to distress you. I didn't mean to. You've got enough on your mind."

"Marie, you are especially important to me. Please tell me what's wrong. If it's money, you know--."

"Ach. No. No money. It's nothing at all." Marie sipped her tea.

"You're not ill, are you?"

"No, no, nothing like that."

Helen tipped her head.

"Honestly. I'm not ill." Marie smiled. "Old, maybe, not ill."

"What's that you're holding?"

Marie looked down at her lap, brought up a worn-out brown and white teddy bear with one eye missing.

"Oh," Marie said. "This is a reminder . . ." She started to cry.

Helen reached out and touched her arm.

Marie wiped her eyes with a damp tissue and sniffed. "Today's the anniversary, you see. Every year I bring Pooky down from the attic to remind me of my sin. To never let me forget what I did." She fell silent.

Helen leaned forward, took her aunt's hands in her own, the teddy bear between them. "I don't understand. What anniversary? What sin?"

Marie looked into Helen's eyes with such sadness, that Helen thought she herself would burst into tears. She waited.

"Joey. It's because of me that Joey is gone. Dead. If I had done the right thing, he might still be alive. And his mother."

"Who is Joey?"

"Don't ever believe the past is dead, Helen. It never dies. It comes back to haunt you again and again."

Helen sat up straight. "Let's leave this for now. Maybe have an early breakfast?" She rose and went to the refrigerator, pulled out eggs, milk, all the while watching Marie. But her heart pounded and her skin felt clammy. There was something about this story she felt was personal. Did it have something to do with her parents?

And who was Joey? She'd never heard of him. Was he a relative she had never known?

Click, click, click. Honey's nails tapped on the wood floor. She sat in front of Marie and laid her head on her lap, burying Pooky under her neck.

The sun rose glorious pink in the eastern sky, promising a beautiful day. It cast a warm glow over the landscape. The greens looked greener, all fifty shades of them. The golds seemed to glimmer in fourteen carat. The reds and oranges blended into a rich shade of rust, like the auburn of a newborn deer.

Sometimes nature was all you needed to banish the anguish and disquietude of the night.

Helen sat under the giant maple with a cup of after-breakfast coffee. Honey lay at her feet. She hoped Marie was in the shower, washing her tears away and getting ready to confide in her.

"We have to confide in Aunt Marie, too, don't we?"

Honey picked her head up.

Somewhere Over the Rainbow sang out on Helen's cell. She looked at the caller ID. Julianne.

"Hi, sweetie," Helen said.

"Hey, mom, how are you?"

"Just fine."

"Really? You're not just saying that."

"Why? Can't I be fine? I'm in the most beautiful place on earth with my wonderful aunt, my daughter who's only twenty minutes away, and a magnificent golden retriever who calls me mom as well."

"What? What golden retriever?"

Helen told her about Honey.

"Wow. Awesome. Do you think you can keep her? I mean, if you haven't found her owners yet, then--."

"Well, it's only been a day." Helen sighed. "I hope so. I'm already in love."

"How is Aunt Marie?"

Helen hesitated. "She's good."

"Doesn't sound like it."

"No, no, she is. Just getting on, you know."

"How old is she?"

"Eighty-seven. Ancient to you."

"Ha. I'm not so young myself."

"Yeah, I said that at thirty-two also. Try fifty-three."

"You're not quite fifty-three yet," Julianne said.

"Hmm. So, how's the bookstore business?" Helen referred to the bookshop her daughter opened in Putney five years ago. She called it *BookStock, the Biggest Little Bookshop in Vermont.*

"Well, it helps to have a mother who's a famous writer and offers me discounts on her books. But, seriously, I'm doing really well. I get lots of customers from all around the state. And guess what?"

"What?"

"We are getting ready to launch an online presence."

"That's great, Juli, really, great. Who is *we*, by the way?"

"I told you about Bella?"

"Yes, this gal you met a few years ago in Burlington?"

"Right. I convinced her to move down here, even though she jokes that southern Vermont is not really Vermont."

"Ahh."

"She helps me run the store and is a tech whiz. I don't pay her much, but she has her own money from a rich mommy or something. So, she's working on the online store."

"Sounds exciting."

"You sound tired, mom. I'll let you go for now."

"Are we still on for lunch Saturday?"

"Absolutely. See you then."

"Love you."

"Back at ya."

Helen clicked off and leaned back against her tree. Her tree. Yes, it was hers. She mused on her daughter, heart hollow in her chest. Julianne was struggling. So much grief, so much loss. Difficult at Helen's age, let alone at thirty-two.

James, she sighed. *Why did you have to go and die on me?* Ten years and she still missed him. So did Juli. Terribly.

She wondered if Bella could be Julianne's partner in more ways than one. What mattered was that she was happy. That's all that ever mattered. Her illness had taught her that.

Chapter 3

Helen regarded the shabby teddy bear staring up at her with one eye. Honey had dropped it in her lap when she nodded off leaning against the great maple tree. Birds sang into the crisp air, welcoming the day. A monarch, a late straggler, lighted on the grass near her feet.

Events of the early morning hours came back with a rush. Helen had no energy to move so she took in a few deep breaths and remained still. She wondered if her aunt noticed the changes in her appearance. Her aquiline nose, once befitting a Roman noble woman, now thin and long on her gaunt face. Her eyes, previously stunning blue, now washed out and pale like a polluted stream. At least her eyebrows had grown back in.

A cardinal landed on a hydrangea bush on the path: a stunning male, red with a spiky plume. He tipped his head to watch her. Since her cancer, she found herself moved by the beauty of a thing more and more. The hills behind the farm seem to wear the weather like a garment, warm purple hazes in the summer, wispy fog in the colder weather . . . changing clothes myriad times throughout a single day. Had she ever observed it before?

Tears welled in her eyes. She sat upright and realized her back did not ache. Falling asleep in an awkward position against the maple, it should be killing her. She pushed herself up with her arm on the tree. Her fingers tingled. The tree seemed warm to the touch. A living, breathing thing.

Helen reached out with both hands and touched the trunk. Yes, it was warm. From the sun? She moved around the tree circumference in a circle, caressing the bark. Were the initials back? They were not visible, but she felt around for them in the place she believed they were. Nothing.

Honey whined.

"You don't see them either, do you?"

"Helen?" The screen door closed with a bang. Marie walked out onto the porch with two steaming cups of coffee. She set them on a small table.

Helen walked up the steps to her aunt and they both settled into rockers.

"I see you found Pooky," Marie said.

"Honey brought him to me." Helen smiled. "You can have him back."

Marie rocked, said nothing.

They sat in tense silence.

"You must think I'm a crazy old woman," Marie said finally.

"Of course, I don't."

A few minutes went by as both women rocked.

"I would like to hear about Joey," Helen said.

Marie sipped her coffee and Helen noticed a slight tremor in her hands. Deep lines etched her aunt's face. Had they been that deep yesterday?

Marie began in an almost whisper. "It was 1945. I was fourteen. The war was ending, soldiers were coming home. I had a series of jobs after school and on holidays, here, at the Inn." She looked at Helen. "You know, of course, this farm was an Inn and Tavern back then?"

"I do," Helen said. "It was an Inn since the Revolution, didn't become a farm until mom and dad converted it in the 50s."

Marie laughed. "Sometimes my memory plays tricks. I seem to forget you're a grown woman and not a little girl. Course you know."

"Go on."

"There was a couple who worked at the Inn. He was a handyman . . . also a talented stone carver. Made all kinds of tiny sculptures for his son." She stopped, drew in a breath. "Angie was a housekeeper. She hired me to help out. It felt good to have a little bit of money in my pocket. Often, I would help her with the cleaning and dusting. Even hoovering sometimes."

"Always loved that expression," Helen said. "So British."

"They had a little boy, five-years-old."

"Joey."

"Joey. The sweetest kid, big brown eyes, dark curly hair, a smile that could move you to happy tears."

Helen grinned.

"He didn't have any friends because we were so far from town and all. I used to babysit Joey and both of us had fun. We'd play hide and seek around the great maple, build log cabins with tiny sticks of wood, read books together." Marie paused, gazing back in time.

"Well, about a year and half before, Joey's dad had gone off to Italy to bring his parents to this country. I heard he joined the resistance there, fighting the Nazis. Seemed like he was gone forever, and the mom was on her own here at the Inn. He was due back any time since VE Day was proclaimed. War was over, thank God. Things could get back to normal." Marie sipped her coffee.

"One day, his mom asked me to babysit so she could go to town and do some shopping. Get ready for her husband's return, maybe buy a new dress, ribbons for her hair, you know."

Helen set her cup down on the small side table.

"But I refused. Imagine that. Shy, mousy little me. I had a date, you see. My first date ever with a silly boy from school whose name I don't even recall. I had to primp and couldn't figure out what to wear and . . . suffice it to say, I pitched a fit and said no." Marie let out a sigh. "I was a fractious, obstinate teenager."

"You were young, at that adolescent age when all that mattered was *you*."

"Upshot is, Joey wound up going into town with his mom. They left after lunch, planning to be home for dinner." Marie paused. "Neither of them was ever seen again."

"What?"

"A neighbor swears a truck stopped for them and gave them a ride. Mebbe. But they never made it to town. No one has seen them since."

"Oh my God."

"I've carried that guilt with me from that day. If I had babysat Joey, he might still be here. Maybe his mother would be too. It's my fault they're gone."

Helen opened her mouth, but Marie shushed her.

"Don't even go there. I feel the guilt and I have a right to feel the guilt. That's the way it is. No one else to blame."

"No one except who was really responsible for their disappearance. I mean, were they abducted or--?

"Some say she ran away with a man and took Joey with her. I say *bollocks*. She left everything behind. All her clothes, personal belongings, Joey's clothes, and toys. He loved his toys."

"And she asked you to babysit, so she wasn't planning on taking him," Helen said. "She would never have left her son behind, would she?"

"Never. She adored Joey. And she adored her husband. He was coming home to her. Never, she never would have run away."

"Was there any kind of investigation?"

"The police were called in and did cursory interviews. But when the father came home just a few days later, he was heartsick. He pushed hard for a full-blown investigation. And he got it. As widespread an investigation as it gets in a small town like Brattleboro. It made the news for weeks. In the papers from The Reformer to The Globe. Went on for months. Searching, searching. But they never found a trace of them."

Helen shook her head.

"It was awful to see him so distraught. He would wander the fields and the woods, drive up and down the roads for miles, day after day, searching. Even hired a private investigator. He turned up nothing."

Marie's voice was hoarse. "He started drinking. No one could blame him, still . . . About a year later he committed suicide."

Helen gasped.

"Oh, they said it was an accident. Car crash. But I know the truth. He drank himself nearly comatose and deliberately bashed that car into a tree. Blamed himself for the disappearance of his wife and child, you see. He should have blamed me."

Helen shifted and her rocker squealed.

"The Inn was a sorry place to be around those days. The war might have been over, but the place had an aura of melancholy that no one could shake."

Marie looked at Helen. "Today's Joey's birthday."

"That's why you visited the attic--to get Joey's favorite toy." Helen picked up the teddy bear and handed it to Marie who clutched it to her chest.

"I never want to forget how I lost Joey."

Helen's mind whirred with questions and notions. Honey moved to sit in front of Marie and put a paw in her lap.

"Looks like she knows how sad you feel," Helen said. "I wonder--."

"What? What do you wonder?"

Helen shrugged. "I don't know. Seems rather serendipitous that Honey would show up now. Out of the blue, I mean, when I come home to rest. Like she was meant to be here. For me. For us." Helen waved a hand in dismissal. "Ridiculous."

"You'll think me a bit cuckoo," Marie said, "but don't dismiss anything you see around here that might seem a bit, um, out of the ordinary."

"What do you mean? Have you seen strange things?"

Marie turned to Honey who sat staring at her.

"The day Joey disappeared, a golden retriever, exactly like Honey, gray around the nose and eyes, same size, same personality, showed up at the Inn. We could not find her owners. She seemed to have appeared out of nowhere. But she was a Godsend and saved my life when I was in the depths of despair. I named her Sweet Pea and that she was . . . and will ever be to me."

Helen felt on the verge of tears. "Marie, can I talk to you about something? It may be related or not, but I--."

"Certainly, you can, Helen. Anything."

Helen was unsure how to broach the subject of the initials. Marie might very well think she was nuts. But she felt sure that there was a connection between her fantastical experience and Marie's story.

Helen told her about the carvings.

"But they're not there now?" Marie said.

"No. That's why you may think I'm crazy or have chemo brain or something. I think maybe I do."

Marie was silent for a long few minutes. "You know, the Indians believe that trees have spirits. They can sense happiness and their leaves perk up. They can sense sadness and they droop."

"I've heard that, about their spirits, I mean. I remember when I was young girl and dad was having a tree chopped down because it was dying, he brought in a *light-giver*, I think he called her, to send the tree off to the next world with a grateful farewell for its life here on earth."

Marie nodded and smiled. "Helen, what were the initials you saw? Do you remember them?"

"I'll never forget. SM-AR with a heart around the letters."

Marie sat very still. "Joey's father's name was Salvatore Martelli, Sal, and his mother's was Angela Rossi, Angie, before they married. They were here for six years working at the Inn."

She turned to Helen, eyes sparking with passion. "I believe they carved their initials in the grand old tree. I believe you saw them. And I believe they disappeared into the bark, just the way you say."

Chapter 4

Salvatore

Sant'Anna di Stazzema, Italy, September 1944

He awoke with that same hole in his heart, the beat slow, fast, slow, fast, *tu tump, tu tump, tu tump.* The emptiness in his gut agonized as if he'd swallowed a heavy stone. This must be what losing someone felt like. Yet, his wife and boy were safe but so far away. It was he who was not safe.

Sal stared at the crack in the ceiling. A spider scuttled across the wall, over peeling paint, and gouges in the plaster. How could this be his home? His boyhood home? How did it come to this? The Fascists were gone, yes, replaced by the Nazis. One monster for another. Worse.

He choked back a sob, kicked his legs out of the filthy sleeping bag and pushed himself up. Every muscle in his body screamed. He was only thirty-two, how could he hurt so much?

"Salvatore?" He heard his mother's voice.

"*Sì,* Mamma, I'm awake." He staggered to the washbowl on the nightstand and threw water in his face. He dried it with a threadbare scrap of towel as he looked in the mirror at his unshaven face, deep circles below his eyes, hair askew.

Today was the day. September 22. His hands shook.

"Salvatore," his mother opened the door. "*Vieni.*"

Sal nodded and followed her to the kitchen where his three brothers sat eating. Funny, how easy it was to slip back into his native language. And his role as eldest brother.

"Hey, the rich American is finally awake," Francesco said with a grin.

"I'm not rich . . ." Sal began.

"We hope you will enjoy our meager offerings," Pietro joked. "Stale bread, rancid butter, and coffee, if you can call this piss water coffee."

Giuseppe offered, "Not what you rich Americanos eat, eh? No bacon, eggs, jam on your toast, right?"

"*Vaffanculo*," Sal said, shaking his head. "Sorry, Mamma." He sat down at the table, edging Giuseppe over.

"I've heard much worse," his mother said.

"Here you go, *fratellino*." Francesco handed him a chunk of dried bread.

"So, what do you have to talk to us about that is so important?" Pietro said, gulping down the hard bread.

"Stop teasing him," Mamma said. "Salvatore, you want to talk to us about something? I don't have a good feeling of this, I . . . uhm, wish you had stayed home where you are safe, with your family."

"You are my family."

"Since when?" Pietro said. "When were you here last, hah? Years."

Sal inhaled. "I know and I'm sorry."

"He was working, sending money to us," Mamma said. "Stop tormenting your brother."

Francesco pushed his chair back from the table. "Tell us, then. What you have to say."

"Oooh, I can't wait," Pietro said.

Sal felt his mouth go dry. "I want you to come home with me."

Silence.

Damn, this wasn't how he planned to tell them. Not just blurt it out, idiot.

"Home? We are home. What home? America?" Giuseppe's voice rose. "You want that we go to America? The land of the rich?"

"The land of freedom," Sal shot back. "Why not? What's wrong with that?"

"All our family is here," Pietro said.

"What about me, and Angie and Joey? You've never even met them."

The brothers averted his eyes.

Francesco said, "No, no, we cannot leave our country. It may be good for you, but not for us."

"Why?"

"For one, we have lived here all of our lives. You left when you were young, a kid almost."

"You could have left too, you know."

"Bullshit. We had to keep the farm going. How would we eat? How would Mamma and Papa eat, ehh?" Giuseppe said.

Francesco held up a hand. "Never mind that. It was a long time ago. Sal had the opportunity and he took it. Good for him. He made something of himself."

"He had the talent," Mamma said. "Cousin Lorenzo said he could carve stone like Michelangelo Buonarroti."

"Michelangelo, my ass," Pietro said.

"Nah, it's true," Francesco said. "Our big brother here has talent. He can turn ugly stone into something beautiful."

Mamma smiled. "Papa wanted that for you, Salvatore."

Sal returned her smile. He missed Papa, regretted sorely that he could not get back in time for his funeral.

"We have families too, Salvatore. Here in Tuscany." Giuseppe stood and paced the kitchen. "What about our wives and children? Do they all come? You must be rich to make such an offer."

"You are *pazzo*, brother. *Molto pazzo*," Pietro said.

Francesco spoke, "Salvatore, *ascolta*. We appreciate what you are trying to do . . . to protect us. But there is much you do not understand. This is our country, our home. We want to fight for it, protect it, kick those fucking Nazis out. We must do this, you see, or we will never be able to live with ourselves."

"But you are not even soldiers, how can you fight?"

"We are the resistance," Francesco said quietly.

"Partisans?" Sal said. He kicked his chair back. "*Dio mio.*"

The air went out of the room.

"Yes, partisans. And we have done much to save our country," Pietro said, eyes flashing.

"What? Throw a pipe bomb at a Nazi jeep. Kill a few Jerries?" Sal spat. "You think that makes a difference in this war?"

Francesco jumped to his feet. "What the hell do you know? Safe and content across the ocean. What do you think war means?"

Mamma spoke. "Everyone, hush, *per favore*. Stop fighting amongst yourselves. Salvatore, sit and listen. Listen. All of you."

They all sat, eyes on their mother.

"This war . . . it was not our war just a short time ago. The fighting didn't touch us even though Mussolini, the pig, was in power. The war happened elsewhere . . . in *Roma*, in *Napoli*, in *Milano*. Not here. Then, a month before you arrived, Salvatore, a terrible tragedy happened." She clasped her hands over her heart.

Sal's three brothers stared down at the table.

"Our little village of Sant'Anna was wiped out."

"What do you mean, it was bombed?"

"Much worse." His mother sighed deep into her chest. "After Mussolini was . . ."

She searched for words.

"Deposed?" Sal said.

"Sì. After that in August, the Germans--."

"The 16th Division of the SS, *Schutzstaffel*," Francesco said. "Fuckers."

"The Nazi police," Pietro clarified for Sal.

Mamma resumed. "The SS stormed into Sant'Anna. They wanted to punish the people for their partisan activities." Tears filled his mother's eyes. "They shot and killed every man, woman, and child in the square."

"Close to six hundred people, all innocents, young children, women, old men. No fighting men, no partisans," Giuseppe said. "As punishment."

"Retribution for resistance activities," Francisco said.

"*Dio mio*," Sal whispered.

"It was a massacre," Francesco said. "We would be dead too except we were here at home. They never searched in the mountains."

Mamma dried her eyes with a damp handkerchief. "You know Carlo, the butcher from Sant'Anna? He managed to survive. He came to tell us. His whole family was murdered . . . murdered." She sobbed. "He pleaded with us to go to the village and rescue anyone who lived or to bury the dead."

"When the Nazis pulled out," Pietro said, "we rushed down there to find the survivors. But all we saw was smoke and a terrible fire."

Sal couldn't swallow.

"The church was on fire," Francesco said.

"They burned them all," Mamma said, crying. "Every one of them. In the church."

"What?"

"The Nazis have a scorched earth policy. Leave no one alive to tell the tale." Giuseppe could barely get the words out. "Especially a crime like this . . . a horrific crime against humanity."

"All those people," Mamma said. "So many children, women, my friends, ahhh."

Salvatore rose and put his arms around his mother, and she cried into his chest. He understood now why his family did not want to leave. They wanted to force the Nazis to leave. Any way they could.

"I remember some of the villagers, from when I was a boy here. Mario Bianchi--"

"Dead," Francesco said. "And his wife and three boys."

"Lorenzo Ricci?"

"Dead."

"Gina Russo? I had a crush on her when--."

"Dead, dead, dead," Francesco said. "Do you get it? They are all dead. Her husband is dead, her children are dead, one only six-months old."

Sal's jaw tightened so much his teeth ached.

"How could they kill infants?" Mamma said, cloth against her eyes.

"The town is like a ghost town," Giuseppe said. "Some of the men returned to find their family dead and gone and now, they just . . . just wander. Lost. Day and night. In what's left of the village, the rubble. In the hills. Down to the river."

"Not all," Francesco said. "Some joined with us to fight."

Mamma took Sal's hands in hers. "You must go home, *figlio mio*, home to your wife and boy. This is no place for you."

Sal pulled his hand away and walked to the tiny broken window in the room.

All he yearned for was peace, nature, and beauty in his life. He'd worked so hard to build a life for his wife and child in the most beautiful place on earth. Would he ever see them again?

Here nature and beauty transformed to ruined landscapes, entire villages of people decimated, animals maimed and scattered from their homes. In his mind, the air was saturated with the smell of death, the briny scent of blood he could almost taste.

A knock on the front door caught them up short.

Francesco put his fingers to his lips to shush them. The other brothers grabbed their rifles and waited while he answered the knock.

They heard Carlo and let out their collective breath.

Francesco fumed as he returned to the kitchen. "It's not enough that they killed off a whole village. Now this." He handed Sal a tattered poster.

Sal read out loud.

The Commandant hereby issues a list of prohibitions punishable by the death penalty:

Trading on the black market

Listening to enemy radio

Harbouring a fugitive

Disseminating enemy propaganda

Possessing weapons

Violating curfew

Sal shivered although it was broiling in the tiny kitchen. "What do we do now?"

The brothers looked from one to the other then at Salvatore.

"We post our own proclamation," Pietro said.

"We will make them pay," Giuseppe said.

24

"Kill the fuckers," Francesco spat. "We will fight back."

"You've *been* fighting back. Look where it's gotten you." Sal stared at Francesco.

"We must plan, stay one step ahead of them at every turn," Francesco said.

"*Combattere in modo più intelligente*," Pietro agreed.

Sal thought about the people of Sant'Anna. They had no chance.

"Yes. We must fight *smarter*," said Giuseppe.

"How do we fight smarter?" asked Pietro.

Silence.

Sal crumpled the list of Nazi prohibitions and tossed it on the floor. His brothers stared at him then at the proclamation on the floor.

"We fight by our own rules." Sal looked from one brother to another. "We devise our own list, a list of . . . of partisan rules."

"*Merda*," said Pietro.

"No, wait, Salvatore is right," Francesco said. "We must have our own proclamation. Our own law. To stand strong against the enemy."

"What would those rules be?" Giuseppe asked. He turned to Sal.

"Principles of partisan warfare. Together we will come up with them."

"We?" Pietro said. "What you mean by we?"

"We." Sal felt a fire spreading in his gut. "You now have one more soldier."

Chapter 5

Milan, Italy, February 1945

The craziest thought crossed his mind. It was Valentine's Day back home. Angie would be decorating the Inn with fake flowers she'd make out of scraps of fabric. Yeah. Joey would be cutting out heart-shapes from paper salvaged from the market and coloring it red. God, he missed them. The last letter he received was months ago, before Christmas. Damn war. He would write them tonight, pray he could get his letter out of the country.

Francesco walked over, flicked a cigarette down and ground it out with his boot. His breath came in spurts of cold vapors. Sleeping outdoors in the cold was taking its toll on all of them.

"Shit, it's cold, man. Not supposed to be this cold."

The two brothers stood side by side next to a jeep that American troops had confiscated from the Germans. Still had some life left in it. Enough to do their job tonight. They turned at the sound of heavy footsteps.

"Hey, Lieutenant," Sal said to an American officer. "Thanks for the wheels."

"You partisans, you do good, you know?" He pulled a pack of Camels out of his jacket pocket, lit one and tossed the match. "So, Sal, tell me. Here you are, fighting for your country, both countries, in fact. How come you didn't join the service?"

"Tried," Sal said. "But I have severe allergies. They said I couldn't qualify."

"Allergies? Like sneezing?" The Lieutenant said. "That's a new one."

"Nah, not sneezing but anaphylaxis. You know what that is?"

"Yeah, I think. Bee stings, right? You're allergic to bees."

"His throat closes up, could kill him," Francesco said. "He has to carry around one of those Ana-Kits, you know for the reaction."

"What's that?"

"It's a dose of epinephrine, kinda' like adrenaline, ready to go, in a shot," Sal said.

"Shit. That sucks." Lieutenant Reggie Wolf threw his cigarette on the ground and stomped it out. "You boys ready?" He rubbed a hand over his stubbled chin, his face raw and chapped from the cold. "Remember, you can run into a German patrol *or* an American patrol on both sides of the line. Either could kill you. One deliberately, one by accident."

"Yeah, we get it," Francesco said.

Wolf looked at his watch. "Still early. Why don't you boys head over to the hotel for some shuteye? Still a few rooms that haven't been destroyed."

"Good idea." Sal climbed into the driver's seat. Francesco hopped in next to him. They saluted and drove off.

"Shuteye, my ass," Francesco said. "Like we could sleep before this mission."

They were to meet Pietro and Giuseppe at the *Grand Hotel et de Milan*, or what was left of it. Allies had bombed it and the fourth floor was gone, its contents settled like a bizarre sculpture in the wrecked lobby.

Pietro and Giuseppe waited for them. Pietro had damaged his leg when a mine exploded near him and now hobbled with a makeshift cane. Francesco, the family jokester, had lost his sense of humor. Giuseppe had become emaciated and his hands shook all the time.

Sal prayed they would come out of this war alive, but he wasn't optimistic. In his early days as a partisan, he hurled homemade grenades at German convoys and barely escaped; he played a major role in a bomb assault on Fascist militia barracks and took some shrapnel in his shoulder for his reward; he devised a strategy to attack German supply lines by disrupting the road system with downed trees and loose boulders. And the nails.

His lips formed a crooked smile. This last act of resistance gave Sal great pride. He didn't invent the object of destruction: four-pointed "nails," but used them to effectively halt the German convoys in their tracks. The device was simple. A pair of iron rods wide and heavy-duty like nails, but longer, with a point at each end that was bent in half at right angles and soldered together to make interlocking vees. The result was ingenious. No matter how you threw them, placing them or scattering them randomly, the "nails" would always come to rest with one point up and three points buried firmly in the ground. Deadly.

Sal had a dark premonition of today's mission. Something would happen to at least one of them. He felt it in his bones. He said a prayer to God, then focused his thoughts on his wife and son. They had kept him alive so far.

The four brothers met and went over their latest plan in detail. Their task was to sabotage the route of the Milan-Torino railway, between the stops of Novara and Vigevano. It was a popular supply route for the Nazis, both north and southbound. All of them recognized the significance of this mission.

Francesco stood, stretched, and wandered over the rubble to what used to be the bar in the lounge adjacent to the lobby. He climbed over debris and hopped over the remains of the bar itself, scrounging behind for a bottle that wasn't broken. Finally, he shouted a loud, "Ooohee," and came back with an intact bottle of wine.

"Vino?" Pietro said. "At eight in the morning. What we are reduced to." He laughed and shook his head.

Francesco managed to find a bottle opener, and, in a few minutes, all had a few sips of the red wine.

"*Coraggio, fratelli,*" Giuseppe said. He began to whistle the song that had become the partisan's anthem: *Bella Ciao.*

The four brothers smiled and started gathering their packs, adding water to their canteens from the fountain trickle at the bar, and grabbing some stale leftover breads and hard cheeses from the hotel kitchen lockers.

A light rain fell at midnight, but the brothers shrugged it off as they made their way across the mountain top. Tripping on rocks and tree roots, they carried their heavy knapsacks over their shoulders and crouched as near to the ground as possible.

Sal worried about Pietro, who insisted he didn't need his cane for this job.

"This is it," Francesco said, standing upright with a groan. "It's downhill from here."

"Literally." Sal grimaced. He peered down the slope to the railroad tracks six-hundred feet below them. "*Merda.*"

"Hey, when we were kids, we'd roll down these hills," Pietro said.

"That's what we're going to do now," Sal said.

"Roll down?" Giuseppe said.

"You think you can stay on your feet?" Sal asked with a grin.

"Watch me." Pietro took in a deep breath and took off sideways down the hill, kicking up rocks. Before two minutes had passed, he slipped on the muddy slope and landed on his side, rolled, and couldn't stop.

"Shit, shit," Francesco said, dancing in place. "He'll kill himself."

Sal, Giuseppe, and Francesco watched, holding a united breath until finally Pietro landed hard at the bottom of the hill. They waited, not daring to call to him.

Pietro moved, rolled over onto his back.

"*Gesù Cristo,*" Giuseppe said. "I thought that was it."

Pietro sat up, then pushed himself to his knees, waved an arm at his brothers and stood. They could see him grinning in the full moon.

Suddenly all four heard it. A convoy of trucks on the road below near the railroad tracks.

"Shit, shit," Francesco said again.

"Hell of a vocabulary you have." Sal said.

"What about Pietro? Can they spot him?" Giuseppe said, crouching behind some bushes.

They watched as Pietro crept to a small copse of trees not far above the road and waited. The noise level rose to a deafening roar as a battalion of trucks, jeeps and armored vehicles careened down the slippery gravel road. It was a convoy of Germans, maybe several dozen, shouting to be heard above the motor thunder.

"They must be meeting the train at the depot ahead," Francesco said.

"How far is it?" Sal asked.

"*Novara Nord*, she's about two kilometers," Giuseppe said.

"All right," Sal said. "We'll wait until they're passed, then we'll give them a surprise."

When the lights at end of the convoy could no longer be seen and the noise had waned, the three brothers made their way down the mountain. All three wound up rolling part of the way down the steep incline but none were seriously hurt.

They limped and rubbed their bruises as they reached the tracks.

"Man, I'm going to sleep for a week after this," Giuseppe said.

"Quit crying, baby," Pietro said.

"Eh, who's a baby, eh?" Giuseppe punched Pietro's arm.

"Knock it off," Francesco said.

Sal was already unloading his pack. He pulled out a railroad spike remover and a foot-long wrench, then hurried to the tracks to examine the rail, bolts, and spikes. His brothers followed his lead.

Within twenty minutes, the four of them had loosened two dozen dog screws and fish bolts.

"The engineer will never know what hit 'em," Francesco said.

They packed up their tools and started back up the mountain.

"What's that?" Sal said.

"What?"

"Is that your wrench, Pietro?"

"Fuck, yeah." Pietro ran back down and picked it up just as a whistle could be heard. The train carrying Nazi supplies and cargo was almost on them.

"Hurry, go, go." Sal prodded his brothers as they climbed the steep slope.

"We won't make it," Giuseppe said. "Let's hide there and wait. I want to see this anyway."

They scrambled behind a cluster of large yews and waited, trying to catch their collective breath. They were only a hundred feet above the train tracks.

The whistle sounded close; lights shone through the misty night.

Sal clenched his fists. The train kept moving. Damn. Did they not loosen the rails enough? Was the train going to make it through?

Then a shrill caterwauling sent a chill down Sal's back. The track was wobbling, metal smite metal and the world shifted. The train shrieked as if in pain. But nothing could stop the cataclysm. Cars jumped the tracks. The rails twisted and jackknifed, sailed across the ballast, catapulting rocks, and debris with them.

The end was horrific. Nine cars derailed and crashed into the hillside below the road, tumbling dozens of feet before screaming to a final stop. Hissing steam billowed in the air. The clanging of hot metal, splintering of wood, shattering of glass permeated the still of night. Then the screams.

Sal gazed down on the devastation. A part of him felt guilt. How many were dead? But they were Nazis, the enemy. No time for soft feelings. Still, he couldn't tear his eyes away.

"Let's go," whispered Giuseppe in a frantic rasp. "Now. While the moon is covered by clouds."

The four men began the climb up the mountain, legs weak, brains numb.

They heard shouts, gunfire. A shot pinged off the rocks near Sal and he ducked. Suddenly, spotlights beamed up the hill. They dove behind a cluster of spindly trees.

"*Stronzi*," Pietro spat. "How could they find us so fast?"

Shouting from below spurred them to motion. All four moved fast, faster.

"Get out of range," Francesco called out.

They pushed their legs to climb, climb. Their lives depended upon it.

A spate of gunfire and they dove to the ground. Waited. Bullets whizzed by their heads with a rush of hot air.

Finally, when they were near the top, the gunfire abated. They climbed up and over the ridge of the hill. They were safe. For a moment.

"It will take them a while to get up here . . . if they even follow," Giuseppe said, words spit out between heavy panting breaths.

"They have their hands full with the train and their dead," Sal said.

"Where's Pietro?" Francesco asked.

They looked around.

"Must be over the ridge and down the other side," Giuseppe said.

Francesco hurried to look. "No, I don't see him. Where the hell . . ?"

"*Dio Mio,*" Sal said. He pointed back down the hill to the way they just came. "Stay here," he ordered. Then he ran down, arms out for balance.

Sal reached his youngest brother, his heart ready to leap out of his chest. "No, no, no." He rolled Pietro onto his back. Too late. His younger brother was riddled with bullets, his face wore surprise, brown eyes open and vacant.

Sal sat down hard, the air rushing out of his lungs. "No, Pietro." He cradled his baby brother's head in his arms. "No."

He heard shouts from below. The Germans were gathering a search team to hunt for them. He had to move, and he had to move Pietro. He would not leave his dead brother to the Nazis.

Sal wiped his eyes and with a rush of adrenaline and sheer willpower, lifted Pietro into a standing position and threw him onto his shoulder.

"Mamma," Sal whispered. "I swear on my life, I will bring your little boy home."

Chapter 6

Helen

Brattleboro, Vermont, September 2018

The day blossomed into a soft blue with wispy fog trailing the ground and Monet-perfect sunrays streaming through the tree branches. An impressionist day. One made for exploring.

Helen stood on the front porch gazing out over the meadows--the landscape of her youth. She could smell the sweet scent of freshly mown grass as a fellow named Josh rode his mower at the far end of the emerald field. Honey barreled up the porch, almost knocking her down.

"I guess you've been out already." Helen smiled. "How about a nice long walk, hmm?"

Helen swung a jacket over her shoulders and she and Honey set off. They followed the low picket fence, which had been freshly painted, no doubt for her homecoming. Honey bounded ahead, then bounded back, keeping a close eye on her.

"I'm okay, honest." Still she smiled. Her eyes roamed the property. A ramshackle barn stood at the far end of the fence. It was approaching decrepitude, listing to one side, the barnboards broken, paint peeling and what was left faded to a pale shade of red. Without farm animals, Marie deemed it a waste of money to fix.

Maybe I'll have it repaired, Helen mused. A shame to let it fall down. The giant barn doors were open and Helen meandered in. The smells brought back a rush of happy memories from her childhood. Horses, leather, hay, manure. At the far end, a boarded-up corner, hidden by a tarp, covered up untold amounts of junk. She stood and gawked around taking in the sights and scents, letting the emotions of her days here wash over her. She spun around and left the barn to continue her inspection.

A few derelict sheds were in need of repair as well. One she remembered vividly. The gardening shed.

"Come on, Honey." She sped her walking to a jog and reached the shed. Opening the door, she whooshed out a breath. Not from the jog but from the smell inside.

"Whoa, that's a might nasty." She threw open the door to let fresh air in and the nastiness out and stepped inside. Honey began a sniffing mission.

"Jeez, I hope there's nothing dead in here."

Helen poked through the dirt and debris near the door. "Wow, this is just like I remember." The shed was packed: shovels, rakes, shears, clippers, trowels, pitchforks, all rusty and worn. "I guess they'd do in a pinch if I decide to plant a garden?"

The idea sounded appealing. Especially since she was brain dead as far as writing her new mystery. She'd written the first chapter six times.

She sneezed and stepped back into the light, away from the dust and the dampness. Her jacket was covered with bits of hay and sticky cobwebs. She brushed them off. It was then she realized Honey was no longer with her.

She walked around to the back of a shed and held her hand up to shade her eyes from the sun that had topped the mountain. She saw something moving in the distance. A tail wagging at the end of a butt. Honey was digging at the corner of the fence.

Helen sprinted toward the dog and called her name. Honey did not stop her excavation.

When she finally came up to her, Helen grabbed her by the collar. "Stop. Now. You'll ruin the beautiful grass."

Honey looked contrite, ears down, and backed away. She barked at Helen and seemed ready to dig again.

"No, this isn't a game." Helen held onto her collar now and the two walked over to the area that Honey was digging in. The grass had been dug up and there was a messy dirt patch in its place.

Helen was about to castigate her canine friend when something in the earth caught her attention. Something white.

"Oh, Honey, did you bury a bone here?" Helen got down on her hands and knees. She began moving dirt to the side so she could get a better look. Suddenly she found herself in the thick of one of her mysteries. She sat up with a jerk and gasped. The white in the dirt belonged to a bone. It was small, maybe an animal. A possum or raccoon.

She gently wiped away more dirt. It was a single bone, barely six inches deep in the soil. Not an animal. She recognized a humerus. The upper arm bone of a human. But small . . . a small humerus.

Honey gave a soft woof.

Helen kept moving dirt ever so gently. The skeleton grew until the arm was connected to a scapula, then a clavicle. As she pushed the earth around, a delicate rib poked through.

Oh God. This was a child. She leaped to her feet, feeling dizzy. She almost vomited. When she turned back and peered into the dirt, she knew what she had found. A grave. With a small child buried in it.

She sank down to the ground. Honey licked her face and Helen hugged her. "You found him, didn't you? How? How did you know this child was here, under the sod?"

Helen moved back to the grave. All her research with bodies and forensics for her mysteries gave her an edge on this discovery. She leaned in and looked more closely. Something to the right of the skeleton caused her to push the earth in the opposite direction. Was there another body?

She gently pushed the dirt until her fingers touched something hard. Carefully, she brushed away a fine layer of earth to uncover what could only be the jawbone of a skull. Realizing this must be a crime scene, Helen quit digging. Two skeletons lying side by side in a shallow grave. A child . . . and an adult.

Joey and Angie.

Helen backed away from the grave with Honey in tow. She had left her cell phone at the house so she would have to return to call the police. Suddenly a wave of vertigo brought her to her knees. She rolled from her knees over onto her back and closed her eyes. God, what was wrong with her? She was not squeamish, never that. It was the chemo, of course. Damn it.

Honey whined and stretched out next to her. Helen caressed the dog's head. She closed her eyes and practiced a few deep breathing exercises that meditation had taught her. The dizziness subsided; her stomach calmed. She blinked open her eyes to stare up at the cornflower blue sky.

A trailing white cloud brought back the image of the bones. Police. She had to call the police. Although she was certain she knew more about bones than the average police officer.

She pushed herself to stand and stared down at the remains once more. *These bones could be a century or more old. They may not be Angie and Joey. Really?*

"Come on, Honey, let's go home and call the police."

Marie was stunned to hear the news and kept asking Helen questions while they waited for the police to arrive.

"Could it be Angie and Joey? Are you sure it was a child? How old were the bones? Maybe they were animals? Were the bones broken? Was there--?"

Helen grabbed Marie's hands. She'd never seen her so agitated. "Calm down, Marie, please. We'll find out soon. I promise." Helen was as anxious as her aunt to find out who the bones belonged to.

"If they are Angie and Joey," Marie said, "how can they be identified? I mean there are no relatives to test against DNA or whatever, now, are there?"

"I don't know. Are there? Did Angie have any relatives, whose descendants might still be alive?"

Marie shot her a quizzical look. "Why yes, that is, maybe. Angie had a sister, I recall, but I don't know anything about her."

"Where did she live?"

"I don't know. . . don't remember."

"We'll find out, relax. The police will track her down."

"If the adult is identified as Angie then the bones of the little . . . little boy can be identified too." Marie seemed in a daze.

"Most likely, but let's wait--."

"It makes sense, doesn't it? That they were both murdered and buried on the property. Angie didn't just run away, I knew it, I knew it." She wrung her hands. "Oh Sal, if only you could've known."

Helen sighed, stood, and went into the kitchen. "Let's have a cup of tea." Or better yet, a brandy. She did not voice this out loud.

Thirty minutes went by before the Brattleboro PD showed up. Not surprising. It was not an emergency.

A tall lanky man Helen guessed to be in his late fifties swung his legs out of a white Ford Explorer. He was agile, dark-haired sprinkled with gray, and handsome. Sam Elliott handsome. The passenger door opened and a police-woman perhaps half his age stepped out more slowly and followed him up the porch steps.

"Hello, Ma'am, I'm Detective Lieutenant Dave Major. This is Sergeant Brenda Pine." His voice deep and throaty.

"Hi, I'm Helen Ainsley and this is my aunt, Marie . . ."

"Right, how you doing, Marie?"

"Oh, you know each other?"

"I think Marie knows everyone in town," Dave said with a grin.

"Can we get you something to drink, Dave, Brenda?" Marie said.

"No thanks. We'd like to get to the reason for this call." He turned to Helen. "Want to tell us what happened?"

Helen explained about the grave.

"I know who's buried there, Dave," Marie blurted out. "I can tell you the--."

"Why don't we take a look at the grave first, then we'll talk. That suit you, Marie?"

Helen smiled to herself. I like him already, she thought.

"Miz Ainsley, care to show us the way?"

"Honey, you stay here now." Marie grabbed Honey's collar and led her inside.

Helen stepped off the porch and the two police officers followed her.

"You're moving back to Brattleboro, then?" Dave said as they walked across the meadow. "To write a book."

Word sure gets out quickly. "Yes, well, I'm not sure how long I'll be around, I mean . . ." Her voice trailed off.

He nodded, shot a quick look at the scarf she wore on her head.

Helen's face heated up. *He knows and he knows I know he knows.*

"It's a beautiful property," he said. "Just needs a bit of TLC."

"Right," Helen said. "I grew up here, loved it."

"When did you leave?" Brenda asked. "If you don't mind me asking."

Helen turned to Brenda who stood about four inches shorter than she, and smiled at her round face, ruddy complexion, and jumble of misshapen teeth. "A really long time ago. Went to school at NYU and just stayed."

"I love your books, by the way."

"Can we chit chat some other time, ladies?" Dave said.

Brenda shot Helen an eye roll.

"Here it is." Helen approached the grave and pointed.

The officers stepped closer and looked down. Brenda took her phone out and began to shoot some photos. Dave snapped on rubber gloves, leaned into the grave and examined the bones without disturbing them. He stood and turned to Helen.

"How did you chance upon them?"

"I didn't. Honey, my dog, did. She started digging furiously. It was all I could do to tear her away. When I saw something white, I thought maybe Honey had buried a bone, an animal bone of some kind. I brushed away a bit of the dirt. It was clear it wasn't an animal."

"Looks like you brushed away more than a bit," Dave said. "There's an adult here as well."

Helen turned pink again. "Yeah, sorry. It's a hazard of my research . . . digging, so to speak."

He nodded. "You know something about bones?"

"Osteology, yeah. It's a particular interest. A writer friend of mine, Patricia Cornwell was able to—."

"Oh, she's terrific," Brenda gushed out. "I've read just about all--."

"Go on," Dave said to Helen.

"Right, Patricia got me into the Body Farm."

"The one in Tennessee?" he said

"You know it, of course." But it was more of a question. *Would the police in Brattleboro be familiar with the Forensic Anthropology Center in Knoxville?*

"Anyway," Helen went on, "I got to intern there one summer. Really informed the research for my writing."

"Interesting," Dave said.

"This is a crime scene isn't it?" she asked.

"Unless a child and an adult buried themselves, yes, it's a crime scene."

Helen grimaced.

"Let me make some calls to the State Police and get a crime team here. Then we'll go back to the house and talk. Sounds like Marie has some ideas about who these bones belonged to."

"She does, and, if she's right, you may need more than the crime team."

He raised an eyebrow over smoky blue eyes she would kill for.

"You might need a forensic anthropologist."

Chapter 7

It started as a gentle rain but by mid-afternoon turned into a gusty downpour, transforming the crime scene site into a quagmire of oozing mud and slime.

"Police still out there, like a bunch of ants crawling over a honey pot." Marie heaved a sigh as she stared out the window. "Rain don't seem to bother them much."

"It bothers me," Helen said. "Evidence could wash away." She poured a third cup of coffee from the pot on the stove.

"You think after seventy-five years, there's any evidence left in that grave?"

"It's possible. Things buried in the earth could re-surface."

"What's all the bother about anyway? We damn well know who's buried there. Why do we have to dig them up? What's that gonna prove?"

Helen cringed as her aunt emphasized the words by pounding her cane on the floor. She opened her mouth, then clamped it shut abruptly as Marie turned to her, red-faced.

"Why not just put a headstone at the top of the grave and leave it be." Her whole body trembled. "Right, that's right, now. A headstone. Say, 'here lies a mother and her son, murdered by a stranger . . . and all because a frivolous young girl wouldn't do the right thing.'"

"Marie--."

"No, unh, unh, don't interrupt me. I mean it. At least then the truth will come out, and they can rest in peace. And I can pay my dues. Goddammit." Her deep blue eyes sparked as if electrified.

Helen stood and approached Marie. But her aunt waved her away and thumped her cane on the floor again.

"Sit down, please, before you have a stroke or--."

"Just what I deserve, to drop dead here and now."

Helen took her forcefully by the arm and pushed her into a chair. Marie dropped her head in her hands.

"Now you listen to me." Helen leaned over. "You did not kill Angie and Joey. Get that crazy notion out of your head. Yes, you made a mistake, a teenage mistake, but you are not the one who murdered them." Helen took a deep breath. "This exhumation is terribly important, Marie. Don't you see? First of all, it proves you were right all along."

"What?"

"You knew--maybe you were the *only one* who knew--that Angie did not run away with some man and take Joey with her."

Marie's breathing quieted. She wiped her eyes with a damp tissue.

Her aunt had aged a few years overnight--her hair whiter, her wrinkles deeper. Helen felt a deep sorrow penetrate her bones. *Please, don't let me lose my dear aunt now. Not now.*

"Do you think he might have, I mean--?"

"No. I don't think he raped her. Remember Joey was right there. They were close to the Inn, outdoors in a field. No, he didn't rape her."

"Is there any way to know, for sure?"

"I doubt it. But he certainly killed her."

"And Joey? Why a little boy?"

"Because that little boy was a witness. He could identify him."

"Oh God."

Helen felt lightheaded but knew she had assuaged some of Marie's guilt. "In a way, it's a good thing that we found their remains. Finally, the truth can come out. We can vindicate Angie. Show the world that she was a victim not a, a strumpet, or whatever people assumed at the time."

Helen rubbed Marie's arm. "I know. It's tough. But they're gone. Angie and Joey are long gone. Now their remains can be laid to rest. Near Sal."

"Do you think, maybe . . ." Her voice trailed off.

"What?"

"Do you believe that Angie'll forgive me?"

"Yes, I believe she will, Marie. I *know* she will."

Marie stood, her back straight and moved to her position at the window.

Helen exhaled and leaned down to rub Honey's head as the dog lay curled in front of the stove. "You're watching over us, aren't you?"

"Thank God, here comes Dave," Marie said. "Let me grab him a towel, he's got to be soaked to the skin."

Helen reached for the door and stood waiting.

Dave strode up the porch steps. The wind behind him swirled the leaves into a funnel. He ducked inside, shrugged out of his rain jacket, dripping onto the wood floor.

"Here you go, dry yourself, then." Marie hung his jacket on a hook near the door.

"Thanks." Dave toweled his face and hair. "That tent doesn't help much with this wind."

"Coffee?" Helen said. "Come into the kitchen."

He followed her in, took the mug she offered. "A hot cup of coffee on a day like this is a very underrated pleasure." His smile made Helen smile.

"You have a nice smile," he said.

"Thank you. I, uh, I--."

"I know, it's hard to smile when you have a murder scene on your property."

Marie said, "Well, what happens now?"

"Looks like we're done for today. The team shot the bones in situ--"

"What's that mean?" Marie said.

"We made a photographic record of exactly how the bones were laid out in the earth, plus anything else that was buried with them," he said. "We want to find whatever evidence we can, in hopes it will tell us how they got there, and, if we're real lucky, who put them there. Once we remove the evidence, there's no going back."

"Did you find something there besides the bones?" Helen asked.

"One thing," Dave said, rummaging through his shirt pocket. "Might help with identification." He turned to Marie. "This look familiar, Marie?" He held out a plastic bag. Inside was a gold band.

"A wedding ring?" Helen said.

"I need a closer look." Marie slipped on reading glasses and leaned against the kitchen table.

"You can touch the bag, but don't take the ring out. There appears to be initials on the inside, but they're near impossible to read, being in the elements all this time."

Marie's mouth worked in silence and her eyes filled. "Yes, it's Angie's ring."

"How do you know?" Dave said.

"See those dings?" Marie sat down heavily in a chair. "I remember that day. Ages ago. Angie was really upset. I heard her in the parlor, wailing like a mad woman. She lost her ring, was all I could figure from her blubbering. It had fallen off, kinda loose, I guess. We searched high and low. Got down on the floor and felt around every inch, even into the dark corners with a torch. Finally, she decided to dump the hoover onto the rug, hoping it had gotten sucked up." Marie shook her head. "She found it, all right. Lord be praised."

"This is when Sal was in Italy?" Helen asked.

"Yup. Angie was so happy to find it again, didn't matter that it was mighty dinged up."

Dave held up the bag to examine the ring. He nodded. "All right. We'll still need to do formal identifications."

"Think you can get DNA from the bones or teeth?" Helen asked.

"Bones, I'd say not likely. Teeth, maybe."

"Is there a forensic anthropologist in town?"

Dave shook his head. "Nearest in Maine."

"Maine?" Marie said with a groan.

"At the University in Orono. State police will determine whether we send the remains there or not. In any case, it will take a bit of time for identification and analysis."

"Analysis?" Marie asked.

"Like an autopsy but on bones. Try to figure out what killed them."

Marie's face drained.

"Sorry to be blunt," Dave said. He swallowed the rest of his coffee. "In the meantime, we will be investigating how the bones got to be buried here. That's where you can help us, Marie."

"Whatever you need."

"Good. I'll have Brenda come by tomorrow and record any information you have. You were here at the time, with--"

"The Martelli family," Helen said. "Salvatore, Angie, and Joey."

"I was just fourteen, but I was here," Marie said, color returning to her face.

"Right. You can help us a lot." He started for the door.

Helen followed him. "Dave, er, would it be okay for me to do a little research?"

He narrowed his eyes as he shrugged his jacket on.

"Just through newspaper articles, I mean. I don't plan on conducting interviews on any suspects, or anything like that." She gave him a faint smile. "Besides the suspects in this case would no doubt be long dead."

"You planning to write a book?"

"You never know."

Helen didn't sleep well that night. The rain and wind kicked up into a storm and continued until three in the morning. Images of bones and dirt, a little boy and his mother, a father unable to save them, looped in her head. By morning, the sheets were twisted into knots and her muscles felt like they were held together with tight rubber bands, ready to snap. She'd been thinking of death too often lately.

She staggered around the kitchen, downed three cups of coffee and a piece of toast. She worried about Marie, who had awakened at her usual five a.m. but went back to sleep.

The storm finally cleared, and the day promised sunshine. Helen and Honey moseyed down the steps to greet it. Helen chucked a ball several times and Honey retrieved it, acting, oddly, like a real dog, instead of an all-seeing, omniscient spirit. She was delighted that no one had come forward to claim her.

Helen checked her watch and decided she could head downtown. The library would open in ten minutes.

After her library coup, thanks to an erudite librarian, and followed by a late afternoon nap, Helen felt rested, energized, even. Now, at the Marina Restaurant, she sat across from Julianne and watched her expression as she filled her in on her research. Her daughter's eyes danced behind her tortoiseshell glasses as she tucked her reddish-brown hair behind her ears.

"So, you spent the morning at the library? What did you learn?"

"One juicy bit of intelligence."

"Well, give," Julianne said.

"I got the name of the police detective who worked the missing persons case in 1945."

"No kidding."

"At first, I wondered whether that was really useful. Even if he were only twenty back then, he would be somewhere in his mid-nineties today. What were the chances he was still alive with his memory intact?" Helen took a sip of her water. "I asked the librarian, and, would you believe, she actually knows him. He's still alive and sharp as a thorn, she said."

"You got his address, then?"

"Ain't small towns grand?" Helen grinned.

"Jeez, mom, this would be perfect for your next mystery. Don't you agree? I mean, a woman and a child disappearing from the Inn, right here in town . . . an Inn that's been in the family--."

"Yes, sweetie, I know the story. And you're right. I'm considering it."

Julianne beamed at her mother. "Missing mother and child . . . found seventy-five years later in a shallow grave on a farm in Vermont. *Yes*. I can smell a bestseller in the works. What does your agent think?"

"Jill? For heaven's sake, I haven't told her a thing about this. Yet."

They ordered dinner and gazed out the window at the West River, which sparkled in the remnants of the sunlit afternoon. Helen wondered for the hundredth time how she had produced such a beautiful child, woman. Juli was clearly James' daughter.

"I guess it's almost time to extricate the Strolling of the Heifer cows from the river, right?" Julianne said.

"I don't know. With this Indian summer and the fall colors . . ."

"Yeah, beautiful."

"I'm kind of looking forward to winter," Helen said.

"You crazy or something?"

"No, I guess I love the snow."

"Maybe, to look at. Try driving in it every day."

"Yeah, but I'll be cozy and warm at my computer. Think about that."

Julianne smiled. "All the fall colors gone. The landscape will be bleak and dark. Winter is death."

"I like to think of it more like nature's break or life's intermission. The trees can rest and regroup."

"You're an optimist, mom." Julianne stirred the ice in her glass. "Sometimes I wish that time could stand still." She looked at Helen with eyes glistening. "That life wouldn't change."

"Ah, be careful what you wish for." Helen smiled at her daughter. "You know, if you hold onto things too tight, they could break."

Their food was delivered and neither woman touched it.

"But if you let them go," Julianne said, "you let a part of yourself go, too."

"Maybe. Some things aren't supposed to last forever. Perhaps they're here to teach you a lesson and then move on."

"For instance?" Julianne said.

Helen thought. "Well, people, for instance. Why hold onto people who don't make you smile? Or why do something you hate like, I don't know, read a book for a book club that you just don't enjoy?"

Julianne stared at her.

"You know, my love, sometimes the things you're fighting for just aren't worth the cost. And sometimes the things you lose, can force you to move on . . . to a happier life."

Julianne covered her mouth with both hands and sobbed into them.

"Oh, Juli, I didn't mean to make you cry." Helen reached out and grasped her daughter's arms.

"Sorry, sorry. I don't know what's wrong with me."

"I do. You've got a heart as big as the moon; you lost your dad who was your mentor; you thought you loved a man who turned out not to be the right one; you adore kids and you have none. And your mom is . . . is sick and struggling to stay alive." She took a breath. "And now, the color has gone from the landscape and you're facing a black and white winter."

Julianne almost choked on a cry.

"But look at the bright side."

Julianne wiped the tears with a tissue.

"I've finally lost those damn ten pounds I've been carrying around for years."

Julianne choked down a new sob.

"Just kidding, sweetie." She reached for her daughter's hand. "We are together, closer than ever. You have a wonderful business that you simply love . . . that the community loves. And I . . ."

"Yes? You?"

"I am so happy to be back home in Vermont, with you, with Aunt Marie, with my new dog, Honey, and my old, enchanted tree."

"Enchanted tree? What tree? Whatever are you talking about, mom?"

Helen smiled, picked up her fork. "Dinner is getting cold."

Chapter 8

Morningside Cemetery on South Main Street has provided a peaceful resting place for about four thousand souls since 1890. Gazing across the street from the meticulously maintained cemetery, Helen studied the house in which former Detective Frederick Lawrence Denning resided for fifty years. Its white picket fence needed a fresh coat of paint and a dozen new pickets. The house itself listed a bit to the left like a tipsy drunk, its shutters tilting toward the earth. The absurdity that a homicide cop looked out his window every day at a graveyard did not escape Helen's sense of irony.

A long wheelchair ramp ran from the sidewalk to the entrance of the house which faced Washington Street. She thought back to their phone conversation of the previous day. He had been cordial when she called to request an interview about one of his old cases, but more hesitant when she divulged the specific case.

Now, she wished they could have met at a coffee shop. The old house gave her the heebie jeebies. Denning claimed he rarely left the house these days, had trouble getting around on the uneven sidewalks with his walker. Hence, the ramp and the reluctance to leave his abode.

Helen strode up the wooden walkway, knocked on the door. She heard a man's voice call from inside. "Come on in, door's open."

She let herself in, expecting the interior of the house to match the exterior. It did not. The first thing she noticed was the fresh scent. The house had been cleaned on a regular basis and as she followed the voice through the hallway to the kitchen, Helen saw furniture in good order, books on side tables, lamps with bulbs burning and a woodstove prepped with paper and kindling. Her shoulders dropped, relieved that she wouldn't be sitting in dust and clutter and

51

inhaling leftover cooking grease. Her stomach had become annoyingly sensitive these last two years.

"Miz Ainsley?"

"Yes, Detective Denning, thanks so much for seeing me."

"Call me Fred. I haven't been Detective Denning for longer than I care to remember." He stood, set his walker to one side, and hobbled to the stove. "Now I don't know 'bout you, but I'm gonna make myself a cuppa' coffee. Even got some cheesecake there." He nodded to the table. "Entenmanns. How about you?"

"Well, how did you know I love Entenmanns?' Helen smiled. "And coffee would be great."

"Ayuh. Everyone loves Entenmanns. What's not to like?"

Helen watched as he prepared the old percolator with coffee grounds and retrieved plates and cups from the cabinets. Fred Denning, despite his age, was an impressive man. About six feet, maybe 180 pounds, slightly stooped, he managed to maneuver well. His craggy face showed signs of drink, but this morning his canny, brown eyes were clear. His hands shook some, but not enough to spill anything.

"So, tell me," he said, when he finally sat down. "What's your interest in the Martellis? Been a long time since I heard that name." He took a bite, sighed in pleasure.

Helen updated him on the grave that was found on her property.

"Jeezum. You actually found, what, the bones? Of the mother?"

"And the child." Helen gazed at him. "You haven't heard about it, then?"

"How would I?"

"Fellow officers?" she suggested.

"They don't . . . I don't keep in touch."

"Oh. What about the newspaper? There was a mention of it in--"

"The Reformer? Never read it. Piece of crap." He drank some coffee. This time his trembling hands sloshed some out of the cup. Neither commented on it.

"You knew the Martellis when you were a policeman at the time?"

"Say, you gonna write a book or something?"

"It's possible. But I'm more interested in finding out what happened."

"How come?"

The question surprised her. "Well, first, it happened on my land. Second, my Aunt Marie has been greatly affected by it."

"Marie, right, right, I remember her. How is Marie?"

"She's good."

"Marie, ayuh. She was about what back then, maybe twelve?"

"Fourteen."

He nodded. "You say she was greatly affected. You mean by finding them bones?"

"Yes. But perhaps more so by the memories the bones stirred up." Helen paused. "Their disappearance in 1945."

Denning stared up at the ceiling. "1945. Long time, huh."

"Almost seventy-five years. What do you remember, Fred?"

"Well now, not sure I can help you there. Memory's shot these last few years."

"Usually it's short-term memory that goes. This is a long-term memory." Denning shrugged.

"How well did you know the Martellis?"

"Didn't know 'em."

"You didn't know them when they worked at the Inn?"

"Why would I?"

"This is a small town, Fred. You were a cop. You must've known when anyone took a leak in town."

Fred grunted but didn't smile.

"How did you get involved with the disappearance?"

"Martelli. The father. He was all hepped up. He called and reported them missing."

"And you went to investigate?"

"Sure."

His abrupt answers were wearing thin on Helen's nerves. "And?"

"And what? I took the report. Had a look, found nothing."

"Had a look at what?"

"Her room, her belongings, the property. Nothin'."

"Weren't all her belongings left behind?"

"Don't remember."

"They were. Which means she left with only the clothes on her back. Isn't that odd?"

"Look," Fred said. "Truth is, there was all sorts of talk 'bout her, the wife."

Helen narrowed her eyes, waiting.

"Everyone knew what happened."

"What happened?"

"She run off with some guy."

"Took Joey with her?"

"Why not? Wasn't gonna leave him behind, now was she?"

Helen leaned into the table. "You really believe that's what happened to Angie Martelli? She took her five-year-old son, left her husband, whom, by all accounts, she loved, and ran off with another man?"

"She was no saint, lemme tell ya."

"I thought you didn't really know her."

"I didn't. Just heard about her from guys, you know, guys she played around with."

"What guys? Can you give me their names?"

"No matter. They're all dead now." Denning rose to fill his cup again.

"Did any of these *guys* disappear at the same time? Any suspicious--?"

"Look here, I answered yer questions. Now, what can you tell me about the bones the cops found?"

Helen blew out a breath. "They're being sent to a forensic anthropologist in Maine. The report will be sent to Brattleboro PD."

"They gonna do an autopsy to find the COD?"

"Yes."

"With the technology they got today, they should be able to figger out what killed 'em, right?"

"Well, there were only bones in the grave, no soft tissue, so it's not that easy, even with technology. But there are a lot of things they can determine."

Denning did not respond.

Helen went on despite his silence, deliberately winding him up. "They can ascertain whether the victims were shot, stabbed, or bludgeoned. Any of those means of death would leave a mark on the bones, even if small."

He stared at her, eyes now wary.

"But we'll have to wait for the final report."

"I want to hear when you get it." His voice rose then fell. "You'll share it, right? I kinda got a stake in the case if you know what I mean."

"Because of your former position, can't you get a copy from the police?"

"Mebbe. But I'd rather not ask."

Helen wondered why but Denning did not look amenable to answering. "I'm not sure they'll let me see a copy," she said. "After all, I'm not in law enforcement."

"You have a right. Bodies on yer property."

"It's a crime scene now."

Denning mumbled something she couldn't catch.

"Fred, you don't seem eager to talk about the case."

Denning's eyes pierced hers as if a laser, and her brain sent out soft alarm bells.

She drank her now-cold coffee. "Are you getting tired? Do you want to continue another time?"

"Nah, not tired. Just not comfortable."

"Why is that?"

"Brings up old memories I'd rather not re-visit, ya know? I couldn't find 'em back then and now they turn up . . . murdered." He wheezed. "And here you are asking questions like it's my fault."

"I never said--."

Denning stood, grabbed for his walker. "I think I am tired. Mebbe you should go."

Helen stood as well, relieved to be leaving, and headed for the kitchen door. "Thanks, Fred, for your time." She stepped outside the house, breathed in the outside air, and reveled in the sunshine. Denning's house, while neat and orderly, somehow felt tainted with dark, hidden memories. She turned to look back and saw the curtains move in the window.

What are you hiding, Fred Denning?

"That old coot still alive?" Marie stopped stirring a pot on the stove and turned to face Helen.

"He's ninety-five, physical health okay, good memory, when he wants."

"I know just what you mean." Marie pulled out a chair and sat. "What did he have to say?"

Helen relayed her conversation.

"Don't trust him, never did."

"Why is that?"

Marie stared into the distance. "I knew Fred when I started at the High School. He'd graduated some years before and was working at the PD as an officer. Came around to the Inn from time to time, said he was making sure all was well, or some such."

"Really? He acted like he hardly paid any mind to the Inn or the people in it."

"Hell, he was here every other day."

"Why?"

"Why'd ya think? He had a crush on Angie."

Helen jerked upright.

"Oh yes. He seemed to know when Sal was away, gone to town, out in the field, that sort of thing. And, when he went off to Italy, well, Fred would be here just about every day."

"Why wasn't Fred in the military?"

"Four F. Something about a bum leg, I think."

"He does use a walker."

"He's an old man, course he does."

"He didn't have problems back then?"

"Not that I saw." Marie shook her head. "Don't think the PD woulda' hired him."

"So, he liked Angie? What did he do? She was married, after all."

"It's coming back to me now that I ponder. He would try to get her out to a movie, for a coffee, like that, you know. She kept saying no and tried to be nice. He was a cop, and she didn't want to get him angry. Had quite a temper, Fred did."

"Temper, huh?"

"What makes me mad, was what he'd say behind her back. He acted all sweet with her and Joey, but then he'd mumble things like tart, or whore . . . when she wasn't hearin', you know?"

Helen's eyes widened.

"But I heard, clear as day. He didn't give a rat's ass what I heard, though. I was just a kid." Marie curled her lips in a sneer. "I heard, all right. He was a two-faced son-of-a-gun and I didn't trust him a whit."

Helen tried to process this information. Was her aunt exaggerating? Was her memory inaccurate? Was she just trying to protect Angie and Joey from a philanderer? She mulled over her interview with Fred Denning. Perhaps it wasn't sadness or frustration he felt about not solving their disappearance.

Perhaps it was guilt.

Chapter 9

When it comes my time to sleep,
I will not wail, I will not weep,
I'll lay my weary body down,
On beds of leaves, both green and brown,
I'll sleep as nature takes its toll,
Reclaims my once embodied soul,
And wraps me in the earth's embrace,
A quiet, peaceful, resting place,
The time outside will still elapse,
But I won't feel my bones collapse,
And I'll return back where I came,
To let the cycle start again.
Erin Hanson

Cancer is a monster, a heartless demon. It robs you of your dignity, your self-image, the very essence of your soul, and, ultimately, your life.

If you let it. Helen would not. Grief and anger had waxed and waned but once her physical symptoms from the chemo had subsided, she'd made her decision. Life was shorter now. Too short to waste on self-pity and regret.

Honey leaned into her as she took in the view outside of her bedroom window. Green fields stretched as far as she could see, rimmed with soft rolling hills. The moon had set, and the sun rose in a sky blooming with gold and red stripes. Central to the scene was the maple tree of her childhood. Tall, noble, sentient. Waiting.

"Today's a big day, sweetie," Helen kissed her dog on the nose. "We have a mystery to solve."

By nine a.m., Helen was sitting on the porch with a third cup of coffee, tapping her fingers on the rocker arm. Her blood sizzled. Where was he? Funny, she mused. The Martelli case was not the only reason she looked forward to seeing Detective Dave Major. She smiled and didn't try to hide it.

"What are you grinning at, young lady?" Marie let the screen door close softly behind her and settled into the second rocker.

"Young lady?"

"You are only fifty-three. Besides, age is relative."

Helen laughed. "I'm smiling because I'm excited to hear Dave's news about the bones."

"Face it. You're excited because Dave's coming."

"Phooey."

"Have you told him about your meeting with Fred Denning?"

Helen's mouth dropped into a frown. "No. I should have, shouldn't I?"

"Knowing Dave, yup. You should've." Marie opened her mouth to say more, then closed it as the police cruiser pulled up the driveway. Dave Major stepped out, followed by Detective Sergeant Brenda Pine.

"Morning," Dave said.

"Morning," Helen said. "Brenda. Please come up and sit."

"Coffee's right there." Marie pointed to a pot and cups on the porch table.

"Love some," Brenda said. She poured.

"Don't keep me in suspense." Helen said. What did the autopsy show?"

"Just what we expected," Dave said. "The boy's neck was broken. Pathologist believes he was shaken—."

"Like a rag doll," Brenda added. "Jeez. Can you imagine doing that to a little boy?"

"You mean someone shook him . . . until his neck . . . snapped?" Marie said.

"Looks like it."

"Damn," Helen said on a sigh.

"Do you think it was deliberate, I mean--?"

"Not deliberate as in murder. More like manslaughter."

"Joey might have been kickin' and yellin' and the killer wanted to shut him up," Brenda said.

"Now the mother . . ." Dave began.

"Angela," Marie said.

"Angela. Autopsy showed no sign of blunt force trauma, gunshot or knife wound to the bones. So, the coroner's best guess is strangulation. Unfortunately, the one bone that could confirm that hypothesis was never found in the grave."

"The hyoid bone," Helen said. "It would have been a miracle for that tiny bone to be uncovered after all these years and under Vermont climate conditions."

Silence prevailed as everyone turned over their own thoughts.

Dave leaned back in his chair. "Here's what we think, some of which is based on Marie's account of that day." He looked at Marie. "You correct me if I'm wrong."

Marie nodded, her face tight, lips compressed.

"Angie and Joey were at the Inn that day in May 1945. It was May, right, Marie?"

"I'll never forget. Few weeks after V-E Day."

"She was probably waiting for word from Sal, who was on his way home from Italy. Angie decided to walk into town to do some shopping, get ready for her husband's return.

"She took Joey and they set off down Ainsley Hill Road."

Helen looked out to the road as if seeing them there seventy-five years ago.

"Someone came along, maybe to offer them a ride. A man, most likely someone she knew or trusted. Angie and Joey got in the car. They barely got a short distance up the road because we know where the grave was found."

Dave took a sip of his coffee, continued. "They got into an argument. Maybe the man wanted a kiss, or more. Angie refused. He got mad. They fought. She jumped out of the car and over the fence, with Joey in tow. Started heading back to the Inn. But the man got angry, grabbed her."

"If there were defensive marks on her body, we would never know," Helen said, "since there were only bones left."

61

"Correct," Dave said. "Maybe he knocked her out, or just threatened her with harm to her son. At some point, Joey started crying. Man got mad, picked him up and shook him. Kid was small, skinny. Not too hard for a grown man to snap a little boy's neck."

"God," Helen whispered.

"And then he went back to Angie," Dave said, fell quiet.

A collective breath all around.

Marie's face drained of blood.

Dave cleared his throat. "That's the one scenario that fits all the evidence we have."

"It's a shame nothing else was found in the grave besides her wedding ring," Helen said. "There's no earthly way to figure out who the killer was."

"Actually," Dave said. "There is. We did find something in the grave that I've kept under wraps until the coroner's report came back."

Helen sat up straight. "What?"

Dave reached in his jacket pocket and pulled out a small plastic bag. Inside was a class ring from Brattleboro Union High School.

"A high school ring?" Marie asked.

"From 1942."

Silence screamed.

"What were the initials on the inside?" Marie whispered. "Every kid had his initials engraved on the ring. Every kid."

Dave did not have to look at the ring. "FLD."

Marie leaped to her feet, belying her age. "I knew it, I knew it. That son-of-a-bitch, Denning. Soon as Helen told me about her interview with him, I was sure he was the one, God almighty."

"Wait a minute, what interview?" Dave looked at Helen. "We haven't even interviewed him yet."

Helen's blood went cold in her body. She held up a hand as if to ward off a blow. "I was going to tell you, Dave, as soon as the coroner's report came back. I only wanted to talk to Denning because he was the cop who investigated the disappearance of Angie and Joey. He was the only one there at the time, and he's still alive, with all his faculties, I might add."

"This is all about your next book, isn't it?" Dave's eyes flashed with anger.

"No, no, that's--."

"Damn it, Helen, you should have told me. Seems to me you specifically said you wanted to do research at the library, not interview suspects."

"I'm--."

"You could have compromised our investigation. In fact, you may have. He could do a runner, cover his tracks or . . . shit, I don't know." He stood, turned, then wheeled back.

"Jesus, Helen, you of all people, with all your experience, should have known. This is a murder case. It may be cold, but it never gets closed."

Helen felt her face go red-hot. Her stomach fisted. What the hell was she thinking?

"Too late, now," Dave said, his lips drawn tight.

Brenda spoke up. "Maybe Helen can tell us what Denning said. I mean, he might have been more forthcoming with her than us as law enforcement. Right?" She looked at Dave.

He sat back down. "Well?"

Helen summarized her interview with Denning. "He was lying, Dave. He told me he hardly knew Angie, but Marie says he was at the Inn all the time, chasing her skirts."

"He was a mean s-o-b," Marie said. "I knew it." Tears filled her eyes.

The four of them sat, spent, on the porch as the wind picked up and worried the tops of the trees.

"Damnit." Dave rubbed his forehead.

"I don't get the problem," Marie said. "You got his ring, buried in the grave. What more do you need?"

"It's not that simple, Marie. A good lawyer could argue that he gave Angela that ring as a token of his affection. That she was wearing it when she died."

"What? You serious?"

Helen asked, "The initials on the ring. Could they have belonged to some-one else?"

"Another FLD? Don't be daft, Helen," Marie said. "Course it was Denning."

"She's right," Brenda said. "We checked the class rosters. No other FLD."

"What happens now?" Helen asked.

"I turn over what we have to the State's Attorney. It's up to her to decide what she wants to do with it."

"You mean to prosecute or not?" Helen said.

"Murder is one of a small list of crimes that we will *always* investigate, no matter what the time frame, as long as the suspect is still alive. Prosecution is another matter."

"Would it help to tell the SA about my interview with Denning?"

"It would be your word against his."

"So, he just gets to go free?" Marie said.

"He's ninety-five years old, Marie," Brenda said. "The State might not want to prosecute a man that old with the circumstantial evidence we have."

Marie dropped her head. "I can't believe this."

Dave stood; Brenda followed.

"Dave?" Helen said. "Will you please call when you know the State Attor-ney's decision?"

He drew in a deep breath. "I will."

She smiled faintly. "Thank you."

Dave and Brenda stepped off the porch and into the cruiser. In a minute, they were gone and, with them, Helen's slender hope for justice for Angie and Joey.

The house phone rang at eleven that night. Helen had not fallen asleep, so she hurried to reach it before her aunt was awakened. Too late. Marie picked it up as Helen reached the bottom landing.

"Hello, hello? Dave? Yes, yes. What did she say? She gonna prosecute?"

Marie fell silent, her jaw clenched.

Helen stood in front of her, hoping to read what happened from her expression.

Honey appeared at her side. Helen put a hand on her head and immediately felt calm. Whatever happened, happened.

Marie hung up the phone and her eyes seemed glazed.

"Well? Will she prosecute?"

"She would have . . . but she can't now."

"What? What does that mean?"

Marie pulled herself up straight. "Fred Denning is dead. Shot himself late this afternoon. Dave's been busy with the crime scene and only now had a minute to call us."

"Dead?"

"I was right, Helen. He killed them, couldn't face trial, jail. So's he killed himself. The coward." Marie sank into the nearest chair.

Helen took her hand. Honey rested her head on Marie's knee.

"His suicide is tantamount to a confession. You were right. Fred Denning killed Angie and Joey. He's gone. It's over, Marie. It's over."

Marie Ainsley rose early the next day, unable to calm her mind with the profusion of thoughts crowding in, she resorted to her old escape. Baking. Now, even as she slid the pie in the oven, her mind was sixty years in the past. Her brain churned, running pieces of the puzzle over and over.

Fred Denning was dead. Angie and Joey were vindicated. But a new heaviness filled her heart. The day was coming when she would have to tell Helen the truth. Or would she? Could the secret remain hidden forever? Was that fair to Helen? Was it safer for Helen? Could Helen handle such a revelation in her weakened state?

She leaned her hefty weight on the stove and breathed in the scent of apples and cinnamon. Nails clicked on the kitchen linoleum and Marie turned to Honey who had come to offer solace. The dog was special. No doubt. She knew when she was needed.

Marie sat down at the kitchen table and Honey sat in front of her.

"You know what I learned, sweet pea?" Marie laid her hand on Honey's head.

"When you are wrestling with something important in your head, the best thing to do is stop thinking about it for a day. Shove it to the back of your mind, pretend it don't exist. Until you're ready. She smiled.

"Like Scarlet O'Hara. I'll think about it tomorrow."

Honey let out a soft whine.

"Then, when you come back to it and face it head on, the solution comes to you, clear as a bug trapped in an ice cube. Yep. Then you'll know the right thing to do."

Chapter 10

Early October in Brattleboro and the curiously relentless heat began to take its toll on the environment. The leaves crisped and fell, overlaying the gold carpet with brown crunch. The grass turned yellow, blades waving in the warm breeze, as if praying for rain. Low humidity caused eyeballs to dry, skin to itch, and tempers to flare.

Helen's was about to erupt with frustration. But it had nothing to do with the weather. Her latest book seemed stalled in the first chapter. She'd written nine outlines and felt positive about the last. Still, the story was not unfolding. Something about the characters didn't work. Maybe a POV change? A plot tweak? Re-work the setting? No. She needed an ending. She couldn't begin without an ending in sight.

A sharp bark startled her. She set her laptop on the side table and rocked herself up to standing. "Honey?"

The retriever bounded up the three steps to greet her, then raced back down, spinning and barking.

"No one can convince me you're *not* a puppy." Helen smiled for the first time that morning. "What's up, girl?" She stepped down to the path.

Honey raced to the giant maple, leaped up so her front legs were five feet up onto the trunk.

Helen felt a chill despite the heat. She moved at a snail's pace to Honey's position, fearful of what she might see. At the exact place she originally spied the initials of Sal and Angie, suddenly appeared the same heart enclosing *SM-AR*. A tiny gasp escaped her lips. Honey stared at the tree then at Helen.

Helen reached up and touched the carving. It seemed warm to her fingers.

"What are you doing, Helen?" Marie came down the porch steps.

"They're back, Marie."

"What's back?" Marie walked over to her.

"The initials. Sal and Angie. They're back. They had disappeared and . . . now, they're--."

"Yes, of course."

Helen locked eyes with her aunt, both sets of eyes intense. "What do you mean, of course?"

"They appeared when the right person came along."

"Me?"

"The tree here--it gave you a chance to figger out the mystery of their disappearance. To right a wrong."

"Why did the initials re-appear?"

"So, Sal and Angie and Joey . . . can finally rest in peace."

Helen realized tears were streaming down her face.

"It's all right, dear," Marie said. "You did a fine thing. A really fine thing, solving their deaths."

The two women linked arms and began to walk back to the house.

Honey barked again. And again. Her paws were up on the tree once more.

Helen shot a quizzical look at Marie, then walked back to the tree. "Now what, girl?"

She followed Honey's paws with her eyes, searching for whatever was causing the excitement. And she found it. Letters, not initials. Carved crookedly about five feet from the ground. A name.

It was not possible, yet there it was.

Tillie.

Chapter 11

Tillie

Brattleboro, Vermont, May 1917

Two young women knelt in a bed of tulips and daffodils, yanking out weeds between the kaleidoscope of colors.

Jane Raymond sat up on her knees and wiped sweat from her forehead with the top of her gloved hand. Her short blond hair curled beneath her hat and her hazel eyes squinted in the sun. "What's wrong with the name Mathilda, for heaven's sake?"

The other woman remained hunched over the ground, working at a frenetic pace, as if it were a race to claim the weeds. "It's . . . stodgy, tedious, boring, dull."

"Hmm. Anything else?"

"Mathilda is an old lady's name. And I'm young . . . I'm--."

"I know exactly how old you are, you're my sister, goodness."

"That's why you should understand."

"Why only now decide to change your name?"

"Because I just turned twenty-five. A quarter century. A turning point in one's life."

Jane studied her younger sister. "And what, may I ask, would you like to be called?"

"Tillie."

Both women stopped their chores and eyed each other under their floppy gardening hats. Tillie grinned showing even white teeth behind full red lips.

Unlike her sister, her hair was long and brunette, streaked with red, and her eyes a deep shade of brown like a newborn colt.

"It's perfect. It's light, it's airy and, well, it's fun."

"But . . ."

"But what, Jane? What's wrong with Tillie?"

Jane shrugged her shoulders. A smile came over her face. "Nothing. It suits you fine."

They stood. Both women were tall, but Tillie's head came to within inches of the top of the Inn's door frames.

Tillie hugged her older sister and laughed. "See, I knew you'd understand."

"Well," Jane said. "Let's say it's just easier than arguing with you when you have your mind made up."

Jane and Tillie stood, brushed off their trousers, stowed their gardening tools in a basket. They linked arms and drifted up the steps to the front porch of the Ainsley Hill Inn.

"Come on, Tillie dear. It's time to prepare for graduation exercises."

Months later, early on a Saturday in late August, Tillie's eyes blinked open to the sound of heavy footsteps pounding up the steps of the Inn. She rolled over and shook Jane by the shoulder.

Tillie scrambled out of the double bed that she and Jane shared and hurried to the washstand. She threw cold water on her face, dried herself and began dressing.

"For goodness sake, Mathilda, why are you . . . oh my God." Jane leaped out of bed and ran to the window. "He's here, he's here. Tillie, oh my word, Tillie?"

"I'm right here, Jane." Tillie stood in front of an antique mirror, squinting into the wavy glass, and adjusting her shirtwaist.

A knock on the bedroom door caused both sisters to start.

Tillie opened it to the housekeeper at the Inn. A frog-faced woman with bulging eyes, Miss Herrick, stood, arms folded. "Why are you girls not ready?"

Jane let out a wail. She pulled on her stockings with shaking hands.

"I'm ready, almost," Tillie said. "There," she pointed. "My bags are packed."

Miss Herrick whirled about and shouted. "Zebula, come up here now."

More footsteps clumping on the stairs, these heavier. A grizzled, stocky man appeared at the door.

"Zeb, thank heavens," Jane said, stuffing a long strand of hair into a quickly made bun.

"Take those bags to the truck," Miss Herrick ordered. "Bobo's' giving Miss Tillie a ride to the railroad station."

"Yes, ma'am," Zeb said. "This the day, then, huh? That Miss Tillie gone 'way?"

Tillie walked over to the old man. "Yes, Zeb. But I'll be back. It's not forever, you know."

Zebula hung his head. "I sure am sorry to see you go, Miss Tillie."

Tillie smiled. "I'll miss you too, Zeb. But Jane will still be here . . . 'til I return."

She grabbed her hat, tied it under her chin and flew out of the bedroom and down the stairs.

Jane followed, carrying a small leather satchel. "Don't forget this, oh, goodness, I can't keep up with her. She's like a tornado." These words were spoken to no one as everyone was downstairs and out on the porch already.

Tillie's bags were being set into the new Ford farm truck. It belonged to the neighbor's farm adjacent to the Inn and was driven by the farm's lead hand, Bobo Johnson.

Jane handed her the last bag and pulled her aside. "Now, do you have everything? Your writing kit?"

Tillie nodded.

"Your toothbrush, comb, paste, makeup . . ."

"Yes, yes. I'm not going to China. I will be able to get everything I need in--."

"But the expense."

"You know very well the Colonel is taking care of all expenses. After all, I am working for him now."

"Oh God," Jane said, her eyes filling.

Tillie turned away to supervise the loading of the truck.

"Wait, wait."

"I'm still here, Jane." Tillie smiled.

Jane clutched at her elbow. "What about, er, you know."

"I know what?"

Jane pulled her sister's head down to whisper in her ear. "The code book."

"Of course. I have it safely stowed. Don't worry." The sisters looked at each other. "What about you, Jane? Do you have your book? We both need it, remember?"

"Yes, I have it and I shall practice so I am ready for your letters," Jane said, her eyes tearing. "I can't believe it. You are really leaving."

"It's a good thing we were forced to hurry so at the last minute," Tillie said. "Then we don't have time for long, sad goodbyes." She clutched Jane's shoulders and pulled her into a hug. "I will be fine. Please, please don't worry. Colonel Pratt will keep in close touch with you. As will I. I will write you daily, dear sister, I promise."

Jane looked about to cry.

"Please, Jane, please don't cry."

"I'm sorry, dear."

Tillie took her sister's hands in her own. "Let us pray that my, erm, mission, is fruitful and I can do some service for my country."

"Which country, Miss Tillie, you talkin' 'bout?" Zebula asked, apparently overhearing the last bit of their conversation.

"Why the country I was born and raised in. Canada."

"But I thought you were born here in Brattleboro."

"Nope. I'm a Haligonian." Tillie grinned. "You know where Haligonians are from?"

Zeb shook his head.

"Halifax."

"Halifax, Vermont? Why that's just up the road a piece."

"No, Halifax, Nova Scotia in Canada.

"Nova Scosha. That's purty far, ain't it?"

"It is," Tillie said. "A truck ride, a train ride and a boat ride, then another truck and, oh, well, yes purty darn far."

She smiled at him then hiked up her skirts, ducked her head, and climbed into the cab of the truck.

Zeb closed the door and said to the driver, "Now, Bobo, you be mighty careful with this here young lady, or you'll have me to answer to."

"Sure 'nuff, Mister Zeb, I be careful, don't you worry none."

Tillie leaned out the window. "Bye, Jane, Miss Herrick, Zeb." She waved.

They all shouted their farewells.

Bobo started the vehicle, cranked the shift into gear, and rumbled off down the dusty dirt road.

Tillie did not look back. She looked forward to her new life.

As a spy.

Chapter 12

Halifax, Nova Scotia, September 1917

Tillie lay in the unfamiliar bed, her stomach fisted into a knot. The house seemed deathly quiet but the blood racing in her veins churned like the rough sea in her ears. Her feet hung off the end of the bed, toes frozen since the covers did not reach. Sleep would never come.

She leaped up, grabbed her robe, and shrugged her arms into it. The freezing naked floor forced her to find her slippers, and still, shivering, she pulled the quilt off the bed and threw that around her as well. She peered out the window. Her view took her down Columbus Street and the four long blocks to the harbour. All appeared deserted in the moonlight.

She had been jittery since she moved into the Barnett's house three days earlier. The Barnett family--father, mother, two little boys and one little girl-- were quite welcoming and insisted she lodge for free in their upstairs room as long as she was teaching at the neighborhood school.

"It's catching up to you, Tillie," she whispered to herself. "Face it, you're in over your head and are scared witless."

Tomorrow she would start her formal job as schoolteacher at the Richmond School. She'd be a substitute until a regular full-time position became available. But Tillie had no intention of staying that long. It was not the teaching job that had her on edge. What made her think she could handle this sort of assignment? Her sister was right. She was impossibly naïve.

"Pah," she spat. "I'll find out what Colonel Pratt wants to know and be ready to return home to Vermont before spring."

The horizon rimmed with a soft reddish glow. Daylight wasn't far away. Tillie could see the shadows of large freighters, hovering like giant black whales on the water, waiting until morning to steer their cargo into port. An anti-submarine net stretched across the harbor entrance from George's Island to protect the ships and while she could not make out the wire mesh which was held to the bottom of the harbor by concrete weights, Tillie could see the large round floats at the surface that kept the nets upright.

She pulled the quilt tighter around her body and lit the gas lamp on the desk in the corner. The house was only partially electrified.

Retrieving the photographs from the desk drawer, Tillie willed her muscles to relax. She picked up a photo, smiled as she held it under the light. It was a picture of Jane and Penny, her golden retriever, both beaming into the lens. Another picture showed a bed of tulips, three in a row, four deep. Tillie remembered the vivid colors: yellow, gold, pink, red. Too bad the photograph revealed only shades of gray.

And the last photo she lifted was that of a tree. Not just any tree, but her beloved maple tree, which stood in front of the Inn, and had been growing for well over two centuries. She had taken the picture from a distance so she could get in all the branches, full of leaves reaching to the sky. Then she had carved her name on it. She and the tree were one. A deep sigh escaped her lips.

The photos were one reason she had been chosen for this job. Colonel Pratt had been impressed with her picture-taking prowess. He had even purchased her a new Kodak, a Number 1, Shutter Pocket Automatic. She could fold it up and hide it in a pocket, it was so compact. And the film, classic 120 roll film, could easily be mailed. Funny, she thought. The film was German, *Agfa-Gevaert*. And here they were at war with them. But then the Germans were masters of technology.

With a few hours of practice, Tillie had mastered its technique. The images were beyond her dreams. Clear, vivid, sharp as a Vermont winter's morning. Even distant subjects were visible . . . you could almost see water droplets flying off a wet dog.

She arched her back and tried to relieve the crick in her neck that seemed to have lodged there permanently. Her thoughts drifted to Colonel Pratt . . . Colonel Walter Merriam Pratt of U.S. Naval Intelligence. Chance brought them together last summer when she and Jane were invited to their home on Fox Farm Road. The Colonel and his wife, Irene, traveled from Boston to Brattleboro to summer each year.

They were a delightful couple and Tillie had enjoyed the soiree very much. Except for the questions that the Colonel had peppered her with once he learned she spoke German and that she was originally from Halifax. Since that party, her life had changed. If she worried that she would forever be a dull schoolmarm, she no longer entertained those concerns.

Tillie started at the sound of footsteps downstairs. The house was awakening. She gathered the photos and replaced them in an envelope in the drawer. Her eyes, stinging from the smoky lamp, spotted a small worn, leather-bound book. The code book the Colonel had given her. She leaned back in her chair, the quilt falling off her shoulders as daylight made its way into the room, warming the dark corners. Her mind reviewed what she had already learned.

The United States had entered the War in April, thanks to a deciphered code by the British, referred to as the Zimmermann telegram. She, Tillie Raymond, would similarly provide coded information to Colonel Pratt and the Allies, on German activities observed in and around Halifax Harbour, a strategic seaport and inroad to Canada and the United States.

She opened the code book now and for the hundredth time reviewed the basic instructions:

The use of this code for regular routine reports should be limited to actual necessities. Such reports should be transmitted by other means than radio or earth telegraphy. In Tillie's case by letter post.

Avoid use of words not in code book when other words with same significance are provided. Words spelled out, letter by letter, not only take time to code, transmit and decode, but they are one of the favorite points of attack by enemy code men.

Messages must be short. Several short messages will be less likely to be read by the enemy than one long one.

Simple word substitutions should be used so final message is unlikely to appear coded. For example, the phrase, 'tulips are in bloom' can be substituted for 'a ship is about to dock.'

Oh God, could she do this? She blew out a breath.

Sunrise was still twenty minutes away. She stood, stretched, and yawned then pulled her clothes from the wardrobe. Sunday, her third day in Halifax, Nova Scotia, was about to begin and she must make it a productive one. The sooner she garnered information on German undercover activity, the sooner she could return home to Vermont.

On the third day of her second month in Halifax, Tillie found herself downtown on an errand for the Barnetts. The day was blustery and she was nearly carried down the street on the wind. Once she found the address she sought, she opened the door and barely caught it before it crashed closed. She feared for its glass, but it held in place. She clutched her parcel and with one hand, brushed hair out of her eyes.

"Quite a day, isn't it?" a man's voice said.

She turned to see a tall, blond-haired man behind a glass counter. She gathered the bundle and walked toward him. "It's a regular hurricane outside."

She set the package gently on the counter and gave him a lopsided smile.

"So, what do we have here?" he said. "My guess is that it's a clock needing repair."

"Now why would you think that, since this is a clock repair shop?" She smiled, unwrapped the bundle to reveal a small mantel clock. "Are you the clock repair man?"

He beamed in return and, nearly eye to eye, he caught her gaze. They were an alpine blue flecked with mica, but they warmed with the smile. "I am the horologist, yes."

"Horologist, of course."

"Let's take a look." He set the protective cloths aside and stood the clock upright. She watched his strong, muscular arms beneath his rolled-up sleeves and followed his long deft fingers as they caressed the clock. She wondered if he played the piano.

"I'm told," Tillie said, "that it is a valuable piece. A Waterbury Mantel Clock?"

"You are correct. It is an 'Engelwood' model, most valuable." He turned the clock upside down and maneuvered the clasp, popping open the back. "Do you see this mechanism?" He pointed to a set of gears and bells.

Tillie leaned forward. "Yes."

"Well, the way this particular gear arrangement is mounted . . ."

She looked at him, their faces barely six inches apart.

"Ahh, never mind, really. Suffice it to say it is special." He cleared his throat. "Tell me what the problem is."

"It loses time. About five minutes every day." She paused, found his eyes on hers.

"Ironic, isn't it? With this new Daylight Savings-Time we just instituted in Nova Scotia. We set the clock an hour behind in the fall, so we gain an hour, but this clock loses . . . ach, no matter. Just my silly wanderings."

"Can you fix it?"

He stared at her. "Of course, yes." He set the clock gently back down on the counter. "It will take about three days, if that is satisfactory, Miss . . ?"

"Raymond. And you are?"

"I am Kurt. Kurt Fischer."

"Kurt Fischer, the horologist," she said. "I detect a slight accent, Mr. Fischer. Where are you from?"

"I am from Lucerne, in Switzerland."

"Hence the German accent," she said.

"Yes, I speak German. You recognize the accent?"

"My grandparents were from Strasbourg in--."

"Ahh, Alsace Lorraine. Yes, there they speak German and French as well, no?"

She narrowed her eyes. The fact that he spoke German gave her pause.

"You speak German and French, Miss?"

"Actually, I do."

"*Wie geht's*," he said.

"*Gut, danke*, Mr. Fischer. I am Tillie Raymond. I teach at the Richmond School."

"That's Miss Tillie, I think?" He smiled again, showing even white teeth and soft dimples in his cheeks.

"Yes, um, Miss."

They fell silent. Tillie wondered if he recognized her accent as American. But then most Europeans could not distinguish Canadian from American English.

"Shall I come back Saturday then to pick it up?" She poked loose strands of hair behind her ears.

He nodded, then grabbed a receipt book from a desk in the rear of the shop and began scribbling. "Here is a receipt for the clock in the name of Miss Tillie Raymond."

"The clock is not actually mine, but, well, that's fine. Do you know how much it will cost to repair?"

"Indeed, I do. It will cost you one dinner at Benito's Italian Café."

"Excuse me?"

"I'm sorry to be so forward, Miss, but I would so much like to see you again. I do not often get such attractive young lady customers. I mean if that is all right--."

"I, erm, I mean, yes, yes, it is all right." Was it?

"Good. That's settled. "I will bring the clock back to you next Saturday at 7:00 p.m. and we will go to dinner."

They stared at each other until, finally, she gave him her address.

Tillie turned with a swish of skirts and bolted out of the shop into a sunless, chilly day that had magically turned spring-like.

Late that night, a million thoughts looped through her brain. They kept returning to Kurt Fischer. She was foolish to accept a date with a man she'd met for a few short minutes. Still, it was only dinner and she wouldn't be alone. Kurt Fischer. She rolled the name over her tongue and it warmed her. Ridiculous.

But the real reason for her angst was not merely her attraction for him. Tillie recognized that her covert operations for Colonel Pratt had produced zero results. In the past month she had even enlisted the aid of her sixth-grade students, under the guise of a teaching exercise, to provide her accounts on the ships coming and going in the harbour. Noble Driscoll, Gordon Robinson, and James Pattison were eager to help. They reported on the cargo freighters, the relief vessels and smaller tugs that steamed up and down the narrows. As well as any questionable activities or characters they made note of on the docks. Tillie took photographs and wrote notes, checked with the dock master on the ship's cargoes and dock workers and sailors. But nothing, no one, proved suspicious.

She'd met several locals of German descent, but her investigations led nowhere and all trails soon went cold. She even monitored the post and had her students on the alert for railroad movements and new arrivals and departures in Halifax.

Then a communication arrived from the Colonel. Short-wave radio messages coming from somewhere in Halifax, had been intercepted by American Naval Intelligence. That was the extent of their knowledge. It was up to Tillie to find out who was sending the messages to German command.

Her mind flashed to Kurt Fischer and her heart sank in her chest.

She jumped up and went to her bookshelf where she had a book of maps and travel photos. She skimmed through the pages and came to Switzerland. Lucerne, a beautiful town on a huge lake. Tillie leaned back in her chair. Was Swiss German like Bavarian German? Could she tell the difference? Yes, she was sure. But then they wouldn't be speaking German since his English was perfect.

Was Kurt Fischer who he said he was? Could she take that chance? Oh, for heaven's sake, Till, you are getting paranoid. Still. She tossed the idea of writing to Colonel Pratt about him in her head. Yes, she should. No, not yet.

Not yet won the argument. Tillie would wait one more day until she dined again with Kurt before she sent off a coded message to the Colonel. After all, maybe Kurt was just the handsome, pleasant, bright young horologist he appeared to be, who had nothing to do with German intelligence or the war at all.

Then again. . .

Chapter 13

I t was early December in what was so far a mild winter for Nova Scotia. Tillie wondered if there would be snow for Christmas. In her mind's eye she could see Jane shoveling the front porch of the Ainsley Hill Inn with Penny scampering about in a foot deep of the white fluff. She wondered if Jane had deciphered her letters, not that there was much of interest in them. More urgent, however, she was despairing whether she would ever fulfill her assignment and catch a spy.

In recent messages from Colonel Pratt, she learned that the U.S. Naval Intelligence Service suspected there was a German spy in Halifax. Short-wave radio transmissions had been intercepted in part on three occasions. They could not pinpoint the location and it was up to Tillie to do so.

To date, Tillie could sum up on one hand how many bits of information she'd garnered about German activities since she'd arrived. There was one harbor pilot that appeared suspicious until she learned he was skulking about trying to hide his stolen booty from the law . . . and his wife. Then, Billy Mercer, one of the sixth graders in her class, loaned her his binoculars to scan the harbor docks. All she observed was the uploading of war relief cargo to the barges and freighters heading to France and Belgium. She kept track of the convoys of merchant ships, escorted by the military and reported those as well.

With the help of another student, Gordon Robinson, her favorite, she was able to reconnoiter the local railroad operation to gather data on the train schedules and passengers coming and going. All this intelligence she forwarded by code to Jane, who, in turn, handed it over to Colonel Pratt. Her replies were disappointing. In Jane's most recent letter, one line, translated from code, said it all: "We are counting on you to track down the short-wave messages emanating from N.S."

Tillie picked up her pace as she strode through the streets of Halifax, trying to avoid the muddy ruts from last night's rain. She'd promised the Barnetts she would purchase food supplies at the market, but her mind whirled in a state of palpable frustration.

Newsboys shouted out the headlines, mostly bad news about the war in Europe and the number of dead that day. Would it ever end? If it did, then her mission would be over and she could go home.

Tillie couldn't help remembering. Besides World War I, Halifax had been central to other tragedies. Five years earlier, the city served as the hub for recovery operations when the Titanic went down in the North Atlantic. She and Kurt had recently visited Fairview Cemetery where over one hundred bodies had been buried after being rescued and identified by Haligonians.

A pang of regret hit her. Kurt. If she left, would she see him again? She found herself thinking of him more and more. His intelligence, their conversations about the war, the world, books . . . his smile, the touch of his hand on hers. He opened doors for her, stayed on the outside of the walkways so horses or carriages or motorcars didn't splash mud on her. The soft way he looked at her. She felt the heat rush up her neck and onto her face.

At Fraser's greengrocer, she stocked up on as much as she could carry, then hurried home back up the long hill that was Columbus Street. It was Saturday and she wanted to bathe and wash her hair for her date with Kurt that night. He promised to bring the photographs he had taken of her and she was anxious to see them. She hoped she looked good so she could send one back to Jane.

Tillie no longer suspected him of being a spy. He was too . . . gentle, kind, sincere. And, oh, so handsome. Why then, did he not want his picture taken? He would always deflect her camera away when she tried, claiming shyness, or distracting her from the object of her camera. She shook her head.

You are reading too much into this, Tillie.

In fact, she had taken a photograph of Kurt with her pocket Kodak, when he wasn't aware. She'd had several copies printed so she could keep one, maybe send to Jane, and perhaps present one to Kurt as a small gift. Surely he would be pleased.

Yes, that's what she would do. Tonight. Wrap the photo and give it to him as a surprise, a token of their friendship. She smiled as she climbed the steps into the Barnett house.

The night ended in disaster.

Tillie paced her bedroom, her heart hollowed out. She had been terribly wrong about Kurt. How could she have believed him to be kind and gentle? When he opened her gift, the photograph of him, he erupted into a violent storm, ripping the image up over and over until only bits of paper survived. His face contorted into an angry red monster and he hissed at her. Like a snake.

Guests at nearby tables at the restaurant stared. He stood, threw money down on the plate in front of him and grabbed her by the arm. They left, Tillie mortified and heartsick.

When she finally screamed at him to stop his ranting, he turned to her. She backed away, now unsure of what he was capable of.

"I have made a terrible mistake. Thinking I could trust you, an American, a Canadian. Do not let me make another. Goodbye, Miss Raymond."

Tillie stood on the street, trembling, tears ready to burst. Kurt stalked off and left her in the dark.

Shaken, she decided not to go home in her current state. Instead she headed for the harbor. The night was mild and she would just wait out her humiliation on the pier.

There was something disturbing that stuck in her mind. It was not merely Kurt's rage, his shameful behavior. Or the spectacle he made of himself in public. Not even the fact that he clearly cared nothing about her as a person, a woman. No. Something more troubled her. But it would not come sharply into focus.

Tillie gazed out to the water, watching the ships as they awaited entry. She spotted the floats hovering like barracudas as they protected the safe harbour. It struck her all at once. It wasn't what Kurt said, or even how he said it. It wasn't even the aftertaste of his deceit . . . or her own recklessness.

They had spoken only in English since they had met. But his malicious tirade tonight . . . was completely in German.

At three in the morning, Tillie arose from a restless sleep. She donned her robe and brought her code book out of its hiding place between several books in a small bookcase. It had been wrapped in a leather binding with the title: *All the Seven Seas* by Harlan Sands. Had anyone looked through it, they would have seen immediately that this was not a novel at all. In fact, there was no such book and no such author. How canny of Colonel Pratt.

She sat down at the desk in the corner of the room. In one drawer was the inkpot that Colonel Pratt had given her. She kept it full so she could write to Jane every day.

Now, she picked up a piece of clean stationery and her Parker pen, also a gift from the Colonel, and dipped the nib into the ink.

6 December 1917

Dear Jane,

I hope this letter finds you well, dear sister, and anticipating the coming of the Christmas holidays. School has been going well, although some of the boys have been rowdy and testing me a bit. Not to worry, I can handle them fine. A few of the boys I've mentioned in past letters have a great interest in the ships in the harbour. They have been helping me observe the goings-on and I have been keeping a diary of such activity. Their sharp eyes see better than mine, I can tell you.

Referring to Colonel and Mrs. Pratt she wrote: *I expect you have heard from the dear couple on Fox Farm Road? I trust they are well.*

Tillie set her pen down and opened the code book. The final paragraph of the letter would be partially in code, including names. Translated, it would say:

I must report an incident worthy of note. The Swiss gentleman I mentioned in earlier letters raised my suspicions last night. I had taken a snapshot of him with my pocket camera and presented it to him as a small gift, a token of my admiration for him. He shocked me with his response. Not only did he not value the photograph as a gift, he ripped it into pieces and began shouting at me like I had done an onerous deed.

To be fair, he had asked me not to take pictures of him, but I believed he was joking. Why would he mind a photo of him when he had taken many of me? But that is not all, Jane. When he flew into this tirade, he fell back to his native language. He yelled and swore at me in German. And, if I know anything about languages, it was 'German' German, not Swiss German.

He stormed out of the café, leaving me in a state of utter humiliation. Now, I ask you again, why would someone be so averse to having a photo taken? Unless he was hiding something.

I have enclosed the photograph of him, since I made several copies, in the hopes he might be recognizable to our friend on Fox Farm Road. My guess is he is using an assumed name.

Tillie stopped writing. This wasn't proof that Kurt was a spy or a secret agent. It only meant he didn't want photos of himself and he had a nasty temper. She needed more. But what? She stood, went to the window, and looked out onto the deserted street, bathed in soft moonlight.

How could she find evidence that would prove what she knew in her heart to be true? Kurt Fischer was not who he claimed to be. The look in his eyes when he screamed at her was not simply anger. It was malevolent.

Tillie ran to her closet and began pulling out clothes. Dark clothes to wander about in the night and not be noticed. In five minutes, she was dressed. She intended to find that evidence. And the first place she would look was in the clock repair shop. *Kurt Fischer, Horologist.*

Quickly, she sealed up the letter, scribbled Jane's name, and address, added postage and slipped it into the mailbox in the upstairs hallway for Mrs. Barnett to send off the next day.

Before she left the house, she had one more task. Back in her room, she opened her overnight bag and retrieved a small bundle she hoped she'd never need. This was not from the Colonel, but from Zeb at the Inn. He had grinned when he gave to her, completely misunderstanding her reasons for the request.

It was a set of tools. Wrapped in a dirty flannel cloth, leaking oil, almost pocket-sized, but ideal for her night's mission. Breaking and entering.

The blood fizzed in her veins as Tillie made her way down Columbus several long blocks to Stanley Street. She turned right, looked over her shoulder and continued to the storefront she sought. Her heart pumped so hard now, it was thundering in her ears. She took in a few deep breaths, reached for the doorknob. Locked. Of course.

She moved to the side alley and tried the back door of the shop. Locked. She reached for her tools. The lock was a simple mechanism and she was easily inside. Tillie thanked her cousin Billy for all the practice she'd received picking locks at the Inn when guests had locked themselves out. Billy never taught her to pick the locks. Rather, he had always lost the spare keys, so the locks had to be picked. She grinned. She was a self-taught burglar!

She found herself in a back room behind the shop. Windowless, the dark enveloped her like a ghostly spirit. Tillie drew in some deep breaths and stood still for a minute to get her bearings. The only sound was the ticking of multiple clocks in the front room. Moonlight beamed in dimly through the shop windows and she made her way into the front. She glanced at the clocks and saw it was already five forty-five. How had so much time gone by? What time did Kurt come to work?

She quelled her panic and concentrated on her objective. She began in the back room. First she retrieved a hand torch, supplied to her by Colonel Pratt, and stocked with D batteries. Shining the light around the room, she spied a desk against the back wall.

Tillie lay the torch down and began going through the papers on the desktop. They appeared to be work-related, clock repair receipts. She opened drawers, pulled out ledgers, but nothing seemed out of the realm of possibility for a small business. Then she noticed photographs. Of herself. These were the photos

Kurt had taken of her. She thumbed through them. What was it? Something. She flipped through them again. It struck her. In every picture, there was a large ship behind her. A freighter, a cargo vessel, a steamer. The names of the ships, their flags were easily discerned.

Kurt was recording the harbour activities. And reporting to . . ?

She tucked the photographs in her coat pocket and stood gazing around the dark room. With the flashlight she combed every corner until she located another door. Leading to where?

Tillie turned the knob. Not locked. She stepped inside with the torch and realized she was on the top landing of a staircase. The basement. The blood in her body seemed to stop running. Her breath came hard. She walked down the steps, clutching the splintery handrail.

She shone the torch around the room when she reached the bottom until she found a light bulb hanging from the ceiling. She pulled the string and the basement lit up. For a frozen moment she listened for any sounds upstairs. None. Then her eyes caught a sight she'd hoped she wouldn't see. It was a large desk with various pieces of electrical equipment on top of it and attached to the wall behind it.

There was a switchboard with wires; transformers and condensers; dischargers, lamps. Tillie knew exactly what this was: a wireless telegraph. She stepped closer and looked down on the manipulating key, the way Kurt would transmit coded messages . . . to a U-boat out in the ocean.

Ice water ran down her spine as she pulled out her camera, took one picture then another. That's when she heard it. Something behind her. She whirled around to face Kurt Fischer at the top of the stairs.

Tillie backed up until she was against a wall. She said nothing but saw his hand come up. In it was a gun. Colonel Pratt had taught her about radios and he'd taught her about weapons as well. It had a four-inch steel barrel, a meticulously crafted wooden grip. It was aimed at her head. A German 9mm Luger.

She considered pleading for her life but looked at his eyes and knew it would do no good. The fear seemed to drain from her and all that she felt was infinite sadness. Sadness that she would never get back home to Vermont, to her sister . . . and to her beloved maple tree. Now why would she be thinking that? A loud boom and she no longer had to think.

Tillie would never know that in a few short hours, the largest explosion in the world at that time would wipe out thousands of lives and wreck to absolute destruction the entire town of Halifax.

Chapter 14

Helen

Brattleboro, Vermont, October 2018

They returned to the farmhouse and Honey began a frantic barking as she approached the maple tree.

"What's up, girl?" Helen followed the damp, red-haired retriever to the tree. Honey stretched her legs high up on the trunk.

Helen's heart ratcheted up a notch. Now what? She moved closer and peered at the bark. Nothing. She felt around with her fingers, even slid her glasses on to sharpen her view. Where was it?

"What are you doing, Helen?" Marie came out onto the porch.

"The name is gone, Marie." Helen shook her head.

"You mean Tillie?"

"Yes, she's gone." Honey whimpered as if she missed her.

Helen turned to Marie. "Did you know a Tillie? Ever hear of one who stayed here or—?"

"Nope, sorry. Can't help you there." Marie turned to go in, spun back again. "But it's not inconceivable that a Tillie stayed here, maybe a long time ago. There were lots of guests at the Inn. And workers."

"Were there any guest books from the Inn in the early days?" Helen asked. "You know when people checked in?"

"Might be, but Lordy knows where'd you find them."

"What about records of the staff?"

"No idea but there might be some paperwork in the attic. And that's a chore for a bunch of days." Marie sallied inside.

Helen looked down at Honey. "Well, we'll have to find out, won't we?" Helen touched the tree lovingly. "You're trying to tell me something again, aren't you?"

The old maple remained mute.

As dinner approached, Marie bustled about the kitchen.

"Can I help?" Helen said.

"No, no. What time is dinner?"

"Six o'clock." Helen studied Marie for a moment from the kitchen door. "It's early but how about I set the table? I'm sure Juli will be early. It feels like a special occasion, somehow."

"Oh, that it is, I promise you." Marie smiled.

Helen narrowed her eyes at her aunt.

A little after five Julianne came through the screen door. She carried a bulky canvas knapsack on her shoulder, which she dropped near the hall table then strode into the dining room.

"Hi sweetie," Helen said as she set glasses down in three places on the table.

"Hey, Mom, how's it going?"

"Great. Got lots to talk about and get your assistance on."

"Yeah? A new mystery, huh?"

Honey bounded into the dining room and Julianne leaned over to pet her. "What's it about? The mystery."

"We'll get to it." Helen watched her daughter rub Honey's belly. Juli wore her hair long and tied back with a clip. Her rust-colored sweater highlighted the reddish streaks in it and complemented her hazel eyes. So beautiful. But don't all mothers think that of their daughters?

Marie came out of the kitchen. "Hello, love," she said to Juli.

Julianne embraced her great aunt. "You're looking fit," she said.

"Pfft, yer jest like your mother. A superb liar."

After dinner, Marie pushed back her plate. Helen rose to clear the dishes.

"Wait, dear, not just yet" Marie said.

Helen sat down.

"I have something to tell you both. Helen, maybe you should pour us all some more wine."

Julianne got up and poured the Chardonnay for them. "You're not sick, are you?"

Marie smiled. "No, I'm not sick."

Helen felt her throat close.

"I have something that should have been said a long time ago, but, well, life kind of got in the way, and after a while, it didn't seem that important. Still, I want you to know." Marie looked at both women with a soft smile on her face. Now, I want you to promise me you won't interrupt for any reason. No questions, comments, nothing . . . until I'm finished. That clear?"

They stared at her.

"I mean it."

"Yes, of course," Juli said.

"I promise." Helen could barely get the words out.

Chapter 15

Marie

Brattleboro, Vermont, May 1945

She was almost sixteen when V-E Day was declared on May 8. The war in Europe was over. But that was not the reason Marie rejoiced. She was in love. For the last semester in high school, she had been secretly dating a senior. Edward Aldrich.

A twinge of guilt skipped over her heart. She had lied to Angie when the housekeeper had asked her to watch Joey one night. She had blamed it on a date with a fellow student. But that was only partly true. It was one of many dates, many hours, days, and nights they'd spent together. Hiding from her older brother, Robert, and his wife, Charlotte.

She could visualize Edward as if he were a photograph in her mind. His blond hair falling over his high regal forehead; his fathomless chocolate-brown eyes; his crooked smile that scrunched up his face; the sexy cleft in his chin. A worldly man, almost eighteen and graduating high school that month. Other boys paled in comparison to Edward. He was intelligent, strong, mature.

And he was leaving.

Edward had enlisted in the Navy, for while the war in Europe was over, the war in the Pacific was still raging.

"I have to do my part, Marie. Do you understand?"

She nodded her head but her heart felt like it had dropped out of her chest.

"Are you sure this is the right thing? I mean the war is almost over and--."

"Not when our boys are fighting the Japs, Marie. They are still dying out there. I cannot let them die and do nothing, ye see?"

He wiped the tears from her cheeks. "It will be all right. I'll be home before you know it and we can be married."

"Will we? Be married, I mean?"

"Of course we will. What did you think?"

She cried harder, thinking of the last three months they had spent together. Those nights in her bedroom, trying to keep her only family from finding out about their secret liaisons. Her face heated up just thinking about them.

"When do you sail?" she said between sobs.

"Well." He pulled her next to him on the bench in front of the old maple.

"My orders are to head to San Diego for basic training, then join the company in San Francisco where the ship will depart."

"San Fran--."

"Course, where do you think ships sail from? Anyway, I will join the men, get some months of basic training and be ready to sail in July."

"Where will you go once you're aboard?"

"Oh, places you might have heard of. Okinawa, Iwo Jima, the Mariana Islands . . . exotic places like that, see? This cruiser is on a mission to deliver some parts or equipment to some place in the Pacific. Don't know exactly where yet. All kind of hush hush. But it sounds important."

"Cruiser?"

"Ayuh. That's the class of ship. It's huge. Six-hundred feet long, 10,000 tons . . ."

He stopped, took her hands in his. "Don't ye see, my girl? I must go. I have to do something for my country. Something important. And then, who knows? With my naval training I may be able to get a good job when I get back."

Marie ceded a faint smile. "I do understand, Edward. Honest. I just, erm--."

"What do you just?"

"I just pray you'll keep your promise and come back to me."

"Why wouldn't I?"

She shrugged. "Maybe you'll meet a prettier girl in California or--."

"There's no prettier girl I want. I want you, Marie, to be my wife."

She leaned into his embrace and they sat like that for a long time.

Then he was gone.

Early in July, Charlotte shouted for her frantically. It was near midnight. "Marie, telephone, there's someone calling. Hurry."

Marie flew down the stairs from her bedroom, tugging on her robe. She took the phone from her sister-in-law, both bleary-eyed with sleep.

"Hello?"

"Marie? That you?" Edward's voice sounded scratchy.

"Edward, oh, Edward, is it really you?"

"Course it is, who else? Sorry, I just realized it's midnight where you are. Only nine o'clock here."

"You haven't sailed yet?"

"Tomorrow, bright and early. To someplace called the Tinian Islands. That's why I called. Wanted to say goodbye. How are ye, my love?"

Marie's heart brimmed with joy. "Fine, really fine. But I need to, erm, want to--."

"What's that? Can't hear you too well. Voice has to carry over thousands of miles, see. What do you want to tell me?"

"I just, um, that, I—."

"Marie, I have to go."

She heard scuffling and voices shouting over the line.

"This call is awfully expensive." His voice faded in and out. "I love you. I will write when I can. Take care of yourself."

The line went dead. Marie whispered too late. "Wait, I'm pregnant, Edward."

She sank down in the nearest chair. What had she done? Why hadn't she told him? But she knew why. She was afraid. What if he was angry? If he didn't want a child? If he decided not to marry her. No, she should have told him. Now he was off to war not knowing he was to have a child.

Marie dropped her head in her hands. Tomorrow he was off to the Tinian Islands on a secret mission. He assured her he would be safe. She believed him. After all, he was aboard the navy's finest heavy cruiser: the USS Indianapolis.

Julianne was the first to speak. "You were pregnant? What happened to the baby? Did Edward ever come back . . . I mean what . . ?"

Helen touched her daughter's arm. "The Indianapolis? Isn't that the ship that was torpedoed by the Japanese? Horrible story. It sank in minutes and the men who did not go down with it were thrown into shark-infested waters. Am I right?"

"Exactly right," Marie said. "Twelve hundred men sank with the ship. About three hundred survived a brutal ordeal in the deadly water for days, trying to stay alive."

"God," Juli said.

"Edward wasn't one of them?" Helen asked.

"No. I never found out until months later when they recovered the bodies they could. But no, he did not survive."

"Oh, Marie," Helen said. "I'm so sorry."

Marie nodded. "Yes, it was tragic. Another grim aftermath of a gruesome war."

Silence.

"Now, you'll be wanting to know what happened to the baby, I expect," Marie said. "This is really what I wanted to tell you."

She took a sip of her wine and sat up tall in the dining room chair. "It took a lot of courage to talk to Robert and Charlotte about it, but I had to, of course."

Julianne said, "Robert and Charlotte, my great grandparents?"

"Yes, and Helen's grandparents." Marie paused. "They were very understanding and we came to a most satisfying arrangement."

Helen leaned forward. "They took the baby." It was not a question.

"His name was Harrison. Yes, they had no children of their own. They became his parents. I became his aunt. Remember I was only sixteen, unmarried, no money. Nothing. It worked out well, really. With Harrison growing up at the Inn, I could be with him all the time."

"So that means . . . that you are really my grandmother, not my great aunt."

"Yes, my dear. That's right." Marie twisted her lips in worry.

Helen blew out a breath. "Whoa. That's a lot to take in."

Julianne looked from her mother to Marie. "But, well, does it really matter? It just means you are a bit closer in blood, right? Still family."

"I think you're exactly right, love." Marie turned to Helen with a look of expectancy.

So did Julianne.

Helen said nothing. She took Marie's hand and lifted it to her lips. She smiled through a veil of tears.

Chapter 16

Helen

Brattleboro, Vermont, October 2018

Foliage season had arrived in New England with a display of unimaginable color. Not all falls were this spectacular and Helen felt it was a portent of things to come. The golds were molten alloys like gaudy costume jewelry; the reds were deep and garish, and the yellows were brilliant and vivacious. All lay at Helen's feet in a soft, plush ground cover beneath her tree.

Honey leaped with enthusiasm when Helen suggested they go for a walk. The two ambled down the road behind the Inn enjoying the sun-sweetened air. The view from the top of a small rise: a vintage painting reflecting colors and shapes as would a Van Gogh. She looked down on the Inn and its surroundings and felt renewed love for her homestead. With her heart full, she called to Honey and they headed back.

Helen felt a tiny flutter in her heart, too, when she thought of her dinner date with Dave Major the next evening. He'd made reservations at Duo in downtown Brattleboro. She hadn't been there in years. But it was Dave she was eager to see. He had forgiven her her *faux pas* with Fred Denning and the Angie and Joey case. Next time, if she could control her natural instincts, she'd think before jumping into an interview in an ongoing investigation.

Watching the light play on shadows outside her window, Helen sat at her computer and, using her elite membership to worldwide newspapers, she scanned through for articles pertaining to any Mathilda or Tillie that might be mentioned in regard to the Inn. One caught her eye.

Brattleboro Daily Reformer

December 9, 1917

Mysterious Death of Brattleboro Woman in Halifax Explosion

Following the disastrous explosion of two ships in Halifax Harbour, the body of a young woman was found in the rubble of what was once the Main Street shops. Thanks to the bravery of a young boy, a sixth grader at the Richmond School, Gordon Robinson, who stumbled across a body of a woman he recognized as his teacher, Miss Mathilda Raymond, of Brattleboro.

The body, however, could not be returned to family in Vermont until a full criminal investigation was held in Halifax, Nova Scotia. Apparently Miss Raymond did not die in the explosion or its aftermath. Rather, a bullet had entered her forehead, instantly killing her. She was soon after buried in debris from the explosion. Authorities in Halifax plan to investigate the murder, but under the circumstances, with dead and injured estimated at over 10,000, plus hospital facilities damaged and a dearth of medical personnel, it will be difficult, if not impossible, to resolve the case.

Mathilda Raymond. This was *her* Tillie. It had to be. How could she find out? Were there any descendants in town? She could check with Marie and Dave.

And the attic. Full of ancient memorabilia from the early days of the Inn begging to be brought to light. That huge task would require help. Julianne had offered and Helen was happy to take her up on it.

One more thing had piqued her interest. The Halifax explosion. Helen knew nothing about it, never even heard of it. Her blood sizzled with the passion of the hunt.

The next afternoon, she joined Julianne in the attic of the old Inn. The plan was to search for evidence of guest books and staff records and rescue them from obscurity. Somewhere in the archives, the name Tillie would appear. Like it had on the tree.

Julianne was already upstairs sifting through cartons and trunks filled with documents.

"Any luck?" Helen asked.

"Not yet but I do have these piles in chronological order."

"That's something."

"With the article you found, we at least know what time period to search. December 1917. Interesting. I'd never heard of the disaster until a book recently arrived at the bookshop. *The Great Halifax Explosion*."

"That's a coincidence."

"I think it was written to commemorate the 100th anniversary a few years ago."

"I'll bet Marie knew about it." Helen sneezed at the dust flying in the air and pulled over a box. She sat on a small chair that was up in the attic and matched Julianne's. In the box were envelopes, folders, logbooks, and documents.

Helen flipped through the ragged carton and pulled out a register of employment records at the Inn from 1915-1920. "Naturally, they're not alphabetical." Helen ran her finger down the pages slowly. "Nothing. Evidently, Tillie didn't work here."

"I think they were guests." Julianne reached for a long green record book, badly beaten up. "Here. Jane and Mathilda Raymond, guests of the Inn for the years 1915 to 1917. Occupation: teachers at West Brattleboro Academy."

Helen and Julianne raised eyebrows at each other.

"So, they stayed as guests at the Inn and taught just up the road," Helen said. "That makes sense. The article says that Tillie's body was found by one of her students."

"So she must have left Brattleboro and gone to teach in Nova Scotia," Julianne said.

"Keep looking. Maybe they left something of themselves behind, letters, diaries, anything." Helen stood up, stretched, and wandered through the piles. "Makes me tired." She spied an old hatbox in a far corner. "What fun, a hat from the early 1900s." When she pulled the round lid off, Helen discovered no hat, but a small shoe box. "Hm, what's this?" She pulled it out.

"Have you come across a Colonel Walter Merriam Pratt?"

Julianne looked up. "No."

"His name is on this box." Helen took the cover off. Inside were two bundles of letters and a small leather-bound book. She pulled them out.

"What's that?"

"Letters. One bundle is addressed to Jane Raymond." Helen opened one. "It's signed Tillie. These must be her letters to her sister from Nova Scotia."

"The other?"

Helen pulled out a letter. "The others are from Jane to Colonel Pratt on Fox Farm Road. Which means the Colonel must have returned all the correspondence back to her."

"Fox Farm Road. I know it. That's off of Black Mountain, isn't it?"

Helen didn't respond. She was thumbing through the small book.

"What's that?"

"If I'm not mistaken, it's a code book. A dictionary of sorts to teach you to write and read in code."

"You mean code as in military?" Julianne collapsed on the floor in cross-legged style next to her mother. "So, does that mean that the sisters were . . . spies? Reporting to this Colonel?"

Helen gazed over her daughter's shoulder at the dusty particles dancing about under the lightbulb. "It was 1917. World War I was raging in Europe and the U.S. had just entered the conflict."

"Why Halifax? Was Nova Scotia involved?"

"Not sure, but it evidently has a significant harbor. Big enough for U-boats to be patrolling, perhaps?"

"Jeez."

"It's beginning to make sense," Helen said more to herself. She glanced at her wristwatch. "I've got to get ready--."

"Yes, for your date," Julianne said with a broad grin.

The women descended the stairs.

"Now don't make more of it than it is. We are colleagues, friends, is all."

"Um hm," Julianne said.

"Um hm, what?" Marie said coming from the kitchen.

"Um hm to her date with Dave."

"Oh yes, um hm, ditto," Marie said.

"Oh for heaven's sake." Helen tromped off to her bedroom. She turned. "Thanks for helping, Juli.

"No problem. Back tomorrow."

"Tomorrow?"

"Yeah, Bella's at the bookstore and you need my help. Besides, I want to hear about your date."

Helen opened her mouth but Julianne was already out the door.

Marie just shook her head and smirked.

At dinner that night, Helen posed the mystery to Dave. She left out the more mystical aspects related to the tree but brought out the article she had printed from the online newspaper. "Any chance you would have records that would give more information?"

"Like who killed her?" He smiled.

"Like that." She smiled back and told him about the letters and code book.

"Code book? What was this Colonel's name?" Dave pulled out a notebook and pen.

"Walter Merriam Pratt."

"Let me see what I can find out. Sounds like quite a puzzle you have. How did you find out about this Tillie anyway?"

Helen debated whether to mention the old maple. What could she lose? Dave would think her bonkers and that would be that.

"Her name was carved on the big old maple in front of my house."

"Really? You mean like Sal and Angie's initials?"

"Right." Helen chickened out and didn't tell him those initials had disappeared and reappeared once their murders were solved. Or that Tillie's name had disappeared and that she hoped it would reappear once she solved her murder. Wow, she really was cuckoo when she reflected on it.

"Sounds like your tree has a thirst for justice," Dave said.

You'll never know how right you are.

The next morning, Helen lay in bed planning her day. The first thing she realized was that her energy level had rocketed up tenfold. She slept better and felt rested in the morning, feelings that she hadn't experienced in months, maybe years. She knew why. Purpose. She had a purpose to her days.

Honey poked her head into the room and began whipping her tail around eagerly when Helen smiled at her. Downstairs, she met Marie in the kitchen and minutes later, Julianne bounded in.

"Goody, breakfast," Julianne grinned and kissed Marie and Helen on their cheeks.

"You're both in a good mood," Marie said, "and I doubt it's my flapjacks."

"It's absolutely your flapjacks. Grandma," Helen said.

Marie scoffed and clunked a large jar of maple syrup on the table.

Helen and Julianne smiled at each other.

"What's the plan?" Marie said.

Helen began. "We know that Mathilda, Tillie, Raymond, was murdered just before the Halifax explosion on the morning of December 6, 1917. The explosion wreaked such havoc that, no doubt, much evidence was lost or buried in the debris. Still, we have to find out what happened to her body. Was she autopsied in Halifax, Brattleboro, or not at all? Where was she buried? Were there any follow-ups to the story on her death?"

"Can Dave check on that?" Marie said.

"Yes, and he will. We talked about it last night."

"Speaking of--."

"Never mind, Julianne. It was just a dinner date, nothing more. We spent most of the time talking about this case."

"Hmm," Julianne began. Marie smiled.

"Never mind you two, stick to the subject."

"Okay, next on the list." Julianne held her pen ready.

"Today we go through Tillie's letters to Jane, and Jane's letters to Colonel Pratt. By the way, Dave is also going to find out who this Colonel Pratt is."

"Do you really think Tillie was a spy for him, for the military?"

"It's the only thing that makes sense."

"All right," Marie said. "Even if you find out what happened to Tillie, how on earth are you going to find out who the perp was?"

"Perp?" Julianne looked at Marie.

"Sure. I watch all those CSI programs. I know what a perp is."

The three smiled.

"That's a good question," Helen said. "That will prove exceedingly difficult. Maybe if we can learn what kind of bullet she was shot with . . ."

"The poor boy that found Tillie's body, her student, what was his name? Her student, right?" Julianne asked.

"Gordon Robinson," Helen said.

"Gordon Robinson?" Marie said. "Really? He was her student?"

"Yes. Why?"

"I know Gordon Robinson. Their family lived in Halifax for generations. I met them on vacations there, summer camp, in fact. Great times. Such a beautiful place. And Gordy was a good friend. We still keep in touch, well, once in a great while."

"Wait, I'm confused. You couldn't possibly mean the Gordon Robinson that found his teacher . . ." Julianne said.

"Oh no, no. His son. The Gordon that found Tillie was much older than me. He had a son, Gordon the second. I had met him, Gordy's dad. I never heard him talk about the disaster, but Gordy told me stories about how it affected his dad. Especially finding his teacher like that. Seems he was never the same. Had sleeping problems, hearing problems, you know?" Marie paused. "Very sad. Gordy said sometimes he would find his dad crying when he thought no one was around."

"I imagine it was very traumatic," Helen said. "I can't believe you actually know the family, the man that found Tillie."

"His son, Gordy's, about my age now and sharp as a tack. Least he was when I last talked to him, around the holidays."

"Any chance you can call him now?" Helen said.

"Ayuh. I will do that." She stood. "It's only an hour later there. Keep your fingers crossed little Gordy's not dead and gone." She stopped. "Nah. I'd know. They would've called me if he passed on."

Helen was on pins and needles while she waited.

Marie came back a few minutes later. "Good news and bad news. Gordy's still alive."

"Bad news?" Julianne said.

Helen held her breath.

"He's out on the farm checking the cows and won't be back home until dinner."

"Well, that's not so bad," Helen said with a sigh of relief. "Maybe we'll have our answers tonight."

Julianne laid her hand on Honey's head which was resting in her lap.

The three Ainsley women fell silent, each in her own thoughts.

A few minutes later, Julianne asked, "What are you thinking, Mom?"

Helen took in a deep breath. "That our wise and venerable maple tree has many secrets to reveal."

Chapter 17

Gordy

Halifax, Nova Scotia, December 6, 1917

Gordon Robinson struggled from the depths of a dream to semi-consciousness. Only to open his eyes and find himself awake. . . in a living nightmare. His head pounded to the drum of a Sousa march and his ears felt hollowed out like a dead log.

Gordy, at twelve years old, was the go-to expert on science fiction at the Richmond School, well, in the whole town of Halifax. He could name twenty famous authors, their books, even their characters. Like Jules Verne's *From the Earth to the Moon*, or H.G. Wells' *War of the Worlds*. He could recite every detail of plot, setting, dialogue, and completely spoil the ending for the listener.

But this. This was not science fiction.

He pushed himself up from the ground, rubbed his eyes and cried out when a burning grease ran into them. Blinking until he could see, he tried to move his legs, but one was caught on something. He looked to find that chunks of cement had his foot wedged. He had difficulty catching a breath, for the air was filled with dust and soot and smoke. Finally, Gordy pulled his foot free and thanked God that it was not broken.

Once again he looked around. How did he get here, on the sidewalk in the middle of . . . the apocalypse. That's where he was. He must still be in a dream. Somehow he knew he wasn't. He sat still, trying to remember. Strange sounds came from all around him. They sounded like they were from far away. Or under water. Or in a cave. They reverberated in his head. Was he suddenly deaf and the sounds came from inside his head? Get up.

Gordon Robinson pushed to his feet, tried to steady himself and get his bearings. He gazed around. Where was he? This was not his school. Not his town. This was another planet. A planet that had been destroyed by some powerful ray gun or accelerator bomb. For the first time in a long time, since now he was almost a grown man, he longed for his mother. He gulped back tears.

He took a few steps despite the dizziness. Looked for something he could recognize. As he moved, he began to hear sounds, more distinct sounds. Crying, shouting, coughing. Whooshing sounds of a fire taking hold. Water running.

He stood still and tried to spot the harbour. It would be straight on and downhill from the school. He was at school that morning, wasn't he? In the direction he felt sure was the water, Gordy saw only ash, grit, and fire. He couldn't see ships for the smoke. He took one step at a time toward the water, not knowing where else to go. The buildings around him were gone and he had no point of reference.

As he stumbled down the street . . . Columbus? . . . he heard crying but couldn't pinpoint the direction. He tripped over debris, not realizing it was the remains of a human body. Kept going. A sign lay on the ground in front of him, Olson's General Store. It had been ripped from its post. So, he must be on Main Street, downtown.

His brain was so hazy, he couldn't begin to work out what might have happened. Just keep going, he told himself, until he ran into someone. Another shop lay in a pile of rubble, shattered glass everywhere. He moved toward it, not knowing why, and tripped over a man lying in pieces. Torso here, arms there. Gordon stared down. Not possible, no, no, no. He squeezed his eyes shut and when he opened them, he noticed something familiar. A red dress. Under what looked like a desk. A woman dead in the rubble.

But not any woman. He recognized the dress. It was his teacher, Miss Raymond. Oh God, he liked her so much. She had enlisted his help to hunt for German spies. Now she . . .

Gordon rushed to her. Maybe she wasn't dead. He reached her and knew immediately it was hopeless. Still he shoved the desk off her and rolled her over. He gasped when he looked at her face, her lovely face. Marred by a hole in the forehead. What? It was the Germans. It had to be. We are at war!

Gordon's brain suddenly clicked in. He looked around. Clocks everywhere, broken and smashed. This was the clockmaker's shop. It dawned on him. Germans. They did this. He spied what was left of a short-wave radio in the wrecked space. What was Miss Raymond doing here? At this time in the morning, right before school was about to start? And why was she killed?

Gordon found himself crying and sending more hot soot into his eyes. He had to get help. Suddenly he felt so tired, he could barely lift a leg. But this was Miss Raymond and he had to move. A cry burbled out of his mouth. He leaped up and began running with all the strength he could summon up the street.

As he ran, he passed several people. In place of eyes they had holes with blood running down; they walked in a stiff gait, arms reaching in front of them. Zombies. From Voodoo land. Gordon ran past them, gasping and crying.

"Help, please, someone, help."

No one answered or even looked at him. He sprinted up the hill in the direction of the school. Would anyone be alive there? A voice called out.

"Here, here." Gordon raced toward it. "Help, please, my teacher, she's, she's . . ."

"Easy now, boy," a man said. Gordon could not see his face, through all the black running in his eyes. "Are you a policeman? Please, I need help."

"We all need help, boy," the man said, and sank to the ground.

"No, don't, please come with me."

The man burst into hysterical laughter and Gordon backed away.

Part of the Richmond School was still standing. Gordon looked up the hill and made his way there. When he reached the brick structure, he realized the front wall was a façade. Everything behind it lay in ruins.

He tore his way through the rubble until he found his classroom. Miss Raymond's classroom. In the far corner, was a small cot used for classmates when they felt ill. Shockingly, it was in one piece complete with thin mattress and pillow. It was covered in soot and dust. Gordon walked over and stared down. Then he lay down on it, curled up like a fetus, and sobbed until he passed out.

"Wake up, kid, wake up." Someone shook him. Gordon awoke swinging his fists.

"Easy now, you're okay, are ye?"

"Who are you? A policeman?"

"No, a teacher. Wait, you. Gordy? Gordy Robinson?"

Gordon threw his legs over the cot. "Yeah, it's me. Who are you?"

"Duncan Ritchey, Gordon, social studies. I hardly recognized ye."

"Mr. Ritchey, oh God, what happened? Did the Germans bomb us? They musta done, yeah?"

"Not sure, Gordy. But there was some kind of gigantic explosion down in the harbour, see? Are you hurt at all? I can't tell, with this black soot all over us."

Gordy grabbed Mr. Ritchey's hand and began pulling. "You've gotta help me. It's Miss Raymond, she's hurt real bad."

"Where is she? Take me to her," Ritchey held onto Gordon and they both jogged as fast as they could down the street.

Gordon stopped short.

"What? Are we going the wrong way?"

"She's dead. I remember now. Miss Raymond is dead."

"Are you sure? How do you know?"

Gordon looked up at Mr. Ritchey. "She had a bullet in her head." He pointed to his forehead.

"What? That can't be right. Maybe it's a piece of shrapnel that flew at her from the explosion. Can't be a bullet, now, can it? Doesn't make sense. Take me to her, come on."

Gordy felt a glimmer of hope.

They picked up their pace and reached Tillie Raymond in five minutes.

Ritchey knelt down and lifted her into his arms, wiped the dirt and debris off her face. Then he set her back down.

"You were right, Gordy. She's dead. Shot. That's no kind of shrapnel. I don't understand. Why would . . ? We need the police."

He stood next to Gordy and man and boy gaped, open-mouthed at their city. Now that the smoke had cleared some, they could see the gruesome destruction. Bodies and parts of bodies lay everywhere. People that were ambulatory were in shock and just wandered the streets, calling for loved ones, unable to be of use to the wounded. Screaming, bawling, shrieking . . . unearthly calls, could be heard three-hundred and sixty degrees around them.

Finally, in the distance, they could hear the wail of a siren. An ambulance, one lone ambulance. Where was it going?

"How will we ever get help?" Gordy murmured to himself.

Chapter 18

Helen

Brattleboro, Vermont, October 2018

That evening, Marie filled Helen in on her phone conversation with Gordy Robinson the second.

"Gordy was eager to talk about it. His father was a hero, had articles written about him and won citations. He found Tillie's body, after all, and uncovered a German spy nest."

"It's fantastic that he passed the story down to his son." Helen poured some coffee and refilled Marie's cup. "I think many people would be reluctant to relive such a tragic event."

"When I think about that explosion, I just shudder," Marie said. "Can you imagine? Poor Tillie."

"Actually, Tillie was lucky in a way. She was dead before she had to experience that horror."

They heard a knock on the front door and Dave Major walked in.

"Evening, ladies," he said.

"Grab a cup," Marie said and Dave did. He sat at the kitchen table with them, smiled at Helen.

"I have some news for you about Colonel Pratt."

"Yes," Helen said leaning towards him.

"He was attached to U.S. Naval Intelligence, high level, and ran the North American Military Cipher Program."

"Cipher?" Marie said.

"Yeah, codes. He was in charge of organizing the agents on the lookout for German spies in Canada and the eastern shore of the U.S."

"Funny," Helen said. "Vermont has no shore except a river."

"His main residence was Boston, so it makes sense. Did you ever find any letters or documents from him to Tillie?"

"Actually, he corresponded with Tillie's sister, Jane, so there was no direct contact between the Colonel and Tillie." Helen got up, left the kitchen, and returned with a small shoebox.

"Tillie wrote to Jane, Jane wrote to the Colonel. These are letters from Tillie to Jane during her time as a 'spy' for the Colonel. One is significant."

"Oh?"

"Tillie gushes on about a Kurt Fischer, a Swiss clock-maker she met in Nova Scotia. They had a bit of a romance, it seems, until she began to suspect him of being a German agent."

"Why?"

"Tillie tells Jane that Kurt slipped one time and spoke *German* German rather than his usual *Swiss* German. Apparently she knew the difference since she was born in *Alsace-Lorraine* where they spoke German from different countries as well as French."

"All right."

"She decided to do some snooping and started in his shop, the clock repair shop, in the downtown area of Halifax."

"And did she find something?"

"A short-wave radio and a book of German military codes."

"How do we know that?" Dave said. "I mean, she couldn't have sent a message since she was dead."

"Gordy saw it too, when he found her," Helen said.

Dave leaned back with an exhale. "Wow."

"Kurt Fischer must have caught her and killed her," Marie said. "Then the great explosion ended the story."

Dave looked down into his cup. "Of course, they had no way of knowing they would both be dead very soon."

"Just a few hours later," Helen said.

"I read about the explosion," Dave said. "Fascinating. Two ships playing chicken in the harbour. One carrying tons of ammunition. Both lost."

"So did about ten thousand people. Two thousand died instantly." Helen shook her head. "The whole town was obliterated."

"Guess there were articles every day in the Daily Reformer," Marie said. "Boston sent huge relief efforts, . . . supplies, medical personnel, food, and all. Don't remember if Vermont ever sent any. Must've."

"Boston receives a giant Christmas tree every year from Halifax, even to this day. To thank them," Marie said. "Quite a beautiful ceremony every year."

They fell silent.

"What evidence were they able to collect on her murder? Do you know?" Dave said.

Helen pulled out another letter from the box. "This is from Colonel Pratt to Tillie's sister, Jane." She read:

18 December 1917

My Dear Jane,

I wish to convey my sincere and deepest condolences to you and your family at the loss of your dear sister, Mathilda. She was, indeed, a brave and dedicated operative. Her government is grateful to her for taking on a covert mission during these dangerous times and providing us much useful intelligence.

Unfortunately, we were unable to confirm the identity of her killer. We know he was a German agent, because of the short-wave radio, the German military cipher book, and the German Luger bullet extracted from her body. However, our records show no one named Kurt Fischer in our archives. The name was an alias.

I hope you are well. Again, I regret being unable to attend the burial service but duty called. I expect Mrs. Pratt and myself will see you in the near future at our home on Fox Farm Road.

I wish you the best and trust you have the consolation of knowing your sister was a courageous hero in service to her country.

Yours truly,

Colonel Walter Merriam Pratt
U.S. Naval Intelligence
Washington, D.C.

Dave shook his head. "Too bad they couldn't identify him but not surprising he used an assumed name." His cell rang and he listened for a minute, then stood. "Well, I'll leave you ladies for now. It's not high-level espionage, but Brattleboro has its crime too."

She watched Dave leave.

"Nice guy," Marie said.

"Yes." Helen blushed and was gratified Marie didn't point it out.

Honey came into the kitchen, nails clicking on the hard floor.

"That's very disappointing, "Marie said. "We still don't know the name of Tillie's killer."

Helen shook her head. "No, and the great maple confirms that. Her name has not reappeared."

Helen spent the next two hours researching newspaper reports following the Halifax explosion. The only mention of Tillie Raymond in the news was a small piece about her body being returned to Vermont and buried in nearby Mather Cemetery.

"We'll have to go visit her, won't we?" Helen said to Honey.

"First, we've got to find out who Kurt Fischer was. Somehow. He killed her, I know he did."

She went back through every letter she could find between the sisters and Colonel Pratt. Nothing.

"Helen?" Marie called from the top of the stairs.

"Yes?"

"Gordy called back. He thought of something he'd forgotten. A photo."

"What?" Helen ran up the stairs.

"Right," Marie said. "He forgot to mention that he had a photograph his father had taken. A photo of his favorite teacher with her beau, standing on Pier 6 in front of the British cruiser, the HMS Highflyer. He couldn't resist, getting a snap of both his teacher and the famous ship."

"Oh my God, Marie. A photograph of Tillie and Kurt Fischer?"

Sounds like Gordon the first took it on the sly, not wanting his teacher to know. His son thought he had a crush on her."

"This may be the answer," Helen said. "Can he--?"

"Before you go on, yes, he is sending it overnight priority, life, or death, or whatever it's called. He heard the urgency in my voice. Plus, I think he wants to get a mention if the story gets into the news."

Helen laughed. "He can get that mention. This is amazing."

"He wants it back, by the way. The picture."

"And he will get it back. Hopefully, with the news that it helped track down a secret German spy."

Helen's mind whirled with possibilities. How can she identify the killer from a century-old photograph?

The answers came quickly. Over the years, Helen's mysteries had taken place in myriad countries around the world. Her research had brought her into contact with experts in many fields: forensics, pathology, art, history, and photography.

Now, through her contact in Berlin, Germany, a professor of Germanic history, the man in Gordy's photograph, alias Kurt Fischer, was digitally matched with facial recognition software to one Gerhardt Franz Koehler, a trained operative for the Imperial German Navy.

"It was easy to see the resemblance between this Kurt Fischer and Gerhardt Koehler in his graduation photo from the Naval Academy," the professor had told her.

"Furthermore, in 1917 Koehler had been assigned as naval communications liaison for U-boat 631, off the shore of Halifax, Nova Scotia, Canada.

After the explosion he never contacted his superiors, and it was assumed he had been killed."

Tillie's killer was identified. Helen felt a joyous vindication.

She pulled on a jacket and called Honey. The two went out to the tree. Helen's eyes and fingers roamed the tree's trunk. Honey stood by Helen's side, calm. Suddenly her ears perked up and she whined.

"What is it?" Helen asked. "What do you see, girl?"

Honey leaped up onto the trunk as if she wanted to climb. Helen followed with her eyes, as Honey's front legs stretched part way up. Helen squinted, the cold wind making her eyes weepy. She could see nothing. Honey kept up her whining, dropped her legs, whirled in a circle. Then she stretched her legs up again and went still.

Helen looked down at the photograph of Tillie she'd been holding, then back up at the tree. Her eyes told her what her mind could not grasp.

As if in slow motion, the name *Tillie* shimmered to life.

Chapter 19

Abigail

Brattleborough, Vermont, July 1856

Abigail Pinn ran 'til her lungs ached and her heart near exploded. The snarling and growling came closer and her feet tripped up in her skirts. She made it to the stream and crashed across, low-lying branches scratching at her arms, sharp rocks slicing at the thin soles of her shoes. Finally across, she sprinted up a rocky incline to the top and stopped short. Below her spread a splendid meadow, lush and verdant, as far as she could see. To the right, in the distance, hundreds of fuzzy white shapes dotted the landscape. Sheep.

Abby turned to her pursuers too late. Two high-spirited, dirty, black mongrels launched themselves, full body, at her, catapulting her into the tall grass and slobbering her with kisses. She screamed and rolled away, which only made them pounce on her again.

"Enough, you crazy beasts." But she laughed too hard for her words to have much effect. "Stop, now, ya hear? Stop." The dogs backed away and began romping with each other. "My gawd, you got me all wet and slimy, durn devils."

She stood up, brushed herself off. The sun had topped the rise and she held her hand up to shade her eyes. The day promised to be hot again. She sucked in the smell of summer in Vermont, loving every minute of it.

In the distance she could make out three long wagons awaiting their loads of hay. Jack Tyler owned the neighboring farm and he and his men had been scything the crop for days. Now, as they whistled *Nelly Bly*, they forked it onto the wagons to carry to the barn. Abby hummed the tune, enjoying its upbeat cadence. She could smell the sweet, sun-dried forage from where she stood. The sounds, sights, and scents made her dizzy.

Gazing down the hill she grinned at the sight of her home. Well, not hers, really, but still. The Ainsley Hill Inn and Tavern. Her home for going on eight years now since she was eleven. She bent down and reached for a red clover to chew on. Bees buzzed around her head.

"Which reminds me, I best be getting back there. Chores starting 'bout now. And Pattie and Hattie will be wakin' up real soon." She hitched up her skirts and started across the meadow. She turned. "Rufus, Josie, let's go now, hear?"

Taking the short trail home, she picked up her pace. The dogs were out of sight, racing home for their breakfast. She was hungry too but would never give up this morning ramble while the weather held.

As she approached the Inn, she sniffed the first hint of honeysuckle and mock orange shrubs, which grew by the side fence. But her eyes were drawn to her favorite living thing in all the world. She had fallen in love with it when she first arrived at the Inn and her love had grown and matured over the years. Her enchanted maple tree . . . ancient and wise, seventy feet tall, its branches spread out over half the width of the house. What did Miz Sara call it? Matriarchal. The mother of all trees.

As Abby approached the Inn, a tall, bony, scarecrow of a woman wearing a red kerchief on her head pushed open the makeshift cheesecloth screen door and barked, "Where you been, heaven's sake, girl? I've already started cookin' and the young ones startin' to wind themself up." She stopped and studied Abigail's smile. "An', what's that grin for? You think I'm jestin'?" Essie Lee shook her head. "I swear, dat girl is moonin' over her tree again. Lawd." The door crashed closed behind her. "Mind you close the screen propoly to keep them bugs out." The words drifted out behind her as she made for the kitchen.

Abigail followed her onto the porch and through the door into the main hallway. She closed the door as ordered then headed into the kitchen where she got breakfast for Rufus and Josie.

"Those dang dogs always come first, don't cha' know?" Essie clucked. But a smile creased her sweat-covered face, the color of chestnuts, and she couldn't hide her satisfaction. She loved those dogs as much as Abby did.

Abby grabbed a bowl and ladled out some hot cereal for her own breakfast, adding honey, a chunk of bread, and a mug of coffee on the side. A thunderous thump sounded overhead and a shrill shriek followed. Abigail gulped her breakfast down and raced up to meet the mayhem. The day had begun.

At noon, Essie summoned Abigail into the kitchen.

"You like to take over this here lunch basket for the boys in the field. Miz Tyler gone for a week visiting her nephew up in St. Albans and there's no one to get them midday meals. So's I offered."

"Where's Cora?" Abby referred to Jack Tyler's housekeeper and cook.

"She's done visiting her sister in Rutland."

"Sure, I'll go." Abby picked up the basket and peeked inside to spy two loaves of bread, a jar of molasses, and a large ham hock, already sliced. Also stuffed in were peaches from the orchard. "On my way."

She took the east-west trail which would bring her close to where she spotted the wagons that morning. The sun heated up the day early. She stopped, wiped the sweat off her face with the back of her hand. As she approached, she noticed there was only one man still working. The others were nowhere to be seen.

The man looked up from his labors and stopped short. He stabbed the pitchfork into a bale and backed away.

"Hey, no, don't go," Abby said. "I just brought you some food." She tried not to let her surprise and discomfort show. He was the first colored man she'd seen in a long while.

They stared at each other.

"Uhm, I can't, I mean, that's not fer me, the food . . ." He backed further away.

"Well, it is. It's for all the workers at the Tylers. That's what you are, right? Worker?"

He didn't answer.

"Okay, look. I'm gonna take out some food for you, then I'll bring the rest into the house. You stay put." Abby pulled out some food and wrapped it in a large cloth, gave it to the man. She brought the basket to the house.

A man stepped outside onto the porch. "Hey, Miss Abby, how you doing?"

"Hello, Mister Tyler, sir. I'm jest fine. Brought some lunch for you, working so hard and all."

"That's right nice of you." Tyler took the basket.

"I, er . . ."

"What?" he said.

"I gave some of it, just a little to that worker over there. Hope that's okay?"

Tyler let out a guffaw. "Why sure, Miss. That's okay." Jack Tyler turned and went back in the house.

Abby smoothed her apron, adjusted her daffodil yellow neck scarf, which for some ridiculous reason she was pleased she wore, and headed back to the wagon where the colored man waited, his food untouched.

"See, Mister Tyler said it fine that you had some food." She smiled at him. "Honest. Go ahead. It's real good. I helped bake the ham myself."

The man blinked, looked down at the napkin filled with food and opened it. He gave a nod and began tasting the ham, gobbling it up within a minute.

She studied his face. Light-skinned, like her, wide-set eyes, lips not as full as darker men she'd seen. His hands caught her interest. Strong, calloused, long fingers. And a ribbon of scars on their backs.

"Boy, you are sure hungry, huh?"

He nodded, took the bread, and stuffed it in his mouth.

"You're supposed to pour the molasses . . . oh, never mind. Try one of the peaches. They are good."

She stopped talking and waited until he finished.

He smiled at her. "Thank you, Miss. That was real fine."

"So what's your name?" she asked, enjoying his dimples.

His eyes dropped to his feet.

"It's okay, I mean, to tell me your name. I'm Abigail Pinn. Abby. I live over there," Abby pointed in the direction. "At the Ainsley Hill Inn. See? Not hard. So who are you?"

"I don't want to get in trouble, Miss. I don't want to get you in trouble."

"Pshaw. You won't. Everyone around here knows me." She waited.

"Elias."

"What?"

He looked up and stared into her eyes. "Elias Turner, Miss."

Abby held out her hand. "Pleased to meet you, Mister Turner." Before Elias could shake, two barking banshees rushed up to them.

"Rufus, Josie, down, stop your infernal barking." She looked to find Elias laughing. He reached down and wrestled with the two dogs to their absolute delight.

"Thank goodness you like dogs, because you will see quite a bit of them round these parts. This here is Rufus, and this is Josie."

"Well, hello. Looks like I have two new friends."

"Three," Abby said softly.

Elias smiled and Abigail felt a rush of warmth come over her.

It was nearing midnight as close as she could tell but Abby felt like pins and needles were poking her all over. She knew she should get some sleep before the next day and all her chores began again. But her mind raced and a peculiar sensation took up residence in her body. Her heart felt tight, like something heavy had settled on it, preventing it from expanding and contracting properly. She'd had this odd feeling before but only a coupla' times. Like when Betsy, the old mare, had a foal in Miss Sara's barn a few years back. And when Hattie got all A's on her report card in first grade. It seemed akin to happiness.

She slipped into her chenille robe and tiptoed on bare feet down the stairs and out onto the porch. The tree waited and she obliged by nestling up to it on the bench that Mister Woolsey had built right in front of it. The stars beckoned and she stared up at the deep cerulean sky twinkling with lights from the far-off universe. Abby wondered if other people had similar thoughts when they looked at the sky. She knew she was different from most folks. Specially most colored folks. Miss Sara said that to her once, in a kind manner, not wanting to hurt her feelings.

"Different is one thing," Miss Sara had said. "Special is another. And you are special, Abigail. Learning to read and write all by yourself. Goodness."

"Don't colored people read and write?" she had asked the mistress of the Inn.

"Well, some, I'm sure. But not many." Sara had smiled at her like she imagined her mother might have when she was a child.

"Why not?"

"Well, whites and coloreds are . . . not the same in all ways."

"You mean whites are smarter?"

Sara scrunched up her face. "That's what some folks think."

"White folks."

"Yes."

"So the color of our skin says something about how smart we are."

Sara sighed. "One thing I know. You have possibilities, Abigail. Real possibilities."

"That's right fine, Miss Sara." Abby turned to face her eye to eye. "What do I do with them?"

Chapter 20

A bby mulled over that conversation with Miss Sara many times. She had possibilities? What did that mean? What could she do with her life? Except continue working at the Inn, cleaning, mending, babysitting, a little teaching . . . writing. Yeah. She liked to write. Anything. Stories mostly, about people around her. She'd written stories about Pattie and Hattie that had the whole household in hysterics. She grinned at the recollection.

But something had happened that day. She couldn't define it but she knew it had to do with that new man, Elias Turner. Deep in her mind, Abby knew who Elias was. Those scars on his hands told her. He was a runaway slave, working his way north. Maybe going to Canada. An idea began to form in her head. It niggled away at her until she could no longer shrug it off. Why couldn't he stay right here? In Vermont. He could be free, like she was, couldn't he?

Aww, what you thinkin', Abigail Pinn? Maybe he don't want to stay here. Maybe he got relatives or friends north. He's just working his way to them. Maybe he's got a wife and children, even. That thought jolted her.

Abby pondered the situation. Jack Tyler owned the farm next door. His wife had health issues and he had only one son. And Cora, of course, thank the lord. He hired men to help him scythe and bale the hay every season. That's how come Elias is there. He's not been the only colored man to work at the Tyler's neither. There's always been least one at haying season. It struck her then how this happened to come about.

Could it be that Jack Tyler worked with the underground railroad to help bring runaway slaves to freedom? Abby had heard about the underground and knew that Brattleborough was a stopping point on the railroad. Maybe Mister Tyler was a station agent?

There you go again, Abigail Pinn, fantasizing all sorts of things about your neighbor. You have no earthly idea that he works for the underground railroad. In fact, the railroad may be just a myth, may not be here in Brattleborough at all. She shook her head. No. It was here. She had seen things. Read things. Heard things whispered by Miss Sara and Mister Jeb.

Something bubbled hot in her blood. There wasn't a soul in the world that didn't know the underground railroad was a perilous undertaking. Essie would have her head if she dared mention it. Wouldn't she?

Abby's mind spun and circled upon itself. Essie. She'd heard her whispering to her husband Wyatt and both would stop short when they spotted Abby nearby. Nah, you're imagining it. Still, the theory stuck to her like Rufus with a prickly thorn in his fur. The more she mused, the more she was convinced. She devised her own narrative:

Elias Turner was a runaway slave, working with Jack Tyler to get him some money to head north. Mister Tyler was a station agent and so were Essie and Wyatt. All three would help Elias escape.

Yer crazy, girl. Then again . . .

Besides, what could she, nineteen-year old Abigail Pinn, a free colored woman, do to help? All at once she realized that anything she did to help a runaway slave could jeopardize her own life . . . and worse, her freedom. The hot bubbling blood in her veins turned ice cold.

The rain fell incessantly through the night and into the morning. Abby knew the mud would be knee-high. Still she loved her outdoor chores. The vegetable garden needed weeding and picking. Tomatoes, beets, green beans, and summer squash were ready and her mouth watered at the thought of Essie's pork stew with pickled beets on the side.

She tied a scarf around her neck to absorb the sweat from the heat and pulled on her long rubber boots. Then she topped her head with a rain hat that wouldn't do much good in this downpour. She bounded down the side kitchen steps and ran straight into Elias Turner.

"Oh, oh, you scared me half to death, Elias." Abby backed up.

"Sorry, Miss Abby, I, er, just, um . . ."

"Well, let's get under the overhang so we don't drown." She pulled him close to the house where a makeshift awning was affixed to the kitchen wall.

"Now, what's all the fuss about?"

"Erm, I need yer help."

"All right. What for?"

"They's lookin' fer me."

Abby was about to ask who when the answer dawned on her. She nodded at him, grabbed him by the arm and they ran across the back field into the barn. Inside, both shook the rain off. Eli looked around, then glanced outside and pulled the barn door closed. "You know what I mean, right? They mean to catch me and take me back."

"Back where?"

"South."

"I know that much. Where, exactly?"

"Chester. South Carolina."

She shook her head. "Not a good state for coloreds."

"Don't I know it." He sank down on a bale of hay and ran his hands through his wiry hair. "I've got to get away. Mister Tyler is gone for two days and I--."

"How do you know they're looking for you?"

He pulled out a crumpled paper and handed it to her.

"You can read?"

"Yeah, well, not really. Some, I can read some. See?" He pointed to the print on the leaflet. "My name."

"Slow down."

"One of the hands, he read this to me. Tole me I better get movin'."

"Let me see."

Eli raised his eyebrows.

"I can read."

Abby read aloud.

Runaway

Light-skin Negro man, goes by name Elias Turner, twenty years old, well-built, sturdy, quick-spoken and smart, left his subscriber in Chester, SC, in April. When last seen he was endeavoring to cross the Sandy River toward Wilksburg, heading north. All necessary expenses plus $100 reward to be paid for his re-capture. Reward will be paid on delivery to me at shop of Asahel Clapp, Carpenter, next door to First National Bank, Main Street, Brattleborough.

Signed, *Colton T. Strange*

"You read real good. Where'd--?"

"Never mind that now. We've got to think where to hide you."

"Uh uh, that's not a good idea. Could get you into big trouble."

"Let me worry about that." Abby went to peek out the barn door. "Listen. I think Essie and Wyatt, they work over at the Ainsley Hill Inn, will know what to do."

"No, hey, what if they turn me in. Folks could get in big trouble for . . . and there's a reward that's--."

"Stop," she said. He shut right up. "They are good people and I know they'll help you. They certainly wouldn't take no reward. But . . ."

"But?"

"If I get any sense that I'm wrong about them, I promise, we'll come up with something else."

"Now, how ya gonna do that? Find out if they'll help me, I mean?"

"I got my ways." Abby touched his arm. "Look, you're safe in the barn here for a little while. Will you give me a chance to talk to them?"

He stared at her, eyes wide and wet. "What choice do I got?"

"My thoughts exactly." She smiled. "I'll be back as soon as I can."

"You not back by nightfall, I'm gonna make a run for it."

Abby turned and squeezed out the barn door then raced to the house to find Essie.

In a few hours she had her answer. Essie and Wyatt agreed to help Elias. They had helped other runaways before. To prove it, Wyatt took Abigail up to a room on the second floor. No one was staying there at the moment. Wyatt stepped over to an old oak wardrobe, its doors stencil-painted with flowers. He pulled open the double doors and waited for Abby to come closer. Then he jiggled the back wall until it swung open.

"Lawd, a secret hiding place?"

"Best we could do," Essie said, as she walked into the room. "Eli can use the room and, if needs be, duck into this hidey hole when someone comes a' searchin' for him."

"Make no mistake, this is temporary and we gots to get him out of Brattleborough and soon," Wyatt said.

"Vermont is a free state. Why can't he just stay here?"

"Because the law here might not want to fight with the law in the south where he *ain't* free. They'll say he rightly and legally belong to this subscriber fella."

"Hmph," Abby said. "A slaveowner."

"That's right," Essie said. "But there's nothin' we kin do about that."

"What about getting him free man's papers. Like I have?"

"That'd amount to a hill of beans to a slave catcher," Wyatt said. "Even free coloreds have been snatched and turned into slaves."

"How do you know?"

"We don't fer sure," Wyatt said. "But many have just vanished."

Abby's jaw dropped. "Vanished?"

"That's right. Here one day, gone the next. No one, not family or friends, not employers ever saw them again."

"But that's--."

"That's the truth of it, Abigail. Better get the stars outta yer eyes, girl," Essie said.

Abby had trouble swallowing. "Then this is really dangerous for you and--."

Wyatt waved a hand. "Don't you worry none about us. You worry about Elias . . . and yourself. Hear?"

"How long will he have to hide?"

"What we've done in the past, see," Wyatt said, "is hang on with him hiding here until the bounty hunter done gone."

"How long is that?"

Essie shrugged. "Days, weeks, probley no more than coupla' weeks. After all he's losin' money every day he hangin' around here."

"So he leaves and Eli is safe?"

Wyatt looked at Essie with a frown.

"Let's cross that bridge later, Abby. First, let's get him settled here." Wyatt headed for the door to the guest room.

"Wait," Abby said. "What about the Woolseys? I mean they own the Inn. What will Miss Sara or Mister Jeb think?"

Essie smiled. "They are station agents, honey. For the underground railroad. They be jest fine."

Chapter 21

Helen

Brattleboro, Vermont, October 2018

Helen had been searching through the attic for bits and bobs of the past life of the Ainsley Hill Inn. She already had a vision of what her next book would comprise: a retrospective of an old, historic Inn in New England, with its mysteries and secrets, riddles, and enigmas. A far cry from her usual whodunnits.

In her explorations into the dusty trunks, boxes, and beat-up satchels, she came across a small valise upon which the name Nathaniel was scratched. Helen touched the letters, wondering their age. Inside the bag, she found a small bundle of items bound together with ribbon. The ribbon, once red, was faded to a pale pink and frayed. Helen untied it and laid out the objects on the window seat.

A cotton shawl, no doubt painstakingly handmade in a soft white cotton yarn. Next, was a bright yellow piece of cloth, the color of daffodils, that would make a fine kerchief.

Wrapped inside the cloth was a ring. Reddish gold, dented, and scratched. No writing on it. A wedding ring, most likely a woman's, since it was small in circumference. Helen tried it on her ring finger and it would not slide past her first knuckle. The woman who wore this was smaller than she in bone structure.

Finally, the last item made Helen light up like a firefly. It was a book. Large, fragile, hand-printed with illustrations. A children's book. Helen ran her fingers over it with reverence. This was no Random House publication. It was one-of-a-kind, bound by heavy jute, each page beautifully scripted and drawn. She shifted her weight on the window seat to get better light. The cover page read:

A Slave No More

By Abigail Pinn Turner, Brattleborough, Vermont, 1858.

Inside the cover were the words:

Dedicated to my dear husband, Elias Turner, and our son, Nathaniel.

Nathaniel. Helen found her eyes tearing. She wanted to turn the page. Instead, she closed the cover and headed downstairs to show the precious book to Marie. This treasure was meant to be shared.

Her grandmother was not in her usual place in the kitchen. Helen peeked in her bedroom behind the kitchen but the room was empty. She stood a moment gazing around the small space and spied several photographs on the chest of drawers. A smile came over her and she tiptoed inside to have a closer look.

Helen set the book from the attic down and picked up one framed photo. There were three people in it. A man, a woman and a child, a little girl, possibly five years old.

"That's me," Helen whispered. "And mom and dad." She had never seen this particular picture. The color seemed washed out in time, and the backdrop was the Ainsley Hill house, a farm back then. Must be almost fifty years old.

The second photo was much more recent. It was in full color and portrayed Helen and Julianne mugging for the camera. Helen knew exactly when and where this photo was taken. It was 2010 in Central Park. Before cancer struck. Julianne was in her twenties. Both were carefree, happy, and healthy. Jim was still alive. What a difference eight years could make.

Helen set the frame back down. She was healthy now and planned to remain so.

"I wish you would take some new pictures, dear," Marie said from the doorway. "I need to update those old ones."

Helen turned with a smile. "Sorry, didn't mean to snoop."

"This is your house, so it's not snooping." Marie walked over to her. "You know, you look just as good today as in this picture."

"Funny," Helen said. "I was just thinking about how good I've been feeling, physically and mentally, these days." She looked at Marie. "Do you think cancer patients go through these times? I mean when they feel they've beaten the monster and will live forever?"

Marie sat on her bed. Helen sat next to her and took her hand.

"I believe it's true . . . for you."

"Just me?"

"You're special, Helen. There's something inside you that touches everyone. A kind of life-force. Sounds silly, I guess, when I say it that way."

"Keep going. I like it." Helen squeezed Marie's hand.

"Think about what you've done just since you've come home. You've already righted two terrible wrongs of the past."

"You can thank the wise old maple tree for that."

At that moment, Honey came into the room, nails ticking on the wood floor.

"The tree and this old girl." Honey lay her head in Helen's lap.

An hour later, Helen and Marie had almost finished Abigail's book. It both saddened and exhilarated them to realize that in the mid-nineteenth century, the Ainsley Hill Inn had been a refuge for runaway slaves.

"Her illustrations were marvelous," Marie said. "Look at this drawing of the big old maple tree in front of the house. Makes me think she loved it as much as you do."

Before they turned the last page, they were interrupted. Honey picked her head up as if someone had called her name from afar. Helen and Marie stared at her as she swiveled her head, eyes wide and expectant.

"What is it, girl?" Helen said. But Honey refused to be petted. She leaped up and ran to the door. "What?"

The two women watched her antics. Honey ran outside the bedroom, then back in, outside and back in.

"She wants you to go with her," Marie said. "Go on."

Helen followed Honey outside to the front porch, where she ran down to the tree.

"I think she's trying to tell us something," Marie said.

Not possible, Helen thought. It's simply not possible. Still, she walked over to the giant maple and raised her eyes upwards.

Honey circled the tree, jumping and spinning.

Helen studied the craggy bark and could see nothing but the old carvings: *Sal and Angie*, and *Tillie*. Names that had reappeared once Helen learned what happened to them in life. They would remain as long as the tree endured, she believed.

Honey slowed down and circumnavigated the tree again as she approached it with something akin to thoughtful determination. She raised her front two legs up, pointing. As if to say, come on, Helen, get a clue.

Helen moved closer and put her hands on the tree above where Honey aimed her paws. There she saw it: *ABBY and ELI*.

Abigail and Elias.

Chapter 22

Abigail

Brattleborough, Vermont, July 1856

On a brutally hot Sunday in July, Abigail began packing a picnic lunch. Essie and Wyatt had left for church only a few minutes ago. The Woolseys and their children would be gone most of the day, visiting Sara's aunt in Guilford. Josh Putnam, the Inn manager was left in charge. He had winked at her when she asked for some time off.

"G'wan, enjoy. You and that nice young man."

Abigail opened her mouth but Josh shook his head and waved her away.

Now she had a large wicker basket filled with fried chicken, corn bread, and fruit jam, plus strawberries and peaches. Enough for an army, she giggled to herself.

A light rap on the screen porch door told her Elias had arrived. She pushed the door open and handed him the basket. He grinned. She raised an eyebrow and his grin faded quick-like into his shyness.

Abby stepped out onto the porch. "Good morning," she said, smiling wide to ease his tension.

"Morning, Miss."

"Call me Abby. Makes me sound like a schoolmarm or somethin'."

"All right, I will. Abby."

"What shall I call you? Elias?"

"Uh, sure."

"What did your friends call you? Or your mama?"

He blinked. "I ain't really had friends. But my mama, when she was alive, called me Eli."

Abby smiled. "Eli. I like that. Eli it shall be."

He beamed at his boots.

Abby started down the path.

"That is sure a fine tree you got in front of the house."

She turned abruptly and he backed up. "Sorry, did I say something wrong?"

Her face lit up. "No, no. That tree, is, well, she's special."

"She?"

"She. She's an old sugar maple, strong, and wise."

He chuckled.

"What's so funny?"

"How can a tree be wise?"

"You think only people got smarts?" Abby walked over to the tree and touched its trunk." She shook her head. "Nhuh, she's smart. Probably smarter than you and me. She's been around a long time, seen a lot of things."

Eli looked up at the tree. "Well, I don't know about smart, but she is mighty pretty."

"Don't you have sugar maples in South Carolina?" Abby bit her lip after she realized what she'd said. Maybe reminding Eli of his days in South Carolina wasn't a clever thing to do.

"No, don't believe so."

"What kind of trees are down there?"

They began walking the trail.

"Well, let's see. There's big oaks, magnolias, dogwoods, and something called the black tupelo."

"Black tupelo? I like that name. What's it look like? Black?"

"No, no. It's mighty fine. Leaves are kinda long and slender-like, real shiny. They's dark green in the summer and got little bluish-black fruit that ripens in late September."

"Can you eat the fruit?"

"I tried once when I had nothin' else to eat. Got a real bad stomach-ache. Found out the fruit's only good for birds and animals."

Abby stopped and turned to him. "Why'd you have nothin' to eat?"

Eli started walking, got a bit ahead of her.

"Did you hear me?"

"I heared you." He stopped. "It was on one of my escapes."

Abby couldn't help the gasp that slipped out.

"Can we not talk about it?"

"Sure, no, we don't have to talk about it if you don't want to." She fell silent, but not for long.

"But . . ." she began.

"But what?"

"Well . . . I'd like to know what happened." Abby stopped, grabbed his arm. "Here's a good spot to have lunch. Look at that view. Ain't it grand?"

The two stood shading their eyes from the sun and gazed at the long meadows rife with wildflowers and the rolling green hills beyond the river.

"Yeah, it is real pleasing."

She shook out a small blanket and set out the meal. "Here you go."

They ate for a while, not speaking, just absorbing the beauty of the Green Mountains.

"You really want to know about . . . my time in South Carolina?"

"I do. See, I've been real lucky. My parents died when I was only eleven and Mister and Missus Woolsey took me in, gave me a home. Even taught me to read and write."

"You were born here? In Vermont?"

"Yep. My mama and daddy were born here too." She frowned. "I never knew about their mommas and daddies, though. I don't know if they were born here or not."

"How come you don't know?"

"Mama and daddy . . . they never wanted to talk about them." She looked right at Eli. "I asked, you know. All the time. But they said 'the past is the past. Leave it lie, Abigail.' So I did."

Eli pursed his lips.

"What?" she said, challenging him to respond.

"I think you do know about your grandmamas and granddaddies. You jest don't want to admit it."

A flash of anger sparked her next words. "What do you mean? What do you know? You know nothin' about me or my family . . ." Her outburst died in the light breeze that picked up.

He said nothing.

"No. You're right," she said. "I do know. Least I think I do."

Eli waited, pulled up blades of grass and chewed on them.

"They were slaves." Abby tightened her lips to keep them from trembling. "I was little, maybe four or five, but I heard mama and daddy talking one day to Miss Sara and Mister Jeb. They were looking to go north, up to the border with Canada. But the Woolseys . . . they convinced them to stay here, work at the Inn. They could protect them, they said. And their little girl. Me. So they did. We all stayed. But they never saw their mamas and daddies again."

"You're real lucky, Abby. You know that, right?"

"Yeah, I guess. But, well . . ."

"What?"

"It's all kind of a hazy picture, slavery, I mean. I got these images in my head about what's it like, but I don't really know."

Eli gave her a sad smile. "What do you think it's like?"

She shrugged. "In my mind, I see coloreds in chains and yokes pulling carts . . . kind of like oxen, ya know? I see them being whupped and left hanging on a post. I see them scarred and beaten." She grabbed his hands. "Like this."

He pulled his hands away.

"Am I right?"

"Yes . . . and no. Depends on the owners, the overseers. Different plantations are different. Some owners, they don't beat the slaves so much. They's a bit kinder." He scrunched his face up and washed it in his hands.

Abby went quiet.

"The hardest part is not being free, you unnerstand? It's hard for you to see, I reckon, since you are free, have always been free." He let out a profound sigh. "Being a slave means not being my own man, not being able to go where I want, do what I want."

"What do you want?"

"You really wanna know?" He lay down on the blanket and gazed up at the cloudless sky. "I want to get my own farm, grow my own vegetables, maybe have a fruit tree or two. Maybe even some cows."

"You know how to milk cows?"

"I can learn." He sat up quick. "I can learn anything, Abby."

"You know, Eli, I believe you can."

Abby looked up at the sky suddenly. It was still a brilliant cornflower blue and the sun still shone. But Eli's face had darkened so much, she thought a storm was coming.

"What's wrong?"

"Nah, let's not talk about it." He jumped to his feet. "Not on such a beautiful day."

"Eli, tell me, what is it?" She looked up at him and he reached for her hand, helped her up. "It's that slave catcher that's lookin' for you, isn't it?"

"Right now, Abby, I'm a free man, here in this beautiful place with a beautiful lady, and I'm gonna enjoy every minute of it while it lasts."

Did he call her a lady? Abby felt her whole body melt to mush. Somehow Elias Turner managed to heat up the blood in her veins. Not for the first time and, hopefully, not for the last.

Chapter 23

Elias

Brattleborough, Vermont, July 1856

That old feeling was back. His heart beat so hard he couldn't hear for the blood rushing in his ears. The sweat spilled out of every pore and his muscles ached from tension. It wasn't over. Would never be over. They'd come to get him.

Elias swiped at his eyes with both hands and leaned against the inside barn wall. He had to get out of the barn. That would be the first place they'd look. Voices sounded nearer. Two men, their horses tied to the post near the Inn. He had but a few minutes.

His body went rigid, bones locked in his skin. Thoughts came at him like musket balls, bringing back paralyzing memories. Of being flogged, branded, doused with pepper water, shamed before the world. The only world he'd ever known.

Something shook him loose. He blinked and fell to his knees, vomited in the dirt floor. Get moving. He studied the barn and saw a window at the top of the loft. Maybe he could reach it and jump out. Pretty far fall, he reckoned. But hiding under the hay bales would only get him stuck like a pig with a pitchfork.

Elias sprinted for the ladder and shimmied up to the loft. He pushed the window out at the bottom and sighed with relief. There was a small roof beneath the window so his jump would be shorter. He slid down the roof, then leaped to the ground, curling his body, and rolling to a hard stop on his elbow. Pain shot through him, but he had no time to think about it. He clutched it and ran onto the north-south trail into the woods. He knew he could find a hiding place in the trees.

Just then he heard exuberant barking. Damn. Rufus and Josie. They would want to play, would follow him. His breath caught in his throat and then he heard it.

"Rufus, Josie, come on in here, now." It was Abby. Beautiful, sweet Abby. Who set his heart thrumming even in calm times. Thank you, Lord, for that wondrous woman.

Eli made it to the grove of cottonwoods and sycamores that had not been trimmed in decades. They were thick and obscuring. Good cover. For a while.

He knew what was going to happen. Colton Strange and his crony would talk to Abby and Essie and Wyatt about the escaped slave. Just like that handbill he had seen, posted in town. They was lookin' for him. He had to leave. But he didn't want to leave. Not with Abby here.

He heard a sound and pulled in his breath, peeked around a tree. Strange and his partner were riding out, heading for town on Western Avenue. Away from him. Elias sank to the ground, dropped his head in his hands. He was safe for now. But for how long? Another sound caught his ear. Barking.

Rufus and Josie came careening through the trees. He laughed and they pounced on him. Abby was close behind.

"Abby," he said, out of breath.

"You okay, Eli?"

"I am now. How'd you get rid of them?"

"Told them I heard there was a colored man up near Putney that someone had seen. He was looking for work, heading north."

"You did?"

"And, funny, he fit your description exactly." She smiled.

He smiled but broke down into tears.

"Hey, it's okay. Really. You're safe now."

"Now, mebbe. But for how long?" He shook his head. "They won't give up, you know."

"I know. That's why I've got to show you something." She turned to head back to the Inn.

Eli followed and the dogs scampered behind.

When they reached the Inn, Essie and Wyatt were waiting on the porch.

Elias felt embarrassed. "Thanks, sir, for covering for me."

"I ain't no sir, just Wyatt."

Eli raised his head and smiled.

"Come on, son," Wyatt said. "Follow me."

The four tromped up the steps to the second floor and into a small back bedroom.

"Now," Wyatt said, "this here is a special guest room. We only allow special guests, like you, to use it."

"Like me?" Eli said.

"Looka here." Wyatt walked over to the oak wardrobe that stood against the far wall and opened the double doors. "Come closer so's you kin see."

Eli stepped closer, peered in. "Don't see nothin'."

"Nothin's good, that's good." Wyatt grinned, displaying tobacco-stained teeth. "See here." He pushed a panel in the back of the closet. It popped open.

"Now in there is a hidey hole, small, but big enough to stand and room for two people for a short stay."

"A real short stay," Abby clucked.

Elias leaned in and stepped into the hidden space. "Wow, this is somethin', really, psshhaw."

"Yeah," Abby said. "That's the word for it."

"Now, you know what they say, Abigail," Essie spoke for the first time. "Beggars cain't be choosers."

"No, no, I know," Abby said, face pink.

"I think it's better than the grandest hotel, I do," said Elias. "Thank you." He turned to Wyatt and Essie.

"Now, listen here," Wyatt said. "Don't have any idea how long that slave catcher fella is in town. But you're gonna stay right here in this room. If'n he comes back, you hide in there. See?"

"I see, yes, I see," Elias said.

"How long do you think he'll keep looking?" Abby asked.

"Don't know," Eli said. "But he won't make any money if he hangs around these parts too long."

"That's right," Wyatt said. "My guess is he'll stay in town two, maybe three weeks then give up. Go hunt another quarry."

"Or head north lookin' for me," Eli said.

They all fell silent.

"All right, I've got to go get some food on the table," Essie said. "Eli, I hope you'll join us tonight."

"You sure about that?"

"The Woolseys are agents for the underground railroad, son," Wyatt said. "They would be mighty unhappy if you didn't join us."

Essie and Wyatt left the room. Elias looked at Abby.

"You okay here?" Abby said.

Eli felt his whole body tremble. He sat down on the edge of the bed. "Yeah, yeah." His voice was hoarse.

Abby put a hand on his shoulder. "You're upset."

He pulled her down to sit next to him. "No. I'm, erm, grateful." He angled toward her. "See, nobody's ever done anything kind like this for me. I mean, Mister Tyler, he's a fine man and let me work and stay at his barn, but this . . ." The words ran out. Damn, why couldn't he spit it out?

"There are lots of people here in Vermont who will help you, Eli. Not all, mind you, so we've got to be careful that—"

"We?"

"What?"

"You said we. *We've* got to be careful."

She smiled. "Sure, I said we. We're in this together, ain't we?"

"Why, Abby? Why would you want to put the life you built here in danger?"

"I don't want anything to happen to you, Eli."

"And I don't want nothin' to happen to you. That's why I'm a mite scared."

She took his hand in hers.

"Not scared for me. For you."

She was silent a few moments. "When I was a little girl something happened that changed my world. Changed me." She stood and went to the window. "We had just moved to the Inn. I was eleven." Abby took a deep breath. "One day, this family came to stay for a while, the father had a job at the law offices in town. They were looking for a place to live so they stayed here. There were two kids, about fourteen and fifteen. I was excited. Now I'd have someone to share things with, you know? Books, poems, stories. I'd teach them how to plant flowers and vegetables, things like that."

Elias did not know how to respond but had a feeling he knew how this story would end. "What happened?

"The same day they showed up, I knew that dream wouldn't come true."

He waited.

"I heard one of them talking to the other. About me."

"What'd they say?"

"The only word I heard for sure was pickaninny."

Elias squeezed his eyes shut.

"So, you see, Eli, you, and me, we share the same color skin; we have to protect each other from those who want to do us harm." She sighed. "I may be living here in this free state, but there are those folks, even here, who still bear ill feelings against coloreds. There's not a perfect place for us anywhere, you see."

Three months later

This was a perfect place, Eli thought. Living in this tiny bedroom on the top floor of the Ainsley Hill Inn and Tavern in the year of our Lord, 1856. He was a married man, married to the most wondrous woman in the world, and by next summer, he'd be a father. And, hopefully, some money to rent a place of their own.

His eyes roamed to the wardrobe. He felt safe, finally, knowing he had an escape route. But he no longer wanted to escape. Brattleborough was his home now, forever. Colton Strange had moved on, to other prey. He wouldn't be back, Eli felt sure.

"Elias?" Abby's voice from downstairs. "We're leaving."

"All right, then," he said. The downstairs door closed, and he watched out the front window as the Inn emptied of all occupants. Both workers, caretakers, and guests were on their way to church. A place that Eli could not go, at least until more time passed. Abby wouldn't hear of it. She did not want him seen in town until all evidence of the slave catcher was erased.

Today, he would work on the new addition to the kitchen and make them all proud. He loved working with his hands and fixing things. It was a big job, the addition, but he could make a dent in it with just a few hours.

He tied up his boots and hustled downstairs. The work area was cordoned off so guests wouldn't trip on the rubble or fall into the huge hole that had been dug. Eli grabbed a shovel and set his back to clearing the rocks and debris for what would be a new kitchen porch.

After an hour, he stopped, rubbed the ache in his lower back and had himself a drink from a ladle in a bucket of well water. Something made him turn around, a sound, but there was nothing. Just a bird, or maybe Rufus or Josie playing. Then his eyes caught the dogs asleep under Abby's maple tree.

He shrugged and drank some more. Another sound. This time when he turned he was rewarded with the sight of a man walking toward him. Not a man he wanted to see. He knew his swagger and a cold dread settled on his heart. The man, tall, muscular wearing a faint smile on a pockmarked face, walked slowly toward him. In the distance, Elias saw two horses tied to a tree beyond the barn.

He should have been more careful, watchful. He should have known the slave catcher would never let him go. It was not just about money. It was personal with him.

Colton Strange had a long memory.

Chapter 24

Helen

Brattleboro, Vermont, October 2018

The day was unseasonably warm so Helen decided to sit outside and read Abigail's book. She reread the story and, again, found herself beguiled by the delicate drawings. Of the house, the tree, the meadows. Fine pencil lines, careful detail but childlike. Colors soft, rubbed with chalk, no doubt. She was about to close the book when she realized she'd missed the writing on the inside back cover. It was a bit blurred so she tilted the book toward the light.

To my darling son, Nathaniel. I met your father on a sunny day in July 1856. Elias Turner was a special man, but he'd suffered much from where he came. We were happy for the short time we had together. We kept him safe. Then, one day, he was gone. I never knew what happened, but I suspected his evil overseer came for him and took him away. Your daddy simply disappeared and left no trace. If you read this when you grow up, remember this name: Colton T. Strange. He is born of the devil and belongs in hell. I hope God sees fit to put him there.

Helen read the words again. Elias was a runaway slave. He vanished from Brattleboro . . . right here at Ainsley Hill. She closed the book and something fell to her feet. She bent to pick it up, a fragile, thin slip of paper. A photograph.

She stared at it openmouthed at the portrait of a couple. In the sepia-toned image, the pretty black woman wore a simple pale-colored dress and the handsome young man wore an ill-fitting suit. No doubt borrowed. This was Abigail and Elias. Their wedding picture. She turned it over. *April 16, 1857. Abigail*

Pinn and Elias Turner. Beneath read: Albumen Print, *Flat Street Photography,* *Brattleborough, Vermont.*

Oh my God. She jumped to her feet, causing Honey to bark.

"We've got work to do." She hurried inside to her computer, Honey at her heels.

"Where's the fire?" Marie said, passing her in the hallway.

"Look at this, Marie."

"Oh my, a wedding photo? Is this . . . are they . . .?"

"I'm sure of it. Abby and Eli."

"Well, isn't that something. Where'd you find it?"

"It was stuck in between the double layer of the vellum cover. Glue has long dried so it just fell out."

"It was hidden?"

"Seems so. I guess Abby felt Nathaniel would find it somehow. Or maybe I just missed it and . . . got lucky when it landed at my feet."

"It's a beautiful portrait. With that yellowed look, historical."

"It is. What surprises me is that it's a print. Not a daguerreotype or ambro-type, you know, on a thin sheet of metal, like many of the Civil War soldiers had," Helen said. "I thought those were the earliest photographs."

"Well, clearly they were able to do this *albumen* print in 1857. What's albumen, anyway?"

"Something to do with eggs, egg whites, I think. Not really sure."

"So what now?" Marie asked.

"Now, I've got to find Colton Strange."

"Who?"

"I think he's the slave catcher responsible for Eli's disappearance." Helen explained as she booted up. She began a search through her historical resources for the name. "Hmm. No information on his name." She kept typing. "Wait. What's this?"

Marie came closer. "More photographs? Looks like from the same era."

Helen zoomed in on the first and blew it up to a larger magnification. The image depicted five people, two women and three men, standing on the steps of a large, palatial, antebellum home.

"What does the caption say?" Marie asked.

"'Tupelo Plantation, Chester, South Carolina.'" Helen said, as she manipulated the image on the screen. "The more I try to blow it up, the blurrier it gets. And why would this image come up for Colton Strange? Is that a whip in that man's hand?"

"I bet you two to one, that man is Colton Strange."

Helen moved on to the second image. Marie pulled over a chair.

They were looking at a picture of a rough-hewn cabin with a family of blacks gathered in front, their expressions grim, their bodies emaciated.

"The caption reads: 'Slave quarters on Tupelo.'"

"What is a *Tupelo*, anyhow?" Marie said.

"I think it's a tree. They probably grow only in the southern climates."

A third photo depicted a man, hands on his hips, hat on his head.

"Now that's a mean grin if ever I saw one," Marie said. "What's the caption say?"

Helen read: "'Overseer Colton T. Strange, prize-winning bounty hunter.' Bingo."

"You can win prizes for bounty hunting?"

"This is the same man as in the first picture. The man with the whip. He must have been an important figure on this plantation. If he won prizes for capturing slaves it was no wonder he pursued Elias all the way to Vermont and didn't give up until he brought him back."

"A lucrative job. Good God."

Helen squinted at the images again.

"Hang on, there's a name under the captions, perhaps the photographer?"

"Maybe it's what's his name. Mathew Murphy. You know that famous Civil War photographer?"

"Mathew Brady, yeah." Helen zoomed in and enlarged the image once more. The letters were fuzzy but readable.

"Not Brady. Someone by the name of Joseph Thornhill."

"Thornhill, Thornhill," Marie murmured. "Now why does that name sound familiar?"

"He might have been a well-known photographer too." Helen leaned back in her chair.

"I knew a woman . . . Sarah Thornhill. We went to High School together, though she was younger. Think she lived up on Sunset Lake. But I'm sure she's dead now."

"Well, there are probably lots of Thornhills."

"Not in the photography business, I reckon."

"What do you mean, the photography business?"

"Sarah had a niece who was a photographer. A famous one, you know that digital-type photography. Worked for the police or something. Can't remember, exactly." Marie turned to Helen. "Do a Google search."

Helen laughed. "You're pretty darn tech-savvy, Marie." She turned and called up the search engine. "What's her name?"

Marie frowned.

"Well, let me search for *Thornhill, digital photography.*"

Helen entered the words and, in a blink, pages of information came up on one Margaret Thornhill.

"Margaret, yes. Maggie, that was it," Marie said. "Maggie Thornhill."

"You were right about her fame. She's helped the FBI and police with lots of cases." Helen kept reading. "Wait a minute." She spotted the words Civil War. "Says she was the great, great granddaughter of the famed Civil War photographer, Joseph Thornhill."

"I knew it," Marie said. Honey blew out a soft huff. "Right, girl? We knew it."

"Darn, if you're not a genius. Both of you. Geniuses."

"Being a genius has plumb worn me out. I'm going to make some fresh coffee if I'm going to help you some more with my exceptional intelligence."

Helen studied the computer screen but no brilliant ideas came to mind. Maggie and Joseph Thornhill. Civil War photography. Fine. Great. What the heck was she going to do with that?

After breakfast the next morning, Helen followed her routine of meditation and journal writing. Meditation grounded her and the words of the yogi calmed her from the maelstrom of life: the tumultuous cancer journey she had embarked on over the last three years. She was filled with gratitude today for being alive, for her home, her daughter, her grandmother, Honey . . . and her beloved tree. She ambled out the door to the majestic maple. Her fingers stroked the trunk where she believed the names *Abby and Eli* had appeared. Nothing.

"I'm going to change that, Honey. Somehow I'll bring their names back, so they can rest in peace forever."

Helen made trips to the library and the Historical Society that day which were respectably fruitful. She learned that Nathaniel Turner, Abby, and Eli's son, was a resident of Brattleboro for many years and was the ancestor of several generations of Turners. Sadly the last Turner had passed on in the 1960s.

With Dave's help, Helen was able to locate a death certificate for Abigail Pinn Turner. Not surprisingly, she was buried in nearby Mather Cemetery, the resting place close by where Helen and Honey were headed right now. She was informed by the volunteer at the Historical Society that it might not be easy to find such an old stone, if one had even been erected. Helen had a stubborn streak that would not accept the answer no. Besides, she believed Honey would find it for her.

The gunmetal sky spit a few drops on them but Helen carried an umbrella. Cemeteries were made for lackluster, shadowy days. Seemed fitting somehow.

They turned on Mather Road, presumably named after Cotton Mather, the Puritan minister remembered for his role in the Salem Witch trials. On one side of the road rested the graveyard which dated back to the 1700s; more recent graves inhabited the other side. Helen stepped into the historic section and began weaving her way through crooked and toppled headstones, many of which were so worn by the elements they were unreadable.

She stopped at a few in the mid-1800s but could not make out the engravings. After an hour and a heavy rain shower, Helen turned to Honey. "Well, I don't think we're going to find Abby today. Let's go home."

Honey whined.

"What? You're not wet enough?"

The retriever barked.

"Do you know where Abigail is?"

Honey spun in a circle.

"Okay, show me. Where is Abby?"

Honey began sniffing and zigzagging between the graves. Helen followed. After about twenty minutes, Helen gave up.

"You don't know, do you? Let's go home now. We can try again another time."

Helen started for home. "Sorry Abby."

Honey whined but acquiesced. It just wasn't meant to be.

That evening, Helen made a spaghetti dinner. Marie opened a bottle of red wine and the two women reminisced a bit before the topic turned to the underground railroad.

Helen filled Marie in on everything she had learned and all that she didn't.

"What's left, then?" Marie said.

"The only clue to follow up right now is the photographer, Joseph Thornhill."

"I think he's long dead."

They both snickered.

"How will that help?" Marie asked.

"I don't know. Probably won't. Maybe he left something in writing. Do photographers take notes or something?"

"You mean, maybe he wrote down that Colton Strange was a nasty S-O-B who should've been shot . . . and not with a camera."

"Yeah, like that."

"Ha."

"Just wishful thinking, I guess. Even if he kept a log of his subjects, maybe I can trace back the dates of Strange, follow him up here to Brattleboro, find out what happened to him here, or--."

"The only one who might know the answers to that is Maggie."

Helen drummed her fingers on the table. "I think you're right."

"Why don't you contact her? I'm sure you can find her address or phone number or something. Ask her, point blank."

"Nothing to lose," Helen said. She looked at her watch. "Still early enough. I'll find an address and email her tonight."

Helen did just that. Maggie Thornhill had contact information at the Georgetown University Digital Lab. Helen shot off a note.

"Well, Honey, if Maggie is the keeper of her ancestor's documents, we may have some luck."

Honey raised her nose in the air and let out an ardent yowl.

Chapter 25

Georgetown, Washington, D.C., October 2018

Helen slung her carryall over her shoulder as she walked toward her destination on the Georgetown University campus: a regal, glass, brick, and concrete structure that housed the science departments. On the fourth floor, Regents Hall housed the computer science classrooms and the state-of-the-art digital photography lab run by Dr. Maggie Thornhill.

Helen had received an email back from the professor almost immediately. And to Helen's delight, Maggie (she insisted on being called Maggie) invited her to visit and discuss the photographs in question.

"I am always thrilled to talk about Joseph," she'd said. "And I am even more thrilled to talk about him with a world-famous mystery writer."

Two days later, Helen had ridden Amtrak from Brattleboro to Washington. The day was sunny, highlighting the fall colors as they unfolded in vividness from north to south. Soon Vermont would be leafless and covered in snow.

She'd checked into The Avery, a boutique hotel in Georgetown that Maggie had recommended. Now, the next morning, she was about to meet the accomplished digital photographer. Maggie's bio online gave her age as close to her own and listed myriad accolades. Helen felt a bit nervous.

When she arrived at the lab, Maggie greeted her personally. Energetic and vivacious, Maggie shook Helen's hand in both of her own, and beamed a magnetic smile. Helen's initial anxiety vanished.

"I am so happy to meet you," Maggie said.

"I was about to say the exact same thing."

"I have read so many of your books and loved them. I was always hoping you'd find a need for digital photography in one of them. Maybe now?"

"Yes, maybe now." Helen smiled. "I have a lot to learn, though."

"Well, let's get started."

Helen followed her into the lab where Maggie explained some of the equipment and filled her in on the type of projects where digital analysis provides assistance. She found Maggie to be intelligent, erudite, but attentive and courteous. A good listener.

"So, I can't wait any longer," Maggie said, as they entered her office. "Please. Sit." She pointed to a small couch against one wall. Maggie sat next to her. "Tell me why you're here."

Helen pulled out a folder from her carryall. She relayed to Maggie her own journey back to her childhood at Ainsley Hill, how she discovered the names of Abby and Eli carved on the maple tree, and her discovery of the suitcase in the attic.

She brought out the children's book, told Maggie the story, and gave her time to look it over.

"Beautiful," Maggie said. "Imagine . . . this was done in 1856."

Helen handed her the wedding photo. "This fell out between the torn sections of the back cover. I'm sure it's the wedding picture of Abigail and Elias."

Maggie twisted a strand of her long red, curly hair as she studied it. "An albumen print. Rare for this time."

"That's what I thought. Wouldn't it normally have been an ambrotype or--?"

"A tintype, yes. Evidently the photographer had the skill to produce it and, my guess is, Abigail asked for it specifically."

"Why would she?"

"Maybe she wanted to secure it in the book?"

"You mean hide it?"

Maggie nodded. "Paper would have been easier to conceal than metal."

"There's more." Helen brought out photocopies of the pictures she took online of Colton Strange.

"What are these?"

Helen explained her theories on Colton Strange and his relationship with Elias. Then added, "The photographer listed under these plantation photos is Joseph Thornhill."

"What are the dates, do you know?"

"Same. 1856."

"Hmm. Joseph had his own portrait studio here in Washington at that time . . . before the war broke out in '61. He was always getting commissions to photograph a wide range of subjects, places, and people. He hated doing portraits. And he had a lot of those. Too many, as he put it: 'of pompous bankers and their persnickety brats.'"

Helen burst out laughing. "Oh, I like him already."

"He wanted something more stimulating, controversial, even. So I'm not surprised that he would travel to South Carolina and photograph a plantation and its people."

"My question is whether he kept notes. A diary, journal, maybe a notebook, to document his photos. I'm hoping that Joseph's notes will tell us first, that Colton Strange was Elias Turner's overseer. Second, that he chased him to Vermont after he escaped and third, that Colton Strange caught him, brought him back, and punished him." Helen paused. "Maybe even killed him."

"You think that's why Elias vanished from Brattleboro?" Maggie flashed green eyes at Helen.

"I do."

"The answer to your question, Helen, is yes. Joseph kept meticulous notes on all his photographic jobs. I've spent years organizing them and I can probably find the ones from 1856."

"That's fantastic," Helen said.

Maggie frowned. "There is something that could throw a monkey wrench into all this."

"Oh. What's that?"

"When slaves escaped, they always changed their names. Usually they kept their given name but came up with a new surname."

Helen's eyebrows arched. "Which means Turner wasn't his real name."

"Right. I can almost guarantee Elias Turner had another name while he was on the plantation."

"Great. How will we ever find him?"

They fell silent.

Maggie stood and walked to her office window, gazed out.

Helen watched her and could almost hear her thinking.

Maggie turned back. "Joseph may have known some of the slaves on the Tupelo Plantation personally. If for no other reason than to solicit help from them to lug all the equipment around."

"Perhaps he met Elias?"

"Perhaps. If Elias was, let's say, a competent slave, he may have been asked to do odd jobs rather than merely being a grunt, a field hand." Maggie sat back down in a chair across from Helen. "Also, Joseph took hundreds of photographs of slaves. I've seen them. Many on the sly, I'm sure, since I doubt the overseers would want those photos to get out. And, from everything Joseph wrote in his journals and letters to his wife, he was clearly sympathetic to their plight."

Helen nodded, fascinated.

Maggie looked at Helen. "There's another reason why Joseph might have taken a photo and made notes about Elias."

"Oh?"

"If Elias was planning on running, he might have sought help."

"Okay. Why Joseph?"

"Joseph was an agent for the underground railroad."

"What?" Helen almost choked. "God."

"Is that so surprising?"

Helen nodded her head. "For several reasons. I mean, what are the chances I would come here, tell you about Abby and Eli, and it turns out your ancestor actually knew him, helped him escape?"

Maggie smiled.

"But, even more astonishing is my own underground railroad story." Helen told her about the history at the Ainsley Hill Inn.

"You're kidding?" Maggie said. "A hiding place on your second floor?"

"I think that's where Abigail and Elias spent their few months together . . . in that bedroom."

"Sad. But romantic, I think." Maggie gave a wistful smile.

"So where do we start trying to find Elias-whatever-his-name was?"

"Let's start by looking at Joseph's notes from that time period."

"Where are they?"

"Well, it just so happens I have a whole storage room in my brownstone."

"A whole room?"

"Yeah, but it's pretty organized. I know just where the boxes are."

"Boxes?" Helen scrunched up her face.

"Only about fifty or sixty."

Helen groaned. Maggie grinned.

"Since we have a photograph of Elias Turner, if we are able to find another Elias in Joseph's files, how will we match them? I mean, just eyeballing them--."

Maggie held up a hand. "Fear not, ye of little faith. That's where magic comes in."

The magic took the form of state-of-the-art facial recognition digital technology. The next morning, on a worktable in the lab, Maggie switched on the large screen monitor.

"Pull up a chair," she said to Helen. "I already scanned the images into the computer so all we need to do is digitally compare them."

Maggie typed commands into the computer and on the screen appeared an over-sized image of Elias Turner from his wedding photo. Maggie manipulated the image so it was just his face and neck and, with a few keystrokes, conveyed it over to the left side of the screen.

She did the same with another image, explaining, "This is the photo of the other slave who looks similar."

Maggie arranged the image onto the right side of the screen next to Elias. Then she began, her fingers flying over the keyboard. She spoke as she worked.

"Every face has a different proportion. The software calculates the diverse distances between facial landmarks, such as the distance between the left and right pupils, and the left and right corners of the mouths."

"And then it scans for similar spans in the other photo," Helen said.

"Exactly."

"There are twenty-seven landmarks I use to analyze a photo, so it takes a little time. There are also a number of obstacles that can impede the manipulations."

"Such as?"

"If the faces are not both in the same position, meaning one is angled toward the right, the other straight-on. Or if the photographs themselves are degraded and have discolorations or scratches on them. I'll tell you now that I already tried about six images last night," Maggie said. "Just for comparison. I saved this one for last so you can see the process. But I really think this is our man."

"The others were no match, I assume?"

Maggie didn't answer, just kept working. "Look at this."

Helen leaned in.

Maggie was mapping out a grid on both faces. "The facial shapes are almost identical."

"Almost? Why not exactly?"

"Elias has his head tipped down a bit."

"What happens when you complete all twenty-seven markers?"

"The computer sets off alarms and money comes flying out." Maggie turned to Helen and both grinned. "We'll know when we hit the jackpot."

Maggie continued the mapping for another twenty minutes. Helen's cell rang and she scooted away to answer. Julianne was checking in.

"Everything okay?" Maggie asked.

"Fine. My daughter wanted an update."

Suddenly the screen went dark.

"What happened?"

"The process is done. Watch."

They watched as the faces began pixelating on both sides of the screen. The images were incredibly sharp for the 1850s.

Helen found herself gaping at the two men on the screen.

Elias Turner on the left. Elias Brown on the right.

"Same man," Helen said. "Same eyes, nose, mouth, skin shade, hair line, even facial shape. I'd swear it."

"More important," Maggie said. "*Technology* swears it."

Chapter 26

Brattleboro, Vermont, November 2018

Helen stepped onto the porch and pulled her collar close. The Indian summer heat had decided to move on and the air was chill but clean and clear. A squirrel screeched at her and Honey took chase. She set her coffee mug on the bench by the tree and studied its trunk. No initials had appeared or re-appeared and Helen let out a sigh. What am I missing, old tree? Give me a hint. The mystery of Abigail and Elias was not solved and the tree was not forthcoming.

Even with the identification of Elias's real name, and with Joseph Thornhill's journal entry, pieces were missing. Where are you, Elias?

A car pulled into the driveway and Julianne stepped out.

"Hi sweetie."

"Hey mom. I brought you that book about Frederick Douglass I mentioned. It has a small section on when he was here in Brattleboro in 1866."

"Wouldn't that have been something? To hear him speak in person?"

"Yeah." Juli sat on the bench next to her and Honey came barreling up the path.

"Honey, how've you been, girl?" A brief lovefest. She turned to Helen. "Where's Marie?"

"Off shopping with an old friend."

"*Old* friend?"

"Old is a relative term."

"You promised to tell me about Joseph Thornhill's diary. I want to know the last things he wrote about Elias."

"I've been going over it in my mind, but it doesn't help in the end. I still can't figure out where Elias is."

"Tell me."

"You know that Joseph worked for the underground railroad. He was the one who helped Elias escape."

"Right. He forged papers and gave him contacts up here in Vermont."

"If he wound up here in Brattleboro, at Ainsley Hill Inn, the contacts must have been the owners here, the Woolseys. Joseph's notes don't say that so that's just a guess on my part."

"We know Jeb and Sara Woolsey were agents for the slave railroad because of the secret space upstairs."

Helen nodded. "Joseph writes that he never again heard from Elias, but he heard rumors that the owners of the Tupelo Plantation received an offer to buy Elias's freedom from someone in Brattleboro." Helen shrugged. "Must have been the Woolseys, right?"

"You could buy a slave's freedom? What a weird concept."

"Desperate times. Anyway, from the confusing notes in the journal that I could piece together, the plantation owners did not want to sell his freedom. Instead, they sent the overseer--."

"Colton Strange."

"Yes, they sent Colton Strange to Brattleboro to bring him back." Helen sipped her coffee.

"We know that Strange arrived here, because Abigail mentioned she found a handbill about a reward for information on a runaway slave."

"So Strange found Elias?"

"I'm pretty sure. He may have killed him." Helen frowned. "Still . . ."

"What?"

"I don't believe it would've been easy to kill him here. With all the folks around the Inn. And Elias being a pretty strong young man."

"If he did, what would he do with the body?"

"Exactly."

"Well, mom. This may be one mystery you may not be able to solve."

"I am not giving up." She gave a forlorn smile. "The old maple is counting on me."

For a while, Helen refused to dwell on her failure to find what happened to Elias. She busied herself writing outline after outline on a new mystery. She spent time with Julianne and had long talks with Marie. She planned Thanksgiving dinner, even went shopping early for Christmas presents and decorations. She also spent time with Dave. Dinners and drives around the area took her mind in new directions. Happy ones.

On the last day of the month, with only a light dusting of snow on the ground, Helen decided to take a walk with Honey. She called her but the dog did not come. She walked around to the side of the house and found Honey chewing on something.

"Hey, hey, stop that. What are you eating?"

Honey immediately dropped it and backed away.

Helen bent to retrieve it and saw it was a ring, a wedding ring exactly like Abigail's.

"Marie," Helen called. Marie stepped onto the kitchen porch, wrapped in a wool shawl.

"Marie, remember this?"

"Sure. It's Abby's ring. How did you get it?"

"Didn't we put it somewhere for safe keeping?"

"In a little box in a drawer in the hallway. Let me go look." Marie disappeared into the house. She returned with the box.

"Nope, still here."

"This must be Elias's ring." Helen's breath steamed in the chilly air. "They must have had matching rings. Wait a minute." Helen ran into the house. She returned with the wedding photo. Sure enough, rings were visible on both bride and groom's fingers.

"Well, I'll be."

"Honey found it."

"Where?"

"Right here by the kitchen porch."

Both women looked around the ground and the porch.

"Maybe we should ask her," Marie said.

"Ask Honey?"

"Sure. Ask her where she found the ring."

Helen blinked in surprise. "Honey," she called. "Come here, girl. You're not in trouble. It's okay."

The retriever came trotting back.

Helen knelt down and held the ring out to Honey. "Where did you find this, girl?"

Honey whined.

"S'okay, really. Show me where you found it."

Honey looked into her eyes and knelt in front of the porch. She stuck her nose underneath and whined.

"Under the porch?" Marie said.

"Marie, when was this porch built, do you know?"

"No idea. Way before my time."

"Looks like an addition." Helen walked back on forth in front of the porch. "Construction different from the original house, you can tell by the roof."

"Too bad there aren't any pictures that go back that far."

Helen grabbed an old blanket off the rocker on the porch and laid it on the ground in front of the porch. Then she lay down and scooted close to the two steps. "Hope I can get myself up again," she laughed.

"Let me get you a flashlight." Marie came back from inside with one.

Helen shone the light under the porch. "Ugh. What a smell. Just old dirt and debris, I think." She slid out and rolled to her knees, then stood.

Honey began sniffing underneath again. She whined, then began digging, kicking dirt back behind her.

"No, don't . . ." Helen started.

Marie put a hand on her arm. "Wait."

Honey kept digging until she could crawl under the porch.

Helen put her hands to her mouth, "No, Honey . . ."

The dog began to whimper, then bark. She continued to bark and refused to come out.

"Something is under there," Helen said.

"I'm going to call Dave and get someone out here to dig." Marie hurried into the house.

By seven that evening, Dave and two of his deputies had torn the porch apart. It was pitch dark by then but no one wanted to stop, so the men brought some night lights in.

Once the floorboards and stringers were gone, there was just open dirt.

"So, what are we lookin' for?" a deputy asked.

"Elias Turner," Helen whispered.

"What? Who?" Everyone ignored him.

"Oh my God," Marie said. "Is that a hand?"

Dave bent closer and gently brushed the dirt away. "Looks like a hand, fingers in a claw-like position. Can't see much else." He stood. "Damn."

Helen turned away.

"We're going to have to wait until morning to fully excavate, Helen."

"I know."

"You think this is that runaway slave?"

"Yes." Helen suddenly found tears streaming down her face.

"I'm sorry," Dave said.

"I'm being ridiculous. If this is Elias, he's been dead since 1856." She turned to Dave, puffy-eyed. "He never vanished. He was here all the time. Under the house."

The next day, the State Police sent out a forensics team to excavate the remains. What they found under the porch astonished everyone. It was the mummified remains of a man, whom Helen had no doubt was Elias Turner.

Marie, Helen, Julianne, and Dave stood by as the coroners van took the corpse away for examination. A sense of relief fell on Helen's shoulders.

"I'm beginning to wonder whether there's something supernatural about this old house," Dave said.

Helen turned away.

"Mom, do you think we can bury Elias with Abigail, at Mather Cemetery?"

"I'd love to but I haven't been able to find her grave."

"You looked?" Dave said.

"Yes, but I'll give it another try."

"I'll get back to you on the remains. There won't be any way to identify him, but they should be able to date the body."

"I did find something that may help," Helen said. "Up in the attic was all kinds of paperwork on the Inn. I found a contract from a construction company to complete a porch addition outside the kitchen."

"Yeah?" Dave said, interest piqued.

"It was dated October 1856."

"Elias was killed and his body placed under the construction debris." Dave stared at the remains of the porch.

"Wouldn't the workers have noticed it?" Juli asked.

"Nah," Dave said. "They wouldn't have paid attention if it was covered well."

"All these years," Marie whispered. "Elias was right here."

Dave left and the three women went into the house to warm up. Winter had definitely arrived.

Over the coming weeks, the mysteries were resolved. The mummified remains were dated back to the mid-nineteenth century, the time of the underground railroad. From the scars on his back, the coroner believed he was a slave. The cause of death: blunt force trauma. Colton Strange never brought Elias back and collected his reward. Elias put up a fight and, unluckily, was beaten to death by his overseer.

With Honey's help, Helen managed to find Abigail's grave. The local funeral home buried her husband next to her. Helen had a new gravestone erected:

> *Here Lies Abigail and Elias Turner,*
> *A Slave no More*
> *Together Forever*
> *1856*
> *to*
> *2018*

One last bit of the puzzle remained. The tree. Had the initials returned? Had Helen brought justice once more to the exceptional residents of the Ainsley Hill Inn and Tavern?

She crept out that night with a flashlight. Her heart beat hard and she had trouble swallowing. The torch beam seemed drawn to one spot on the tree. There, where she remembered seeing the names for the first time, were the engravings: *Abby and Eli.*

Here to stay.

Chapter 27

Daniel

Brattleborough, Vermont, May 1776

Daniel Noah Ainsley stood on the porch of the Inn, untied his barkeep apron, and wiped his brow with it. He peered up at the maple tree, grateful for its shade on a day so unusually hot for early spring.

"Yer work is done, then?" a soft voice spoke at his elbow.

He felt an arm slip around his waist, a slight arm that didn't reach but midway around him. He wondered how a man of considerable height and girth like he, ended up with a tiny lass whose head barely reached his shoulders.

"My work never be done unless the queen of the manor finds it acceptable." He leaned down to kiss her. "My Susan of the black eyes and yellow hair."

"I, erm, will allow you a few minutes before you get back to your chores." Susan Pritchett Ainsley untangled herself from her husband and walked down the three porch steps. She sat on the bench that encircled the tree. "Come, rest a while."

He joined her. "Now aren't you glad I decided to keep this lovely old girl?" he said, patting the gnarled trunk. When he built the Inn and Tavern ten years before he considered chopping the maple down. Without it, he would have been afforded more options for where to set the structure. But the stately maple was too handsome, its lofty shape, its artful branches . . . and its leaves, their vibrant color, but more . . . their sound. A feathery sigh, a blustery whoosh, followed by a whispering demise. No, he would keep it. She seemed happy about that decision. She. What was he thinking? It was just a bloody tree. His wife seemed happy about the decision as well. Ah, women. They tend to hew together.

"I would never have let you cut her down. And look. The shade is wondrous cool."

Ferocious barking broke the quiet of the morning and two dirty, wet yellow dogs barreled around the corner of the house.

Husband and wife looked at each other, smiling.

She stood. "Nothin' like dogs smelling of pond scum to brighten yer day." Susan stood, bent down to kiss Daniel again and headed into the house.

He leaned back into the tree but before he could decide his next move, he saw dust rising in the distance. A horse. He had a visitor.

Daniel heard footsteps behind him.

"Hey, Da, s'pose that's a guest?"

Daniel squinted into the distance. He burst out with a loud guffaw. "No. That's an old friend, son. An old friend."

A man rode in on a fine gelded, Virginia-bred quarter horse, dirt flying, as he reared up short.

Daniel nodded to his eldest son, Peter, who quickly took the horse's bridle and held him while the man alighted.

"John Stark, as I live 'n breathe," Daniel declared. "You are a sight I din't intend to see again."

Stark brushed off his shirt and held out his hand. "Now why may that be? Course you'd see me again, my friend." He laughed." How long has it been, then?"

"Don't know, mebbe twelve, fifteen years."

"Can't be that long."

"When the war ended, 1763."

"That long. By God, man." Stark turned to Peter. "This is your son?"

"Aye. Peter, meet my old compatriot, John Stark."

The men shook hands.

"*The* John Stark?"

"Uh oh, *the*? What's this?" Stark raised sardonic eyebrows. Daniel noted the gray streaking his dark hair. Much like his own mane.

"I mean, well, you're famous, sir." Peter's words began to tumble out of his mouth. "You outflanked General Howe in Boston, I mean, building a breastwork along the beach, well, damn, it sent those British scum scurrying." He sucked in a breath. "It was brilliant and you are--."

"Stop, desist, my boy." Stark put a hand on Peter's shoulder. "How old are you now?"

"I'm sixteen, sir. Well, almost. In a month."

"Or three." Daniel laughed.

"No, but you're a hero, sir, you--."

"All right, please, do not go on," Stark said. "You must be reading the leaflets my wife writes."

The two friends burst out laughing. Peter looked perplexed.

"John, you are a hero, make no mistake," Daniel grabbed Stark by the arm. "Come inside and let's celebrate our reunion."

Stark followed Daniel into the Inn while Peter led the horse to the barn, around the left side of the Inn and past the sign newly engraved by the middle brother, Isaac. It read: *Ainsley Hill Tavern* and featured an arrow pointing the way.

Within a few hours, John Stark had met Daniel's family: wife, three sons, and a daughter. He was fed a hearty mutton stew and given a room for the night.

Other guests arrived and were settled by the Inn manager, the youngest of the Ainsley sons, Jonas. After a brief respite and wash-up in his quarters, Stark joined Daniel in a corner of the Tavern to share war stories. Or so Daniel thought. He soon discovered that Stark had other intentions with his unexpected visit.

It was nearing eleven and the Tavern was still in full measure although the noise level had subsided with the departure of a muster of the Green Mountain boys.

Stark drank from his mug of ale. The two men eyed each other over the years.

"Been a long time, John."

"It has that, Daniel. I noticed your leg has never gone right since that musket ball in '62."

"Nope, it hasn't. Least I can hobble around."

"You were right, not letting them take the leg at the knee."

Daniel nodded, drank some. "Aye. Don't think I'd want a wooden one instead."

"It could've killed you, you know."

"Reckon so. But my Susie deserves a whole man."

"Sure. She might've had a dead one."

"How is Molly?"

"Ah, she's fine. Don't see enough of her."

"That's not what I hear."

"What do you mean?"

"Do you not have enough kids for your own army?"

"Only eleven." Stark laughed. "Hmm, I see what you mean."

"Oy, tell me, John, what are you really about these days?"

Stark's face lit up with a fervent passion that Daniel had seen all too often during their fighting days in the French and Indian war. He leaned in. "I have a proposal to put forth to you, my good man."

Daniel stared at his friend, his heartbeats intensifying. Somehow he had expected as much. Whenever John Stark was near, the air seemed suffused with lightning.

"Have you been to New York?'

Daniel frowned at the change in conversation. "I have not. Why would I?"

"Why indeed." Stark stretched his neck on his bony shoulders. "There are those who feel you are the right man for an important job. I, for one."

"I'm listening."

Stark leaned back in his chair and Daniel knew he was in for a bit of story-telling.

"After the rout of the British in Boston . . ."

"In which you played a major hand . . ." Daniel grinned. "Wish I was with you."

Stark nodded. "As do I."

"It was a masterful drubbing."

"Nothing they didn't deserve. In any case, the bastards retreated to Nova Scotia. However, Halifax is only a short stop on the way . . ." Stark paused.

"On the way? To where?"

"New York. Well, not on the way literally but the next stop in their strategic plan. New York is where we expect them to repair. They could regroup, restore their troops, replenish supplies, and spread out across Brooklyn, Long Island, then Connecticut, and New Jersey, and the real prize--."

"The Hudson River," Daniel added.

"Indeed. In New York, they could incarcerate or hang every patriot within their sights and spread fear and insurrection that could transfigure the northern colonies. And, in an astoundingly short time."

Daniel felt the hairs on his neck bristle. The patriots had won Boston, but if they lost New York, the war could be irrecoverable. "How do you know all this? That the British will take New York?"

Stark forced a weak smile. "The man who takes this job will be one who believes fiercely in our cause. He has the fortitude of a hungry bear after his prey, the stomach to kill the enemy when necessary, the backbone to stand up for what is right and to not be swayed by argument." He clasped his hands together on the table. "His purpose is to live free . . . or die. "

"You think I'm this man?"

Stark nodded.

"Well, I guess I'm a real saint, then. What is this job, which you refuse to define?"

Stark laughed but it died on his lips. "A bartender."

"Oy?"

"You will run a tavern in the heart of New York, where you will gather information and pass it on."

"A spy? You want me to be a spy? Never going to happen."

"Don't dismiss it out of hand, Daniel."

"I do dismiss it. First, how can I leave here, this Tavern, the Inn, my wife, kids and--."

"From what I've seen, your wife and kids run the place. We could supply help for them when needed."

"What? Yer crazy, man."

"We would make sure the Inn made a profit, that your family was in good stead, taken care of. They would always know your status."

"You mean whether I'm alive or dead?"

"Yes."

"Oh, now that makes me feel better." He waited. "And how would I gather information, as you say? Me a known patriot."

"Ahh, but you are only known as a patriot here, and to only a few at that, seeing as how the Tory sentiment runs high in Vermont. In New York you will be a dedicated loyalist."

"No, no, never, cannot do that."

"It's for the cause, Daniel. Our cause. Think, man. You are a genial and capable barkeep. What you could pry out of your patrons is immeasurable. They will confide their deepest emotions, thoughts, dreams, and woes, to you. It would be easy pickin's for ye to learn about the troop movements and intentions." He paused. "Be assured. You are the perfect man for the job."

"Me. A perfect spy?" Daniel slapped his head with his palm. "Susan will never have it."

Stark finished off his ale. "We can let her decide."

"What? Fuck, no. Yer not gonna tell her anything about this."

They fell silent.

Stark exhaled. "There is an esteemed man coming here tonight. He wants to meet you, to determine if my choice for this job . . . you . . . shall be his choice as well. He will want to meet Susan. If he can convince her, will you consider taking on this urgent mission? For the patriots, for the Continental Army. For your family . . . and for the future of this country?"

Daniel narrowed his eyes. "Who is this *esteemed* man, then, who has so bloody much influence?"

"George Washington."

Chapter 28

Late that night, Daniel sat with Stark over glasses of wine. He watched Peter, who was tending bar, throw the rag with which he was wiping down the bar into a basket and look up. His son's eyes widened and his mouth dropped.

Daniel turned to see what had shocked his son so. The door to the Inn opened but it was not near tall enough for the visitor. The giant had to duck under the doorway to enter the parlor. There was no mistaking the man. General George Washington.

The commander of the Continental Army wore a dark blue epauletted coat with buff rise-and-fall collar, buff cuffs, and lapels. Yellow metal buttons ran down each lapel. His waistcoat and breeches were also buff in color with gilt buttons. Long black boots reached to his knees. His hair was dark and smoothed back. He did not wear a wig, but Daniel could detect a powdery residue. More impressive was his countenance. Earnest, grave, severe, without a hint of humor.

Stark introduced Daniel to Washington.

Daniel called to Peter for more drinks.

"John has told me a good deal about you, Daniel," Washington began. "You men were soldiers in the war, I understand. Got to know each other well?"

"As well as you can know any man who is bleeding next to you in a ditch," Daniel said with a smile.

Washington parted with a faint smile, showing no teeth.

"John says you are the man for this job, Daniel. I very much wanted to meet you and discuss it if you are amenable."

Daniel was mesmerized by Washington's lilting Virginia cadence.

"Of course, General."

181

"We are at a fateful crossroads, sir. The British and the loyalists are swarming over the northeastern colonies. Once they take hold in New York, by God, we will be hard pressed to rid ourselves of the swine." He stopped to sip his Madeira, a bottle that Daniel kept for special guests. "We have an opportunity to turn the tide of the conflict. In New York City. But we need a special, erm, soldier, for a particularly delicate mission. Now John has convinced me that with your personality and talents, you are a perfect fit for this occupation, sir."

Daniel felt his body tingle with both exhilaration and trepidation. He yearned to help his country but he feared for his own livelihood, his family, the Inn. A thousand thoughts crisscrossed his mind and tied up his tongue.

Washington nodded. "I understand your hesitance, Daniel. I believe John told you that we would ensure the safety of your home here. And your family, of course. As best we could."

"The war is not being fought here, Daniel," John said. "No one even needs to know you're not here."

"Daniel," Washington said. "Might I ask your permission to speak with your wife? It sometimes helps to have all the players involved to make a momentous decision such as this."

"Players?" Daniel said. "As actors in a play?"

"Exactly. Is that not what we all are, in fact? Acting out our part in this dramatic and decisive stage performance? *To be or not to be?* As Shakespeare said. *Our* question is: To be free or to be forever subjects of the crown? Will the colonies remain under British rule or become our own sovereign country and govern ourselves? That is the question we can help decide. You and I. Right here."

The men fell silent.

Daniel's head was spinning in directions he had not anticipated. His blood fizzled with passion for this stunning proposition and his whole body seemed on fire with it. The aches and pains he experienced just that morning were somehow gone. A new energy overtook his limbs and he felt like dancing. Insane, ridiculous, senseless.

A female voice interrupted his reflections. Susan.

"How did you . . ?" Daniel stuttered.

182

"I asked her to meet us, Daniel," Stark said. "I hope I haven't overstepped my bounds."

Susan spoke, her voice soft. "It is all right, John. I am privileged to be included." She smiled at Daniel then turned to Washington. "I understand you wish to speak to me, General. I am happy to oblige."

"It is my pleasure, Missus Ainsley, I assure you," Washington said as he stood. Daniel grinned at the general's six-foot-two height towering over his wee wife.

"It is my honor, sir," she returned.

For the next thirty minutes, the General explained his proposal to Susan Ainsley. As John Stark had assured Daniel, his home and family would be under the care of the Continental Army and the direct orders of Washington himself.

"Tell me, Missus Ainsley," Washington said. "What do you think of this notion?"

"You mean do I think Daniel can do the job for you?"

Washington nodded.

"I think he would be the man best suited for the job, better than any other you could recruit. If it's information you are after, my husband could . . . connive a turtle out of his shell."

Stark and Washington laughed. Daniel turned red.

"Joking aside," she said. "Daniel is the man you want for this job." She paused. "I do have one stipulation, however. You must bring him back to me. It will *not do* if he doesna' return."

"I understand." Washington gave a solemn nod.

"All right, then, General Washington," Susan said. "If my husband can help the patriots in this fight for our country, I am agreed."

"Thank you, Missus Ainsley, that is the right decision," Washington said.

"Anything to help this country achieve independence is the right decision, sir. I will leave you, gentlemen, to your business." She rose.

George Washington spoke. "You are a brave woman, Madam, and I admire your courage. I shall do my best to safeguard your husband. You have my word."

"Your word is a precious commodity, General. I am relying on it. Good night."

Hours later, with his illustrious guests, Stark and Washington, abed in their rooms, Daniel lay next to Susan who breathed heavily in sleep. He found sleep a futile endeavor. He gazed out his window at a navy blue sky bejeweled with stars and other celestial objects. New York. His life was about to change on a grand scale.

Daniel started at the scratching sound at his bedroom door. Dawn was still hours away. He opened the door and his two friends jostled their way in, wagging their tails.

"Ach, boys, my loyal warriors, come here, then."

"What's going on?" Susan mumbled.

"Go back to sleep, me love."

Daniel sat on the floor and the two dogs fell into his lap. He felt his heart slow and the tension ease from his muscles. His mind drifted off . . . to the past, to the future. In a few minutes all three were asleep on the rug in front of the bed.

On a night, several weeks later, after the supper guests at the Inn retired, Daniel rode out to meet two men at the only other tavern in the area. The Arms Tavern was one of the earliest buildings in town, even older than his own family's Inn and Tavern. He and John Arms had been friends since childhood. John's wife, Susanna, took over running of the place when John died five years ago.

As he approached, Daniel noticed two horses tied outside. He hoped they belonged to the men that Stark had introduced him to by post: Benjamin Tallmadge and Nathan Hale. Both men had attended Yale and gone on to become schoolteachers in Connecticut. Both were ardent patriots.

"You Daniel Ainsley?" one of the men said as both stood to greet him. "I'm Ben Tallmadge. This is Nate Hale."

Daniel shook their hands and they sat down to mugs of beer.

A barmaid came by for his order." What can I get the competition, eh?"

"Same as them," Daniel said. "How are things, Franny?"

"Ach, quiet. Not like your place, ye know. But then your place has *you* as barkeep. Here, they've got only me." She cackled and wandered away.

Daniel turned to the men. "You rode up today, then?"

"We did and booked a room at the Inn here for the night," Benjamin said.

Franny set his drink down and left to tend a new customer at the bar.

All three men eyed him. Daniel shook his head. "Just the local greengrocer. Anyways, yer probably better staying here rather than taking a chance on arousing suspicion at my place."

"Must say, I was surprised at the rough ride from Wethersfield to Brattleborough," Nathan offered.

"Aye, could be treacherous in the dark." Daniel drank his beer and studied the men. Benjamin, tall and lithe, kept his face clean-shaven. Stark had told him he attracted girls as bees to honey. He was no doubt right, Daniel thought. Girls would love his long blond hair which he tied back in a leather thong. He wore a blue jacket and dark breeches, both worn and dusty from the ride.

Nathan Hale, the other man, also wore a blue coat. Slightly shorter than Benjamin, and also fair-haired, Daniel didn't think Nathan would attract the fairer sex as Benjamin. He wore a somber expression and rarely smiled. But his flawless light blue eyes shone with a brilliance that bespoke an uncommon intelligence. Not simply book-learning, according to Stark, but a quickness in perception and judgment.

"What did John Stark tell you about this meeting?" Daniel asked.

"Very little. He chooses not to put too many ideas on paper, if you know what I mean," Benjamin said.

"He only said to meet you here," Nathan said. "That we would learn more from you directly."

Daniel drank from his mug before speaking. Quietly he told them about his visit with Washington and what the General wanted him to do.

Benjamin and Nathan exchanged glances.

"He asked you to go to New York City, where thousands of British and loyalists are expected to take up residence, and become a spy? Good God. And you're good with that?" Benjamin smiled.

"What exactly did Washington say?" Nathan asked.

"He said that Congress had made it clear that New York must be defended to the death. John Adams said the city was 'a kind of key to the whole continent.'"

"A key?" Benjamin said.

"That it is a post of infinite--he used that word--infinite importance."

"The thing about New York," Nathan said, "is that it is an island, which means it is surrounded by water. It is a strategic city in that regard."

"Aye," Daniel said. "Washington said that should the British take over that town and command of the North River, they can stop the interchange between the northern and southern colonies . . . upon which depends the safety of America."

"Makes sense," Benjamin said. "Whoever owns the sea owns the town."

"It's going to be a hard press to fight a Royal Navy assault," Nathan said.

The men fell silent, each reflecting on his own thoughts.

"Another risk worthy of consideration," Daniel said, "is the fact that Brooklyn's high ground looms above lower Manhattan."

"Indeed," Nathan said. "If the British gunners seize those heights they would have an advantage similar to the Continental Army in Boston, when they seized the Dorchester Heights."

"Bloody hell," Benjamin said. "You will be in the thick of it all. You will have to find out when the troop ships are arriving, exactly where, how many troops aboard . . ."

"Yes, yes, I know." Daniel felt his palms begin to sweat.

"Tell me. How does a dedicated patriot pretend to be a loyalist?" Nathan said.

"He would have to be a great actor." Benjamin grinned. "But then if John Stark and George Washington are convinced that you can pull it off, Daniel, I believe them."

"What do you know about spying?" Nathan said.

"Not a fooking thing," Daniel said, clunking his mug on the table. "That's where you come in."

"How?" Benjamin said.

"Washington will need to be informed of the British movements, plans, dates, and any other piece of scuttlebutt that comes along. Once I find out something of importance . . ."

"As the genial barkeep everyone confides in," Nathan said.

"I will pass the messages along to you and you will ensure it gets to the General."

Benjamin's eyes popped. "To us? We don't know much more about spying than you do."

"What?" Daniel said.

"Hold on," Nate said. "The point is that, together, we can work it out. Figure out how to get messages to the General. Right?"

"Yeh, right," Benjamin said. "Do you know what bar you will be keeping?"

"The Black Horse Tavern. I believe it is on William and John Streets."

"Where will you live?"

"There's an apartment upstairs."

"Yes," Nathan said. "Perfect. The Black Horse is popular pub with the loyalists. Once the Brits arrive, they will frequent it as well."

"Why? Because the loyalists do?"

"No. Because right up the street is a playhouse. The John Street Theatre. British officers love the theatre, you see, so they will visit the Black Horse after the play."

Daniel's mind flashed to Washington's comments about the theatre. "Meanwhile, the British are not in New York," Daniel said.

"Not yet. If you're good at ferreting out information, you will learn when they will be in New York. And where they will alight. "

"When are you bound for the City?" Nathan asked.

"In two weeks' time." Daniel stood. "How will I get word to you there when I need to?"

"How is your memory?"

"Good."

"I will be at 344 Pearl Street, second floor. Remember that. But the safest way to reach me is not to send messages or even visit."

"Oh?" Daniel said.

"Put a lantern in the window of your apartment after the tavern closes. Leave it there for thirty minutes, then put it out. Just a man getting ready for bed. No one will be suspect."

"Who will see it?" Daniel said.

"I will. Or Nate. We will make it a point to keep watch. If you have a message, leave the lamp on past the thirty minutes. One of us will sneak upstairs."

Daniel fell back into his chair. This whole business began to make him nervous. Benjamin and Nathan were presumably capable, but they seemed rather offhand about it all. This was a dangerous game but these men took it lightly. Perhaps he should not have accepted this assignment.

He stared into space. There was nothing for it now but to move forward. Surely he could handle this undertaking. He would, by God. There was much at stake. If they lost this bloody war, his whole world would change. His home, his family. . . his country. Yes, his country. America. His country should not be ruled by a tyrant across the seas. It should be ruled by its own people.

Daniel recalled reading a pamphlet called *Common Sense* by a man named Thomas Paine in the early days of 1776. One of his memorable quotes was something so simple, but it struck him in the heart and he could never forget it: *These are the times that try men's souls. The summer soldier and the sunshine patriot will, in this crisis, shrink from the service of their country; but he that stands it now, deserves the love and thanks of man and woman.*

He would stand for his country. For if he foundered, he would lose his own sense of self. If he turned back now, he would always brand himself a coward, a turncoat, a defector.

And Susan. What would she think of him? No. He could not fail her or his children. They counted on him. He would make them proud. Contribute in any way to the cause, whatever the cost.

At this moment, he suspected, that cost would be profoundly high.

Chapter 29

Helen

Brattleboro, Vermont, December 2018

Her old maple tree stood in glorious black and white relief against a luminous blue sky. Denuded of its leaves, Helen crunched on them as she sat on the bench, thinking of Khalil Gibran's words: *Trees are poems the earth writes upon the sky. We fell them down and turn them into paper, that we may record our emptiness.* Our emptiness. In her mind, she flashed to the pages of her new novel. Devoid of words. Empty.

On hold. Her novel, her life. Her body and soul. All on hold. Oddly enough, it felt good to not have deadlines. So what if her next book took a year, or two?

"What are you thinking about?" Marie came down the porch steps. More slowly these days.

Helen smiled and patted the bench for Marie to join her. "I was just thinking how free it feels to not have any time constraints. I can simply . . . be. Do what I want and not what I must."

"And what do you want?"

"Honestly? I want to search this old house and uncover its history."

"Haven't you done that already? With the stuff you found in the attic and the mysteries you've solved about the Ainsley Hill occupants over the years?"

"A bit, I guess. But there's more here, I know it."

Marie gave her a faint smile. "What do you know?"

Helen shifted her position to face her grandmother. "This old tree told us stories about the residents of the Inn dating back to the 1850s. But the place was built before the Revolution. That's almost a hundred years earlier."

"Right."

"There must be more stories in that first century of existence, don't you think?"

"Has the tree given you any clues?"

"No. That's just it. I think I have to find something first . . . before the tree--."

"Before the tree confirms it."

"Something like that."

"You want to tear this old place apart looking for a new mystery? I get it."

Helen took Marie's hand. "Yes. Now that you said it, that's exactly what I want to do. Need to do. And not just the house."

Marie raised her eyebrows.

"The barn too. I feel, erm, I feel as if it's been calling to me." Helen laughed. "God, I am really going nuts, aren't I?"

"No. I think you should follow your instincts. You've been right every time so far."

Marie tilted her head toward the old red barn. "It's been many years since I was in the barn. Fond memories as a teenager."

"Really?"

"That's where my sweet Jasper was kept."

"Who was Jasper?"

"An old, gentle gelding who would let me ride without a saddle. We'd wander about the fields and woods, cross over the brook. He was a dear, loved apples."

"All horses love apples."

"No. Jasper *really* loved apples." Marie smiled as she gazed back in time. "The barn, yup. That's where you should start."

Later that morning, Helen drove to Julianne's bookstore in Putney. Her daughter had two unusual books to show her and insisted she come up right away.

When she arrived, Helen sat in her car looking at the storefront. Juli had decorated it with seasonal colors and the latest best sellers were in the window. A special display in one corner was dedicated to Helen and included some of her most famous mysteries. Two of which had been made into movies.

Inside the store, several customers browsed and a number of women pushed strollers with preschoolers. Helen smiled as Julianne's partner, Bella fussed over the little ones.

Julianne greeted her with a hug and kiss and pulled her into the tiny office in the back. Her eyes danced and her face shone with a pink glow. "The place is hopping since we've started our marketing campaign for soccer moms. They've been bringing their kids in by the busload."

"That's wonderful. Congratulations. By the looks of it, you're giving away books for free."

"Hardly. Bella is terrific with the customers, isn't she?"

Helen watched her daughter's face. "Yes, she really is. And she's very pretty." Julianne blushed.

"So. What's so special about these books to make me run up here?"

"First, I want to tell you how I came to find them."

Helen scrunched up her face. "Sounds dramatic."

"Down in the cellar, there are several crawlspaces. I began to clean them out—should have done a long time ago--and was shocked to find this old leather satchel." She held it up.

Helen could smell its age and knew the cracks and creases in it had a story to tell. "It was just lying in the crawlspace? Waiting to be found?"

"Not exactly. I had set some mousetraps, you see, the problem was getting untenable, and well, we caught one . . ."

"Yes?"

"It got away. Dragged the trap with it." Julianne blew out a breath. "I felt bad. You know that it was probably maimed and I--."

"You were responsible. I understand. You get that animal obsession from my side of the family."

"Ain't that the truth. Anyway, I started digging around to find it. I never did. But I did find the briefcase."

"You think someone hid it there?"

"It's possible. This place dates back to the early 1900s. Maybe it was used for cold storage or something." Julianne shrugged.

"And it was simply forgotten over time."

"Maybe."

"What was in it?"

"Two things I think you'll agree are an incredible find."

Julianne leaned over to her bookcase and picked up a thick leather volume. She handed it to Helen.

"*Annals of Brattleboro Volume 1 of 2, 1681-1895 by Mary Rogers Cabot.*" Helen looked up at her daughter. "Is this--?"

"It's an early edition, published in 1921, not a reproduction, which you can get now, by the way. Isn't it beautiful?"

Helen thumbed through the pages. "It is. More important, her historical research dates back to before the Inn was built."

"When was the Inn built?"

"Not sure but I believe around the mid-1700s. I'll have to research it."

"At the library?"

"No. In the barn."

"What?"

Helen paused. One more thing to convince Julianne she was losing it.

"What, mom? You know you can tell me."

"For the last few nights now, I've dreamt of the old barn. That there's something hidden in it that will give me answers to, to . . . I don't know what."

"I don't get it. What about the barn? Isn't it a big empty space with farm tools hanging on the walls and dried up old cow pies on the dirt floor?"

"Actually, yes . . . and no. On the west wall there's a large storage area, covered by a giant tarp and partly boarded up on one side."

"You're kidding."

"I have no idea what's there. But I do recall it being there when I was a kid. Just never found it interesting enough to ask, I guess."

"What do you think is there?"

"No idea. I do believe that there's one more story that hasn't been exposed yet."

"The tree hasn't given you any more initials?"

"No. That's just it. I feel like I have to make the first move this time. Find something that will unfold a new mystery. And, for some peculiar reason, I'm sure the answers are in the barn."

"What do the dreams tell you?"

"All I remember is colors. No characters, no plot, nothing else."

"What are the colors?"

"Red and blue."

Helen stood, trying to force her brain to recall more. She looked down at the book in her hands. "Did you look through this? For the Inn?"

"I did but didn't find it mentioned. I'm not sure what that means."

"I'm going to check with the Historical Society and the Library to see if there's any history on our old place."

"You think there are answers in the barn?"

"Yes. It's crazy, but I do." Helen sat down. "What else did you find?"

"Maps. Hand drawn of Brattleboro, spelled *ough,* by the way, dating from 1745 to 1912." Julianne reached for a folder and handed it to Helen.

"These are amazing," Helen said. "Look, here's Fort Dummer on the west side of the Connecticut River. The first settlement in Brattleboro and the first English settlement in Vermont."

"When did Vermont become a state?"

"Not until 1791, but Brattleboro was chartered back in 1753. New Hampshire and New York fought over it as their territories."

Julianne caught her mother's eye. "What is it? I've seen that look on your face before."

"I just remembered something else from my dreams."

"What?"

"Sounds."

"Like music, voices, what?"

"No. At first I thought it was thunder. There were loud, percussive booms but it was deeper in pitch than thunder and seemed to have residual waves or . . . something, I don't know."

"If you had to guess, what would you say it was?"

Helen hesitated but then said, "A cannon firing. It was the sound of war."

Minutes went by before either woman spoke.

"War," Julianne said, gazing into space. "I think we can rule out the Civil War, because Abigail and Elias lived at the Inn before that war."

"Right. And we're going further back in time. It has to be the Revolution. Red and blue. Redcoats and bluecoats. Cannon fire. What else makes sense?"

Julianne shook her head. "But the war wasn't fought in Vermont."

"No, but the *warriors* could have come from here."

"When do you plan to tear the barn apart?"

Helen laughed. "Why? Are you going to bring a ten-pound hammer and an L-bar?"

"Why not? I'd love to help. Now, I'm dying to know what's under the tarp in the barn."

"Make you a deal. This afternoon, I'm heading straight to the library. I've already got a call into the Historical Society. Surely, they'll have records of when the Inn was built and who built it."

"You could also try the Town Clerk's office. Don't they have all the property records?"

"Good idea."

"I'll get some time off and join you at the demolition tomorrow."

Helen stood and pulled her daughter in for a hug. "Call me tonight. I will have some answers."

By five that afternoon, Helen did have answers. But not the ones she expected.

Chapter 30

By mid-morning the next day, December 4, Julianne had arrived wearing work clothes and bearing a ten-pound hammer. "Sorry, I didn't have an L-Bar."

Helen laughed as she zipped up her hoodie. The barn felt chilly.

"It's okay. Hopefully, we won't be ripping anything apart. Except for the partial wall and that's already pretty broken down." Julianne rubbed her hands together. "By the way, what did you find out at the library?"

"Nothing much. The Inn was built in 1766 and remained an Inn for many decades after. That's about it. But I'm not discouraged. Still have a lot of research to do."

"What do you hope we'll find here in the barn?"

"Something that will tell us more about the history of this old place. We know it goes back to the American Revolution, which in itself is astounding. I mean, that it's actually been around this long."

"Maybe that's why you're dreaming about it."

Helen tapped her daughter on her back. "I hope we're not disappointed. All we may find is a bunch of old junk furniture and farm equipment."

"It's worth a look."

"Well, let's get crackin' if we're going to search this old barn and unearth a mystery."

Julianne rolled her sleeves up and slipped on gloves.

In two hours, the women had pried off the broken boards that had separated a corner of the barn from the rest. Helen got splinters for her efforts.

"Told you to wear gloves," her daughter said.

"I had all intentions of *you* doing the work."

"Ha. You can't keep your hands off."

"Got that right. Okay, let's get this tarp off."

"Yeah, I'm dying to see what's underneath."

"Grab a corner. One, two, three, ready. Go."

They pulled the old tarp down and dragged it into the middle of the barn. Dust flew up as did a couple of birds. Both women screamed, stepped back, and started laughing.

"Ugh, what a mess. How many years of dirt just came down?"

"A guess?" Helen said. "At least thirty. When dad took over for his parents who actually bought the Inn in the 30s, he turned it into a farm. But by the time he was fifty, he no longer did any farming, so he shut up the barn."

"Want to hear my guess? A hundred and fifty or more. I doubt grandpa cleaned this out even when he did use the barn."

"You might be right. Let's see what's here that could give us some clues." Helen touched Juli's arm. "Wait, I've got an idea." She walked across the barn and picked up a leaf blower.

"Brilliant."

"Okay, put on your sunglasses and step back." Helen put her own glasses on and, after three tries, managed to fire up the blower. She started at one end of the space and blew untold years of earth, grime, and dirt, into the air. She then followed the billows outside until she was satisfied that was all the blower could get.

Both women went to stand outside and gulp the clean air. Honey came racing up from the house, barking like mad.

"S'okay, Honey, just us," Juli said.

Julianne dusted herself off, shook off her hair, and retied her ponytail. Helen brushed off her denim shirt.

"I hope we have enough light in there," Helen said. "Not sure if the electricity in the barn can be hooked up at this point. We may have to cart stuff out into the daylight."

"Or into the house."

"Ready?"

They donned their gloves and headed back inside. Windows over the corner space afforded them light enough to identify several large objects right away.

"Hey, look at this. An old bicycle," Julianne said. "Looks really old . . . maybe old enough for it to be yours."

"Very funny."

Julianne grasped it by the handlebars and rolled it into the middle of the barn.

"Oh my God. It's one of the early Schwinn's."

"How early?"

"1950s. Must have been dad's or mom's."

"Wow, a collectible."

"Look at this," Helen said. "Even had a luggage rack. What's it say? Phantom? This is a Schwinn Phantom."

"Swell," Juli said.

Helen stuck her tongue out at her daughter. "You don't appreciate quality."

"Hm, let's keep looking." She moved back to the corner. Next, she rolled out an old wooden swivel chair and pushed it aside. Then she pulled out a side table, two lamps and another small chair.

"What era do you suppose?" Juli asked.

Helen looked down at the items. "I'd say forties, maybe even thirties. Don't think they're valuable, though."

"You may have to look through those banker boxes, but since they're a modern invention, I doubt there will be anything of ancient history in there."

"We can browse through them in the house later." Helen pointed at an object. "That's what I want to search through."

"Is that a desk?"

"A secretary, I believe it's called." Helen ran her fingers over the dark cherry wood then gently pulled at the edges, bringing down a flat writing surface. "Stunning," she whispered.

"I thought they had roll tops back then."

"Those came later. This writing desk was early."

"Like how early?"

"Like Daniel Ainsley early."

"Ainsley, like us, Ainsley?"

"Yup. Your ancestor about eight or nine generations removed."

"So he built the Inn . . . when?"

"If the Historical Society is correct, 1766."

"Ten years before the Declaration of Independence. Jeez."

Helen nodded, still running her fingers over the wood. "Look at all the storage space—the drawers below, the tiny compartments above. Even a compartment behind this little door over the writing surface."

"Now the question is, is it empty?"

Helen lifted the writing surface and latched it closed so she could pull open the lower drawers. All empty. Next she pulled down the writing desk once more and tried the small upper drawer in the center above it. Inside were blank envelopes and paper, bottles of dried ink, and stiff-quilled pens. She stared at these objects with her mouth open.

"You'll catch flies."

"Do you know what we have here? This is a slice of early colonial history, right here in our barn, Juli." She turned to her daughter. "This is a precious gift, such a treasure . . ."

Julianne said nothing but picked up the ink jar. "Daniel Ainsley may have used this."

At that moment, a car pulled up into the driveway and someone beeped a horn.

Both women started and hurried to see who the visitor was.

"Ah." Juli grinned. "It's your new beau."

Dave Major stepped out of the police car. Helen walked over to him, brushing her hair with her hands. They both smiled.

It took Helen a long time to fall asleep that night. When she finally did, it wasn't for long. At three in the morning, she bolted upright in bed. Honey whined and raced around to her side of the bed, tail down, fearful.

"It's okay, Honey. There's something I need to do." Helen dressed as quietly as she could then stole down the stairs. Marie had good hearing for her age and she didn't want to wake her. In the kitchen she found a flashlight and headed out in the night. Honey followed.

In the barn, she headed straight for the old desk.

"There's something here. I just know it." Helen pulled out the bottom drawers again and searched behind and underneath. No secret compartments. She slid them back in. She tried the upper middle drawer again where she'd found the writing tools. This time she searched below and behind the drawer. Nothing.

Now she reached for the upper cubbies on the left of the writing desk. She pulled open the two tiny compartments on the left. Both empty. She slid them out and searched.

"Damn."

Finally she tried the two on the right. They would not come out. Blowing out an exasperated breath, she walked around the barn looking for a tool. A screwdriver would do.

Helen tried to pry the obstinate drawers out. "God, Honey, the Historical Society would have my head if they knew what I was doing to this antique." All of a sudden she realized the tiny drawers weren't individual drawers at all. They were fronts for one larger drawer. She wiggled the screwdriver into the bottom right, then the bottom left. Finally, a popping sound and the drawer came free. She pulled it out, trepidation mixing with exhilaration. The double drawer was completely closed on all four sides. A sealed box.

She sat on the dirty barn floor and poked and prodded the drawer to find a way in. The back began to slide with effort. At that very moment, the flashlight died.

"Nooo." She shook her head and laughed. "Serves me right. Come on, Honey. Let's go look at what's inside this prized box like civilized people."

Helen stood, brushed herself off, and hurried back to the house.

"Ssh," she whispered to Honey. "We don't want to wake Marie."

Helen set the box on the small desk in her bedroom and brought the lamp closer. She firmly wiggled the back off of the drawer and gently slid the contents onto her desk.

Inside was a small stack of papers. Softer than modern paper, more like a cloth or cloth parchment. The writing on the pages was nearly illegible after so many years and Helen had trouble deciphering the print in the dim light. As she thumbed through the pages, she came across what appeared to be a newspaper article. The *New York Gazette*. Why New York?

It was dated June 7, 1776. She would need a magnifying glass to read the small type, but the headline brought her up sharply. It read: *The Black Horse Tavern Reopens Under New Management.* Below in smaller type it said: *New York Welcomes Loyalist and Tory Party Leader, Daniel Noah Ainsley, as Tavern Keeper.*

That can't be right. Daniel? A Tory? Wait, wait. If she remembered correctly, Brattleboro at the time was a hotbed of Tory sentiment. In fact, she recalled a story in the Reformer about Ethan Allen. He gathered his Green Mountain boys and fully armed, rode into town and arrested the political leaders and carted them off to prison in Westminster. They were tried and found guilty and fined for opposing the newly formed republic.

Well, hell. My ancestor was a loyalist. Helen sank back onto the bed, folding her arms across her forehead. That notion did not sit well with her. She wanted him to be a hero of the revolution, a patriot.

Honey began a low growl in the back of her throat. Helen sat up. "What?"

The retriever pranced around the room, her growls more guttural now. Helen went to the window and looked out. She saw nothing. But Honey was insistent. She ran from window to door and back again.

"All right. Let's go." Helen followed her downstairs, sliding her arms into her sweatshirt. She grabbed a new flashlight from the hall table and stepped outside onto the porch. A chill greeted her and she zipped up her hoodie.

Honey was standing at the tree looking up.

"Oh God, not again." Something was happening. Helen could feel it even if she couldn't see it. She joined Honey at the tree and looked up, shining a beam on the trunk. There, about seven feet high on the ancient maple, she watched as new letters chiseled themselves into the bark. She could almost taste the smell of burning wood. If she could reach them, she knew they'd be warm to the touch.

These initials were different from the others. They were sculpted in a beautiful italic script, a fine-point calligraphy that might have been used in the early days of the Inn.

Helen stared at the letters and could swear they had a bluish cast. The blood rushed to her head and she leaned on the trunk for support. She knew, almost expected, what the initials would be even as they formed.

D N A.

Chapter 31

Daniel

New York City, June 1776

The Black Horse Tavern sat on the corner of John and William Streets in lower New York. It was surrounded on both sides by like-wooden and-brick buildings sucking up every inch of space on the tiny island once called Manahatta by the Indians.

Early on the morning of June 29, Daniel strolled the cobblestoned streets and sidewalks of flat stone. He'd been happily surprised to find many trees lining the lanes. No maples but beech and locust, linden and elm providing shade from the unrelenting sun. Still he could feel the moist heat rising from the stone beneath his feet.

His new role as barkeep in the populous city caused him no end of bane, his working nights at the bar filled with apprehension, his dreams with disquietude. He called upon his reserves of exuberance and geniality, necessary virtues of a tavern owner, to draw in the locals and earn their trust.

Daniel enjoyed this time of day to perambulate the city. It unstiffened his maimed leg and helped him gain his bearings and find new sights. Few folks besides laborers and dock workers could be found on the streets this early.

He ambled down Fulton Street and turned left on Broadway toward a splendid view at the tip of Manhattan. He stared at his favorite spots from that vantage point . . . Richmond and Brooklyn. They were only dimly visible today with a heavy fog laying low on the water.

Soon he reached number one Broadway, the Mortier house, a mansion of massive architecture, with a lofty portico supported by Ionic columns. Not at all to Daniel's taste.

"Oy, Daniel," a voice called.

"Hullo, Ben. What are you doing up at this hour?"

"Aye, it is early, isn't it? I'm stopping to see the General today. Get some instructions for me and the boys."

Daniel pointed at the upstairs windows. "I assume General Knox and his wife are having breakfast as usual."

"Seems likely." Benjamin Tallmadge laughed displaying unusually straight and white teeth for a soldier on the move. "I hope General Washington is at the mansion as well. How are things going, then, at the Tavern? Been about three weeks?"

"The neighborhood's warming up."

"Yeh? Starting to confide in you?"

"Little things only, marital or money woes. Some a bit hostile but they like their drink so they come in. It's a slow process."

"You living upstairs?'

"In the apartment above the Black Horse."

Ben nodded. "Going down to the water, eh? Yeh, a pretty spot, she is."

"I'm always wondering if this will be the day to see them."

"Them? Ah, you mean the British Royal Navy sailing into the harbor."

They walked together a while. As they neared the docks, Daniel's breathing ratcheted up and his body drew tight. So far, there had only been a few cargo ships and schooners on the bay. All quiet in the city. He squinted into the murk. The quiet felt like a pall, the air heavy, and Daniel held his breath.

Benjamin walked ahead of him, rested his hands on his hips and stared out into the mist.

"Do you hear that?" Daniel said.

"What?"

"Listen, the waves are cresting near the docks . . . growing larger, louder."

"Oh shite." Ben began to run toward the water.

The day was about to take a turn for disaster. Suddenly, what had been a calm and quiet morning erupted into bedlam. At nine o'clock to the mark, warning guns began an incessant barking from the Grand Battery. Ships, sloops, and schooners began reversing course and piloting their way across the Upper Bay toward the Hudson, in a mad rush for refuge.

People poured out of the houses nearby and began shouting and conferring with neighbors. Within minutes, carriages were hitched and residents were riding or walking in haste, north, out of the city. Daniel had a fleeting thought they were rats deserting a sinking ship. Blue coats appeared out of nowhere and rushed into the Mansion, intent on reporting to Knox, he imagined.

Daniel rushed to the docks on the Bay and watched, heart pumping blood so fast his ears were about to burst. He peered through the remains of the morning fog and choked out the breath he was holding when he saw them.

"Are those troopships? Heading for Richmond?"

"Holy fooking God," Ben said. "Aye. That's where they're going."

The sun made its way from under the blanket of fog as Daniel stared at the ships: ten, twenty, more. And more again, crowding the waterways.

"Look, the pennants," a man running by him shouted.

Daniel spied pennants flying on their masts, some blue some yellow, each with an insignia he couldn't make out for the sun shining on the sea not only burned off the fog but created a blinding sparkle on the waters.

Several men gathered around him staring into the harbor.

"There are over a hundred, mebbe a hundred and twenty ships," one whined.

"Which could mean upward of 30,000 troops," another added.

Daniel turned to the men, recognized some as loyalists that patronized his bar.

"All right, boys," one loyalist said. "We always knew the British were coming."

"It's 'bout time, I say," another piped up. "Now we can kick the patriots' buttocks outta here."

"Let's go welcome them, why don't we?" They took off scurrying down to the water, whooping and shrieking.

Daniel turned to Ben who seemed frozen in place.

"Well, at least there'll be no more chanting "the British are coming, the British are coming," Ben said, smirking with irony.

"Nope," Daniel said. "They're here now. God help us all."

The city emptied out. From twenty-five thousand inhabitants to barely five thousand. It felt like a giant clock was ticking and the entire city held its breath waiting to see who would make the next move.

Meanwhile, Daniel carried on as usual in the bar, learning a few bits and bobs of information but nothing worthy of a true informant. If he couldn't be of value to the Continentals, then what good was he?

Barely a week passed when late on July 9, Nathan Hale stopped at his apartment, out of breath and covered with sweat from running but bearing the bright smile of victory.

Daniel ran to the window.

"No one saw me. It's safe."

"What happened?" Daniel asked.

Nathan collapsed into a chair at the table. "General Washington . . . he spoke on the Commons . . . there were hundreds of people. It was a sight."

"Yes?"

"He read part of a, a . . . declaration that the Congress sent."

"A what? Declaration? What did it say?"

Nathan whisked away sweat from his forehead with the back of a hand. He pulled out a crumpled notebook and set a quill and powdered ink jar on the table to refill.

Daniel shook his head in disbelief. "You carry that with ye?"

"I must if I'm going to pass on information." Nathan ignored Daniel's bewildered expression. "I wrote as fast as I could but could only get a few lines."

"Tell me."

"It was composed by the Congress, well, mostly Jefferson and--."

"Go on, read."

Nathan coughed, cleared his throat. "In Congress, July 4, 1776: We hold these truths to be self-evident, that all men are created equal . . ."

Daniel sank into the chair, his heart warming to the words.

" . . . that they are, something, couldn't get the word, by their Creator with certain inalienable . . ."

"Inalienable?"

"Inalienable rights . . . and listen to this . . . that among these rights are *life, liberty, and the pursuit of happiness.*"

The tension in Daniel's body began to drain. "What else, son, what else?"

Nathan looked down at his notes. "That to secure these rights, governments are instituted among men, deriving their power from the *consent of the governed.*" He stopped. "Did ye hear that? We, the people, *we* give the government power. Not the other way 'round."

"I hear you." Daniel stared into space. "It's everything I dreamed about. The way this country, our new country, should be led."

"I couldn't write fast enough, but there was something about denouncing royal despotism." Nathan jumped to his feet and pranced around the room. "We will have a fight on our hands, by God, but we will win. We will kick those British fookers out of our country."

Daniel listened to Nate's words and recognized the same fervor in himself. Yes, he thought. And I am part of it.

"And then, you'll never guess," the younger man said. "A half-crazed crowd took off down Broadway to Bowling Green."

"Where the statue of King George the Third stands," Daniel said. "They defaced it?"

"Better. They tore it down and carted the head to the Mortier, proudly displaying to the General."

Daniel let out a whistle. "I guess there's no going back now."

Nathan frowned. "Do you want to go back?"

"No, I don't. We cannot go back. We're in the thick of it now, my boy."

209

They fell silent for a long while, each absorbing the momentous impact of the words of the declaration of independence.

Nathan packed up his goods and left Daniel with much to contemplate. His brain would be engaged in interpreting what it all meant. But of more consequence . . . his heart was bursting with hope.

Three broiling hot weeks went by with nary an incident in the heart of the city and one night at the Black Horse, Daniel happened on his chance to make himself useful to the patriots. As he wiped down the bar he spotted a couple of loyalists at one end.

"Gentlemen, what may I get you?"

"How about some of that special Madeira, me man? I hear you keep it behind the bar, eh?"

"Are ye celebratin', then?"

"What's it your business?" one of the men said. As a working man, he was clean-shaven and dressed in a leather vest, torn shirt, and cheap breeches.

"Ahh," Daniel said. "Tell me the cause for celebration and it's on the house."

"Why should I tell ye anything?"

"Because if the rebels are gonna get a whuppin', I want to know. So's I can celebrate."

"Here, here," the second man said. "Besides, if'n it's free, what do you care, Freddy?"

"Shut yer yap, Booty," Freddy said.

Freddy eyed Daniel. "All right, then. Just a bit of gossip, is'all." He leaned in while Daniel poured the expensive wine. "We all know that General Howe is waiting for reinforcements, eh? I've heard today that his brother, what's 'is name?"

"Howe, ye dolt," Booty said.

"I mean what's 'is title?" He looked at Daniel who narrowed his eyes.

"Don't ask me. This is your story."

"Admiral or something like that, Howe. One's a General, one's an Admiral. Hmph," sniffed Freddy. "Anyways, the General here got word that his brother's on the high seas backed by the whole Royal Navy."

"Now surely that's an exaggeration." Daniel chuckled.

"What ye mean?" Freddy spit out.

Daniel poured more wine. "I mean the whole Royal Navy? Here in this town? Bah."

"Yeah, what ye mean, Freddy? That ain't make any sense," Booty said.

"Well, I heard it from me brother who works down the docks haulin' cargo from them freighters. He knows everything what happens on the wharf."

"What'd he say?" Daniel asked.

"He said twelve thousand sailors coming," Freddy nodded. "Sounds like the whole army to me."

"Must be reinforcements," Daniel said, almost to himself.

"Reinforcements, yeh, that's it. To back up the soldiers they's already sailed in."

"Sailors or soldiers, Freddy? Soldiers the army, sailors the navy. Which the hell is it?" Booty said.

"Fuck off and drink yer wine. What the hell difference? Sailor, soldier. They's gonna whup the rebels, that's all that counts."

Daniel forced himself to smile. Too bad dumb Freddy was right.

In the apartment after the Tavern closed, Daniel told Benjamin what he'd learned.

"Got to get that intelligence to General Washington."

"Now? At three in the morning?"

"I'll pretend I'm drunk and head down to the Mortier, sneak in the servant's entrance below."

Daniel opened his mouth to argue.

"That's my job, Daniel. It will be all right. I've got a great drunken singing voice. All the constables around here know me." He grinned and patted Daniel's arm. "Don't wait up for me." Then he was out the door.

Daniel hurried to the window and watched the young man stumble down the street. He heard him bellowing in song. God damn. At least the street was empty. Or was it? The gas lamps flickered on the houses, every seventh one. Was that a shadow he saw? What would make a shadow in the dead of night under lamplight?

Daniel squinted into the dark but could not see any movement. Had he imagined it or was there someone else wandering around the desolate streets besides Washington's agent? Had someone seen Benjamin visit him in his apartment? Do they know who he is? And why he is associating with a tavern keeper who's supposed to be a Tory?

He turned back and sat exhausted on the edge of the bed. Like he could ever sleep now. He fell back onto the pillow and his mind drifted to Susan and how displeased she would be with this plan. Unbidden, a poem came to mind. One that reminded him of his beloved wife.

> *Though battle call me from thy arms,*
> *Let not my pretty Susan mourn,*
> *Though cannons roar, yet safe from harms,*
> *Daniel shall to his Dear return.*
> *Love turns aside the balls that round me fly,*
> *Lest precious tears should drop from Susan's eye.*

Chapter 32

Daniel's composure was fit to explode. The sight of redcoats on every barstool in the Black Horse, their coats damp and stained with drink; the sound of their coarse swearings, bleating laughter, back-slapping bawls; the stink of their chewing tobacco bulging in their puffy red cheeks followed by their gruesome hacking and spitting onto the sawdust floors. They made him sick. Acid rose into his throat and his belly roiled incessantly.

Once upon a time, he had imagined the British to be a civilized people who partook in literature, theatre, art, and music. But this was a crude and boorish lot. On the other hand, Daniel prided himself on the fact that these buggers crowded his bar with frequency, so much so, that he had to hire a second cook and barmaid. With the approval of the General, of course. Indeed, he had done the first part of his job well: enticing the Tory scum to his lair. Now he had to coax information from them. A more delicate charge.

Both barmaids were skirting around the tables and mingling with the crass blokes who groped and pinched them. Of course, the maids too, were loyalists so it was no difficult feat for them. At that moment, a slight hush fell on the crowd, much as if a high priest had entered a church. Daniel squinted through the murky fog of the tavern.

Ahh. Only one man had the power to draw that kind of regard, other than King George himself. That man was Major John André.

Daniel watched as the British officer strode through the Tavern. He stopped at a table in the corner and with the wave of a hand, dispersed the current occupants. He sat and faced the bar. As always, he had a sketching pad with him.

He laid it down on the table and set out his drawing pens. Daniel had come to think of the table as André's since it afforded him the best light to do his work.

André settled and looked up, his eyes catching Daniel's. The men nodded at each other and Daniel got the special Madeira wine out for him. He brought it to André personally.

"Sit, Daniel," André said.

Daniel sat.

André held up a hand and studied it as he said, "*Cowards die many times before their deaths; the valiant never taste of death but once. Of all the wonders that I yet have heard, it seems to me most strange that men should fear. . .*" He smiled as he delivered his lines.

"*Seeing that death, a necessary end, will come when it will come,*" Daniel finished with a flourish.

"I should have known you'd be familiar with *Julius Caesar,*" André said.

"Why is that?"

"Somehow you would be drawn to powerful leaders."

"Oh?"

"Like King George," André said, a dry smile on his lips.

"Indeed." Daniel wrinkled his brow. "Can I get you some of our famous mutton stew, Major?"

"In a little while. I want to talk to you about something."

"Besides Shakespeare?"

André stared at him. "I like you, Daniel. I think you are clever and, erm, well, cultured. Thing of it is, I don't know if I can trust you."

"Trust me? To do what? Serve your wine?"

André smirked. "I need men like you." He turned to the bar crowd. "Not like these rabble."

"Need me? For what?"

"Oh, this and that."

Daniel burst out into a loud guffaw and stood up. "I'm needed at the bar, Major."

"Shall we continue this conversation later, then?"

"If you wish."

"I do wish." André turned to his sketch pad, and Daniel was dismissed.

By one in the morning the bar had cleared out. André still sat in the back corner. During the night, many soldiers and officers had visited with him. Women went back and flirted. Still he sketched away. Daniel would like to see those sketches. Perhaps he could convince André to show them to him.

The cooks took their leave and the barmaids were cleaning the tables. In a few minutes they were done.

"Shall we lock up, Governor?" one shouted as she approached the door.

"Yes," Daniel said. "I'll let the Major out myself."

The door slammed closed and the bolt was shot into place. He was alone with John André and Daniel felt a cold snake slither up his back. He wanted to hear what André had to say, but the man set every nerve in his body on high alert. André was an unusual man for an officer. Well-liked, admired, even. Always dressed immaculately. Educated, well-read, clever, attractive to the ladies. And dangerous. Tallmadge suggested that André was really a spy for the British. That he garnered information from locals and sent it on to General Howe.

Daniel wondered if this was why André wanted to meet with him. He sighed long and deep. No sense second-guessing. He mopped up the last of the bar stains and went to see what the Major wanted.

Daniel sat across from André and stared down at his illustrations.

"You like them?" André picked one up and showed it to Daniel.

"Not bad. Actually pretty good."

"Does the subject look familiar?"

"Aye. It looks like you."

André laughed. "It's a self-portrait, man."

"I have a good eye."

Both men laughed.

"Here, bartender," André said. "This one is for you."

Daniel picked it up and held it under the gas lamp. "Why this is me."

"Yes."

"Why would you draw me?"

"I think you've an interesting countenance."

"Interesting what?"

"Countenance, my man. Face. I like your face. There are lines of sense and reason. Intelligence." André stopped and leaned over the table. "I would think women fancy you."

"Bah. I have no time for women, Major. This Tavern takes every minute of my time."

"Where are you from, Daniel?"

"Grew up in Setauket. Long Island."

"No family there now?"

"Dead and gone."

"Never married?"

"Once. She died."

Daniel began to feel uncomfortable, as a butterfly being studied under a magnifying glass. "What did you want to talk to me about, then?"

"Ah, yes. A few of the men in my regiment have good things to say about you."

"Yeah? How nice."

André smiled.

"So, you've been askin' questions about me?"

"I have to know I can trust you."

"And what do your men say?"

"They say yes. That I can trust you."

"To do what? You want me to spy, eh?" Daniel knew he was playing with fire.

But André did not blink. "Exactly. To spy."

The two men stared at each other across the table.

"Are you up to it, then?" André said.

"What's in it for me?"

"There will be small remuneration. But the real reward . . ."

"Is *fooking* the rebel bastards," Daniel almost spit. "Yeah. I'm interested."

"Oh, this is what I was hoping for. Tell me, Daniel, why are you so eager to *fook* the rebels, as you say?"

Daniel didn't answer. He looked down at his hands.

"Tell me."

"They killed my son."

A quiet rap on his apartment door woke Daniel at three in the morning. He opened it to a worn and drawn Benjamin Tallmadge. Once inside, Daniel poured him a glass of rum, strong and dark.

Benjamin unslung the pouch from his shoulder and collapsed in a chair by a small table. He sucked in a long draught.

"Easy now, Ben. You'll founder."

Benjamin set the glass down and rubbed his eyes.

"Thanks for coming so quick."

"I took off as soon as I got your message. Tell me."

"You know Major John André?"

"Who doesn't? Probably the only British *gentleman* in the colony. What about him?"

"He's gettin' cozy with me if you know what I mean. He even gave me these." Daniel showed Ben the sketches of himself and André.

"Did he write you a poem now, too, eh?"

Daniel smirked. "Wants to recruit my help."

Benjamin narrowed his eyes. "For what?"

"To spy for him."

"You joking?"

Daniel shook his head.

"Spy on who? And for whom?"

"He wants me to spy on his own men. Thinks he may have a turncoat in the dragoons."

"Shite, that's beautiful." Benjamin whispered the words. "A British officer . . . a traitor? Did he give you any names?"

"No. Just wants me to keep my ears and eyes open for a drunken sod who can't help but blather on."

"What did you tell him?"

"That I would, of course."

"Bloody hell, man. You'll be spying for both sides."

They fell silent for a long moment.

"Listen, Ben, I'm worried. This is getting complicated with André meddling about. I don't want to bugger it up."

"I'm still not sure why you picked Setauket."

"I couldn't tell him the truth, for God's sake. I don't want him to know about Susan and the kids."

"Yeah, right."

"He believes that I hate the patriots. I'm sure of that."

"The story about your son? What did you tell him?"

"That he was set upon by a band of rebel highwaymen who took his money and killed him."

"You're a smart man, Daniel." Benjamin squeezed Daniel's arm. He stood, gathered his things. "I've got to go or I'll be missed in the morning."

Before Daniel could open his mouth, Benjamin Tallmadge was gone.

Daniel spent another sleepless night trying to calm his agitated mind. One thought kept him from quietude. He was a traitor to his countrymen . . . now a traitor to the British. He felt very much alone.

The next night he spied John André entering the Black Horse with another well-dressed gentleman. He swallowed to wet his gullet.

"What can I get you gents?"

"Daniel, you know Richard Woodhull, of course."

Daniel didn't respond.

André turned to Woodhull. "This is the man I was telling you about, from Setauket. Daniel Ainsley. Farmer, wife dead, son killed by rebels last year?"

Woodhull stared at Daniel and shook his head. "Don't know him."

"I told you I knew very few people in Setauket," Daniel said.

"Right, you did," André said. "But surely you would know Master Wood-hull?"

Daniel scrunched up his face, all the while his heart threatened to pound his ribcage to splinters.

"Richard Woodhull is the Magistrate in Setauket. He knows everyone there."

Chapter 33

Helen

Brattleboro, Vermont, December 2018

Fall melted into winter early in December with a second dusting of snow. The Indian summer seemed long forgotten as temperatures dipped into the thirties and forties. Helen didn't mind. She exchanged her summer tee-shirts for fleece sweatshirts, her capris for jeans and long silk underwear.

She'd been engrossed in reading about the American Revolution and didn't hear the doorbell until Honey started to bark. She crossed the living room to answer it.

A tall, thin man, perhaps mid-fifties stood on the porch.

"Ahh, you must be the stone mason."

"Ayup, that's me. Joe Putnam."

"Come in. I'm Helen Ainsley. Marie told me you were coming." She led him into the living room where his job would be to repair the large stone fireplace.

"So what's wrong with her?"

Helen loved that he referred to the fireplace as 'her.' Made it human.

"Well, I can't open the flue," she said. "Seems to be stuck or broken. And it probably needs a thorough cleaning. Marie hadn't been using it, but I really would like to."

"She's quite a beauty, ain't she? Old."

"Old is right. We were hoping to get the flue fixed before the cold really set in. Think you can do it?"

"I'll take a looksee."

"Mind if I watch?" Helen asked. "I love to see things taken apart and put back together."

"Okay by me." He began checking the flue and damper. Then he started tapping the stone on the hearth.

Helen sat on the chair near the fireplace. Honey ambled in and sat down at her feet.

In a few minutes, Joe said, "Looks like I gotta take part of the hearth out as well as some of these stones. Mortar is just about turned to powder. The damper is pretty well shot. Probably need to replace the whole flue from what I'm seeing . . ." Joe kept going.

Helen's eyes began to glaze over.

"Good thing you're doing this now. You'd never get it to work when ya need it."

"Great." Helen pulled a face at Honey who whined.

In a few minutes, she was asleep on the chair with Honey stretched out on the floor.

"Lookee here," Joe said. "Just pried this up."

Helen jumped. "What?"

"Buried in the hearth stone." He handed her a coin. "A ha' penny? Looks old, real old. When's this place built?"

"1760-something."

"Ayup. Like I said, real old."

Helen rolled the coin over in her fingers. "Why was this embedded in the hearth?"

"Usually the mason who built it would put that in. Gives the fireplace a date, for future reference, you see."

"Wow, what a find." She reached for her glasses on the desk and held it up to the light. On one side in the center was a man's profile. Above him, it said: *The Restore of Commerce* and below: *No Stamps 1766.*

"1766," she said aloud. "That's when it was built."

"Told you it was old," Joe said. "Even older than me." He barked. Helen assumed it was a laugh.

On the flip side of the coin was a large ship which appeared to be an old, tall ship with four masts and many sails. Unfortunately, she could only read a few words: *Thanks to the . . .* at the top; *America* to the right of the ship; *. . . and trade* at the bottom. She stared at the ship and could hear Marie asking if it was the Black Pearl and where was Jack Sparrow. Helen tried to suppress a giggle.

"Now here's somethin' you don't see oftentimes."

Helen went to look at what Joe was pointing at. "What is it?"

"Looks like a hiding place. Several stones around an empty box or somethin', see? Kind of like a safe deposit box, colonial-style."

Joe was pulling out one of the stones in the inside wall of the fireplace when the whole side caved in. Helen grabbed Joe's arm as the avalanche started and pulled him back to safety. The sound of the toppling rocks sent Honey running.

They both waved at all the dust that had spewed in the air.

"Ugh, what a mess," she said.

"Not to worry. Mortar's all dried up. These stones were meant to come down. Just not that fast." Joe barked again. "I'll clean up later with a heavy industrial vac. You won't even notice."

"What about that hiding place? It's gone now."

"If there was anything in it, it's buried in this rubble. Be real careful, though, going through it, cause there might be nails or wood splinters or sharp stones to get yourself cut on. If you're going to look through this, wear gloves."

"Good idea."

"I'm going to get some tools in my truck. Be right back."

"Okay." Helen went off to search for gloves in the hall cabinets. She found some suitable and came back before Joe returned. She studied the crumbled stone on the drop cloth covering the floor. Honey had returned and was sniffing around the stones. She began to whine.

Helen watched the dog who seemed attracted to the ruins of the fireplace. Old smells, perhaps. She thought back to the retriever's unearthing of the mummified remains of the runaway slave, Elias Turner, and the buried bones of Angela Rossi Martelli and her little boy, Joey. She could not deny that Honey had magical detecting capabilities.

Before Helen could stop her, she was digging her nose into the debris and yanking on something.

"No, Honey, don't . . ." She ran over and pulled the dog away. That's when she saw it. A leather strap. "What on earth is that?"

Joe came back. "She find something?"

Helen was bending over the debris. "Look, Joe, what is this?"

Joe got down on his knees. "Let me see. Some kind of strap, maybe a belt. Okay, let me move some of the rubble out of the way."

Helen backed up, Honey at her side.

Joe dug through the remains of the fireplace. "Well, hell's bells." He pulled out a leather pouch by its strap. "Looks pretty darn old, wouldn't you say?"

Helen looked down at the small, square pouch, covered with dust and bits of stone and mortar. Joe brushed it off and handed it to her. She brought it over to the light and studied it. Definitely old. She turned it over, looking for some clue to its age or identity.

"Wait, what's this?" she whispered. But Joe was back at work.

There were numbers stamped into the leather. C XIII. Roman numerals? One hundred and thirteen? What did that mean? When did this bag get hidden in the fireplace wall? Back in the 18th century when the Inn was constructed?

She took the pouch out of the dusty room and into the kitchen to examine it. She set it on a towel on the kitchen table. When she opened it and peered inside, she saw something whitish colored. Whatever it is, don't destroy it, she warned herself. She held her breath and reached in.

By a miracle, she pulled out two small, maybe five and a half by four and a half inches, soft pieces of a cloth-like paper. They were not letters or documents as she expected. They were sketches. Sketches of two men.

"What have I found?" she murmured to herself.

Under one it said, *Self-portrait: John André.* Drawn in pen and ink, was a man seated in a chair, one leg crossed over the other in a casual stance. He clearly wore a uniform, although the color was indeterminate. One arm was stretched out, the hand resting on a table where a pen sat in an ink jar. His face was boyish, almost pretty, and he wore a neutral expression.

The second sketch was labeled: *Barkeep: Daniel Ainsley.*

Helen felt every nerve fiber in her body hum until she was tingling all over.

She stared at the barkeep. The drawing depicted a handsome, rugged-look-ing man with thick, dark hair marbled with occasional strands of white. His penetrating dark eyes looked right at you, and he wore a tight smile on his lips. His shirt was open at the neck and his shoulders stretched across the width of the paper.

Oh my God, this is Daniel. My ancestor.

Helen spent the evening researching. First she found that the image on the coin embedded in the hearth was a depiction of William Pitt, who served as Prime Minister of the United Kingdom twice from 1756-1761 and again from 1766-1768. The dates jived with the time the house, ergo the fireplace, was built.

According to auction sites, there was nothing particularly unique about the coin and perhaps worth up to a thousand dollars. She tucked it away in her desk drawer.

Next she Googled John André. Even with her resources as a writer, she came up with contradictory information about him, except for two facts: one that he was a high-level British officer residing in New York City. And two, that he was an artist and a poet. How unusual for a military man.

Still, it gave her chills to think he knew Daniel, they might have even been friends. After all, he drew a sketch of him. Did it mean that Daniel was, indeed, a loyalist? She flashed back to the New York Gazette and was reminded that her ancestor may very well have been a Tory.

As to the Roman numerals, C XIII, stamped on the leather pouch, she found nothing.

Frustrated, Helen grabbed her cell and starting scrolling through her contacts. Who did she know that was an expert in the Revolution? She chewed on her lower lip. "I know, I know. Sylvia Holscomb, where are you?"

Marie came into the parlor. "What's going on? Is it about those sketches?" Marie picked up the sketch of Daniel by the corners. "Handsome, wasn't he? I can almost see Robert in him."

Helen turned abruptly from her contact search and looked at Marie. "Really?"

Oh, this is so exciting, Marie. Sit down. I'm trying to find out more about John André but there's a surprising dearth of material on the Internet. I did learn that he was a poet."

"As well as an officer . . . and an artist?"

"Yep. He's even got a statue to honor him as a poet in Westminster Abbey."

"Well, that's quite a coup."

"I'm going to call my old friend Sylvia at the British Library, kind of like our Library of Congress, to see what she can tell me."

"Not now, you're not."

"Why not?"

"Well, I would say everyone in London is asleep now."

Helen threw her hands up. "Oh for heaven's sake. What was I thinking? Darn, now I have to wait until morning."

"Waiting is not something you're good at, my dear." Marie snorted. "But I love you anyway."

"Phooey. Let's see, there's a five hour time difference, so I can probably call early our time."

"Do you think this Sylvia knows a lot about the American Revolution? The Brits lost that war you know. She may still be in a snit."

"Ha. Yes. Let's hope she doesn't hold it against us. It would be great if she knew what the stamp on that pouch means also. A hundred and thirteen. Must have some significance."

Marie stood up. "I'm going to bed, sweetie. Let's hope your London friend knows the answers. Now *I'm* really curious." The two women smiled at each other.

Helen grabbed a sweater and walked out on the front porch, her mind zig-zagging at a furious pace. Honey took off zig-zagging in a similar manner for a late night lap around the field.

Joe would be back in the morning to continue work on the fireplace. He had checked to see if there were more treasures hidden in the stone. Alas, no. But two treasures, the coin, and the pouch, were enough. For now she had an actual drawing of her great . . . times eight . . . grandfather. Long before photographs existed.

A weak wind had a hard time moving the heavy damp air. Rain was coming. Snow not far off. She walked over to her tree. Funny, I think of it as mine. But it was Daniel's, too. She knew deep in her bones that the tree was here before the house. Daniel loved it perhaps as much as she did.

The porch lights made it visible. She could see all the carvings now. *SM-AR* with a heart around them. The lone name *TILLIE*. *ABBY and ELI*. Now *DNA*.

But wait. Where were Daniel's initials? She walked around the tree several times. Honey sat and looked at her, let out a soft woof.

"They're gone, Honey. They disappeared. This just proves I'm right about Daniel. He wasn't a traitor. He was a hero. And I'm going to prove it."

Chapter 34

Hours later Helen lay in bed unable to fall asleep. In a few weeks she had a doctor's appointment down in the City. It was a full year since her last chemotherapy treatments had ended and she felt grand. Not a twinge of discomfort, no aches, pains, dizziness, queasiness, or any of the other symptoms she'd experienced the first time around. Brattleboro was good for her. Her body, her mind, her heart, and her soul.

"It's gone, Honey," she said to her dog sleeping at the foot of the bed. "My cancer is gone. I know it. I used to feel it inside me. I don't feel it anymore, haven't for months now." A laugh bubbled out of her mouth and Honey wagged her tail. Helen kissed her on the snoot. "You're one of the reasons it's gone, you know." The two gazed at each other. Helen got out of bed. The clock read three a.m. The stars were in all their glory, dotting the indigo sky outside her window. Her tree seemed to catch the moonbeams and send them to her.

At eight the next morning, Helen rolled over. She didn't even remember going back to bed. She only remembered the moonlight shining on her and her beloved tree. She smiled and stretched.

"There's work to do, Honey. Let's get this day rolling."

After breakfast, she placed the call to Sylvia in London, hoping she wasn't out of town or otherwise occupied. A million questions had lined up in her mind. Helen grabbed a pen and a pad.

Sylvia's secretary confirmed she was there. Helen tapped her foot setting the floorboards to crackling and waited for her old friend to come on the line.

"Helen."

"Sylvia."

They spent a few minutes catching up. When Helen lived in New York, Sylvia often flew back and forth from London. She was always conferring with the librarians at the New York Public Library, one of Helen's favorite research places. They kept in touch but not as often as Helen would like. She vowed to be better about that.

"First," Sylvia said. "You must tell me about any men in your life."

"Oh, for heaven's . . ."

"No, no. If you want me to give you information, you must come clean. Quid pro quo."

Helen grinned. "Well, there is one man, but he's really just a friend."

"Aha, I knew it. A friend, indeed. Tell me more."

"Honestly, Sylvia, he's a sweet guy that I met when I moved back to Brattleboro and he--."

"What does he do? Is he a lumberjack?"

"Lumberjack? Why on earth would you--?"

"It's the wilds of Vermont, right? Aren't all men back to nature, the earth, the woods, and all that?"

"Good grief. He's a cop."

"Perfect," Sylvia burst out. "A cop and a mystery writer. I love it. What does he look like?"

Helen knew she would never get her questions answered if she didn't provide the information. "He's tall, athletic, dark hair with a bit of gray, deep blue eyes, handsome. And smart."

"Ahh, I picture Sam Elliott."

"No mustache. But he does have a deep voice."

"I like him already."

"You are a nutter, my old friend. Now, can we get to business?"

"All right, all right, spoil sport. So what can I help you with, lovey?"

"Sylvia, how much do you know about the American Revolution?"

Sylvia laughed, a tinkly sound. "Well, let's see. You people in the colonies like to think you won the war, but, in fact, we just got tired of it all and cut you loose."

Helen smiled. "Oh, I rather believe that."

"Is this for your new book?"

"Might be. Getting background details before I decide."

"So, what is it about the Revolution you want to know? I am a bit of an expert."

"I thought so. Excellent." Helen gave her a synopsis, ending with the discovery of the old pouch in the fireplace.

"That's beautiful. You were able to track down your ancestor like that, wow. I can do some research here and see if his name appears anywhere in our documents. But John André . . . now *him* I can tell you about." Sylvia paused. "By the way, I very much want to see those sketches. You know they'll fetch gobs of money?"

"I guess they would, wouldn't they? I can take photos and send them to you if you like."

"I would like. Very much."

"Deal. Tell me about André."

"You are right about Westminster Abbey. There is a poet's corner within the South Transept. And alongside greats like Tennyson, Shakespeare, and Chaucer, is the statue of a little known poet named John André."

Helen sat down on the couch and pulled her legs up under her as Sylvia told the story. She jotted notes on her pad as Sylvia spoke.

"In 1771 André bought a commission to the Royal Welch Fusiliers. He studied military engineering until 1774 when he sailed for America to join his regiment. He used his personal charm and command of foreign languages to rise to position of adjutant to the British commander-in-chief, Sir Henry Clinton. To make a long story endless, he wound up as head of British intelligence . . ."

"A spy?"

"*The* spy. Spy master, in fact. A regular James Bond." Sylvia paused. "That may be the way he and your ancestor met."

"Both were spies?"

"Just a thought."

"Or maybe both liked to drink? Remember Daniel ran a tavern," Helen said.

"Hmm. Anyway, André did some spying, then got himself in trouble with a woman, don't they all, and wound up on the gallows."

"He was hung?"

"Indeed. For consorting with one of your traitors, Benedict Arnold."

"Really?"

"Thing of it is, George Washington really liked the man, André, that is. But he couldn't stop the hanging, wouldn't actually. Trying to set an example, I suppose. And all that time, André was sketching, writing stories, and poems."

"And spying. Incredible."

"Yes, he was quite the ballsy Renaissance man."

"Do you have any of his poems?"

"Of course. Would you like me to read you one?"

"How about just a verse or two and then email it to me?"

"Hang on, let me pull one up. Ahh, here's a delightful one you'll like, called: *Yankee Doodle's Expedition to Rhode Island:*

From Lewis, Monsieur Gerard came,
To Congress in this town, sir,
They bowed to him, and he to them,
And then they all sat down, sir."

Sylvia went on, "Wait, one more snappy verse:
So Yankee Doodle did forget
The sound of British drum, sir,
How oft it made him quake and sweat,
In spite of Yankee rum, sir."

"And," Sylvia said, "it could be sung to the tune Yankee Doodle Dandy."

"Wait. When was that written?"

"Well, it was quite a bit before the Hollywood movie with James Cagney. It was written in 1755."

"No kidding." Helen shook her head. "So for that little ditty, they erected a statue of the man."

"We Brits like to celebrate small victories."

Both women laughed.

"He should have been hung for his poetry, you ask me," Helen said.

"What happened to your ancestor? If he was a spy, he, too, might have dangled from a gibbet."

"Actually, he must have made it home since we found these sketches and he would've been the one to hide them here." Helen asked her friend about C XIII but Sylvia had no idea what they stood for.

"Well, my dearie, sounds like you have your work cut out for you. I'm off to a meeting now, but it was a delight hearing from you. You will let me know what you find out?"

"Of course."

"And keep me apprised of your copper."

Helen laughed. "Thanks so much, Sylvia. Cheers, old friend." She clicked off, turned to Honey who was lying on the couch next to her.

"Well, Yankee Doodle Dandy to you."

Later, Helen fired off an email to the Brattleboro Historical Society asking what they could find on Daniel Ainsley. They had records of him building and running the Ainsley Hill Inn, but nothing of him being in New York. Apparently the New York Gazette article had not reached Brattleboro. Also, they had no official record of his death, or so the volunteer thought. But Helen received an email from the same person an hour later.

Dear Mrs. Ainsley,

I was not able to find any obit for Daniel Ainsley but am happy to tell you that with a little more digging (excuse the pun) into cemetery records, I did locate a gravesite for him at the Mather Cemetery. From what I can tell, the stone is pretty much crumbled to dust, so I doubt you'll be able to locate it. More of a patch of dirt and rubble.

Best of luck,

Debbie

Helen went to find Marie and filled her in on both conversation.

Marie summed it up. "Sounds like Daniel left here to go to New York City sometime around 1775 or 1776, run a tavern there as barkeep, according to the sketch. Then he returned home, brought the sketches with him, and lived for who knows how long beyond the Revolution years. No telling without a death certificate or an obit." Marie frowned. "That about right?"

"That's about it."

"Do you think he really was a redcoat?"

Helen shook her head. "No, I don't, Marie. Neither does our old maple tree."

Helen meandered her fields with Honey late that afternoon, listening to birdsong, hearing the brook gurgling behind the barn, and watching squirrels run the old stone walls. Red squirrels, the same color as Honey, which she did not often see. The temperatures were dropping but fall hung on. Quiet descended with evening. She loved this time of day.

After dinner, she brought her coffee onto the porch. A few minutes later, headlights jounced up the gravel drive.

"Am I under arrest?" she asked Dave, as he alighted.

He grinned. "Only if I could lock you up at my place." He walked toward her, took her in his arms and placed a gentle kiss on her lips. They stayed, arms wrapped around each other for a sweet moment.

"Wait, I forgot something." He hurried back to the car and returned with a heavy book.

"Come inside. It's getting chilly now."

"Where's Marie?"

"She's playing poker with some friends in Guilford. They picked her up."

"Poker?"

"Yeah, she's a real card shark. She won fifty bucks last week."

"Why am I not surprised?"

"How about some coffee?" She walked into the kitchen and Dave followed. "So what's the book?"

"I thought you'd need to read the definitive history of the American Revolution. Rick Atkinson. Terrific author." He laid the tome on the table.

"*The British Are Coming*?"

"It's a trilogy and this is the first book. His World War Two trilogy was riveting."

Helen served coffee with Marie's homemade coffee cake.

"But there's a reason I brought it over. First, you told me about that pouch you found in the fireplace? Can I see it?"

"Of course." Helen left and returned with it, handed it to him.

"Yes," he exclaimed with excitement. "Here, let me show you." He flipped through the book and began to read: "So much thievery plagued the army in New York that Washington, on Tuesday, June 18, ordered the quartermaster general to stamp every tool with 'C XIII,' denoting the thirteen colonies. That proprietary brand would soon be amended to 'United States,' and subsequently shortened to 'U.S.'"

Dave looked at her. "You can close your mouth now."

"My God, Dave. You are a genius."

"You noticed, good."

"I suspected the C was not for one hundred. But *colonies*, wow."

"Now you know." He picked up the leather satchel, ran his hand over the stamped letters. "This is quite a gift. Can I see those sketches?"

"Yes." Helen scurried into the living room and came back with a folder. She handed it to Dave.

"Jeez, these are incredible. So this is Daniel Ainsley and the other is the artist, John André?"

Helen told him what she learned about André from her friend, Sylvia.

Dave slid the drawings back in the folder and handed it to her. The pouch slipped off his lap. "Sorry," he said.

"Wait, what's that?"

He bent over. "Looks like a tightly-folded piece of paper. You didn't see this before?"

"No," she whispered. "Must have been stuck inside the folds of the leather."

He handed it to her. "Whatever it is, it belongs to you."

She licked her dry lips then bit by bit unfolded the paper and flattened it on the table. She settled her glasses on her nose. "Can you hear my heart pounding? God." She took in a deep breath and looked up into Dave's eyes. He smiled his okay at her.

Haltingly she read the tiny script: "*Whosoever finds this, and, at the time of my death, the three articles in this satchel are bequeathed to my wife, Susan, and my three sons and one daughter. Two of the articles are sketches by my good friend and, he would say, best enemy, John André. The third article consists of two parts: one sworn affidavit by the General . . .*"

"What General?" Dave asked.

"*. . .along with a small token of recognition. These last two are sheathed in goatskin to last through time and clime and are hidden securely in the heart of the venerable one for safekeeping.*"

"Venerable one?" Dave said. "Sounds like a tribal elder."

"The heart of the venerable one," Helen repeated. "What does that mean? And who is the General?"

Dave shook his head.

"Daniel's family never got this," She held up the pouch. "Why?"

"They were hidden, maybe too well?"

"Wouldn't he have left a clue for them?"

"Maybe his death came too suddenly or . . . I don't know. In any case, you have two of the articles now. You just need to find the third."

"Easier said than done."

Dave smiled.

"What is that sly little smile for?"

"*You* are his family."

"What?"

"These are bequeathed to Daniel's family. It's eight generations later, but that's you, Helen."

She felt her eyes well. "Yes, I am his family, aren't I?"

"And now you have to find the missing pieces," Dave said. "Just another day in the life of a mystery writer."

Chapter 35

Daniel

New York City, September 1776

Fire. A small word that flares dread in every heart in the city. Daniel felt his own heart slam into his ribs. He threw down his bar towel and rushed to the Tavern door. Screams, wails, and cries erupted from the street. Horses brayed in terror, their hooves thundering on the cobbles. The vibration of dozens of feet pounding the boardwalks.

Major John André and the Magistrate, one Richard Woodhull from Setauket, Long Island, followed as did every other patron. Outside the Black Horse, he could spy a red and gold glow to the west beyond the buildings across the street. Smoke rose above it. If it weren't for the imminent peril, the scene could be almost picturesque . . . a fine museum painting. A Gainsborough perhaps.

Other sounds reached him now. Glass breaking, planks and beams crackling, stoves exploding. And more menacing sounds: the low whooshing when dry tinder catches then a swelling roar as the blaze grows and spreads. Within seconds, every incendiary object within its reach is aflame.

"It's close, mebbe two blocks," someone yelled. "Could be Broadway."

Men began running west toward the fire.

"Damn . . . the theatre." André took off at a run behind them.

Daniel looked at the Magistrate, who shrugged and turned, heading in the opposite direction. Probably home to Long Island. Daniel felt the tension ease across his back and neck. A close call . . . for the moment.

He hurried after André toward John Street and the John Street Theatre. The smoke thickened and he felt his chest constricting. Where were the fire wagons? He caught up to André in front of the playhouse, which had, so far, escaped the fire. Daniel understood why the theatre was so important to André. It was under André's direction that plays were staged to keep up morale during the British occupation. Besides his patronage, the Major was admired for his *scene painting*. An artist at heart, thought Daniel of his enemy overseer.

Both men turned now to the melee of the fire, several streets west. Fire meant catastrophe in a city built house upon house, structure upon structure, with little space between.

It was after midnight on September 21 and rumors were already flying about how it had started.

"I tell ye, it was some kid playin' in the doorway and he looked like trouble, he did," one said.

"Nah, kids, bugger that. It was at the Fightin' Cocks. Punters always brawling there. Probly tipped over a lantern."

Daniel agreed. The most likely genesis was at the Fighting Cocks Tavern where a mob of drunken revelers could've easily started a small blaze by accident, or not, and were unable to stop it from spreading. Now it was an inferno threatening half the city.

A group of redcoats stood watching when André approached. Immediately they ran to help the bucket brigade, to little advantage. One would seize a bucket and the strap would break, another and the bottom fell out.

"Nah, it's useless," Daniel said, coughing, and moving back from the dense smoke.

Someone shouted, "This is Washington's doing, I swear it."

"Whad'ya mean?" another said.

"He ordered it, he did."

"Bugger off."

"No, think about it. Why are there no bells?"

"What?"

"Why aren't the bells ringing to rouse the town and get people marshaled?"

The other man looked at him. "Why?'

"Cause of Washington, dummy. Where ye been, man? The fooker ordered the bells from all the steeples removed to melt down for ammunition."

The man gaped at him.

"It's true, by God."

André shouted at them. "Get on with the work, men, and quit yer blathering."

"Aye, sir." They ran off.

André looked at Daniel, who shook his head.

"Don't think Washington would've burnt down the city. To what advantage?"

"I agree. This is beyond the rules of normal engagement." With a cheeky smile, André added, "Makes for good story telling, though."

The fire had spread from rooftop to rooftop until hundreds of houses burned. A quarter of the city. A thousand residents stood on the streets, far as the eye could see, gazing with vacant eyes, lamenting their fate. The old, the sick, babies, children, women.

Daniel ran to aid an old woman who had fallen. An old man on a cane hobbled over as he lifted her to her feet. The old man nodded to him and took her arm. Both teetered off, moaning. But the sounds of their misery added to all the other sounds of despair and ate through to Daniel's heart.

"What will happen to all these people?" Daniel said.

"They'll be seen to."

"Oh? By who?"

"Not Washington, I can assure you."

"Then who?" Daniel furrowed his brows.

"My question is, where are the patriots, then? Why aren't they helping fight the fire?" André poked a finger into Daniel's shoulder. "I'll tell you why. They're all cowards. They've skedaddled."

"Nay. They all joined the Continental Army and are off fighting somewhere."

André smiled. "Ah, heroes are they?"

The two men continued up Broadway. Cinders and soot flew in the whirlwind created by the inferno.

"Let's get away from the smoke. There's nothing we can do here," Daniel said.

They came to a sight that almost brought them both to their knees. Trinity Church, the Anglican Church that the British soldiers and officers attended, was entirely engulfed. Flames shot up the hundred and forty foot steeple and seemed to hover there, as if ensuring it was destroyed in no uncertain terms.

"Do you think it could be sabotage?" Daniel asked.

"Why say that?"

"No warning bells, pumps broken on fire engines, bucket handles torn, buckets broken, people running in and out of buildings . . . I don't know. Doesn't really make sense they'd burn the city."

"They?"

"That's just it, who?" Daniel said. "Red or blue, neither makes sense."

"I think it's safe to say it was an accident, plain and simple."

They stopped walking and looked back over the horror. People were now stumbling towards them, women crying, jostling babies and children, men hauling what was left of their belongings.

"My men will put up a tent camp for the night. I'll see to it," André said.

They began the long trek back. André stopped a number of times to give orders to his men for the tent camp. Redcoats could be seen scurrying in all directions. Daniel felt a little better, knowing the residents would have some place to bed down for the night. But winter would soon be upon them. He didn't want to think that far ahead. For now, he couldn't bear watching the scenes unfolding in front of him.

"Look," André said. "Saint Paul's Chapel hasn't been touched."

"Thank God."

"No, thank the wind, blowing in the other direction," André said.

"At least the folks who remain will have a church to attend."

"Many will leave the city now. What's left for them here?"

The men stood in silence for a long moment contemplating the fate of the New York City inhabitants.

"The wind is in our favor," Daniel finally spoke. "Not likely the fire will reach the tavern. Shall we go back and imbibe?"

The two men dragged their emotionally drained bodies back to the tavern, which they now had to themselves, and indulged in a new bottle of Madeira.

He knew it was a dream but he had a desperate need to watch it unfold. It was New York City. The sun beat down with a brutal glare turning the sky white and devoid of clouds. It pained his eyes and he shaded them with his hands. He stumbled along, searching for something he knew was important. But what?

Daniel came upon the greengrocers and moved toward the fruit carts in front. He gawped at them, dead and desiccated berries, apples, oranges. The greengrocer stood smiling at the front door. Yet it was not Mister Finley, it was a haunted scarecrow of him. A dog looked up at him, panting in the heat. A dog or a mummified corpse of a dog?

Daniel pushed on. A man stood at the far end of the row of shops. He knew his uniform, his stance, his smile. John André. Yes, it was André. Thank God. Who was that standing next to him? All in black? A preacher? His blood turned cold despite the heat of the day. Not right, it was not right. He stumbled on a cobblestone, fell to one knee, rose, and continued. He could see the preacher now. Not a preacher. A judge. He wore the costume of a magistrate of the courts.

Something gnawed at him. A premonition of gloom skirting around his brain. Still he kept on, even when the man in black pulled out a pistol and aimed it directly at him. From the corner of his eye he could see André smiling.

He heard it first, saw a puff of smoke, then felt something punch into his chest. And again. Two guns, two enemies. His heart bounced around his ribcage then turned cold in his chest as it absorbed the lead.

The sun flared in the sky and the heat became an inferno. Daniel felt light as a feather as if he were floating. The two men were still there, talking. He heard words that ripped through his brain . . . his soul: *Susan, Brattleborough, Ainsley*

Hill Tavern. A smile came to his lips. Towering over him was his beautiful maple tree, tendering him shade from the unrelenting sun. He was home.

He could not die now. Not now . . .

The pounding on the door finally dragged him from the depths of his nightmare. The sun streamed into the room, its rays piercing his eyes. Daniel rolled over in bed feeling as if he'd been trampled by a horse. He lifted his head from the pillow and dropped it back in agony.

More pounding, shouting.

"All right, hold on."

He forced his body to rise and unlock the door. He found himself looking at a disheveled Benjamin Tallmadge.

"Jesus, God, Ben, what in the almighty are ye doing, pounding like that?"

"What's wrong with you, Daniel? Did ye not hear me? Were you caught in the fire? Are you hurt?

"No, no. I got caught in a fookin' nightmare, couldn't rouse myself." He staggered over to the wash basin and threw water on his face. "That's what Madeira will do to you. Ach, God."

"Daniel, you've got to leave New York."

Daniel wiped the water dripping from his face and hair with a thin towel. "What?"

"You've got to leave the city right away."

"Sit down, Ben, calm down."

"There's no time for conversation, Daniel. You've got to get out. Now. It's not safe any longer. Ye've been compromised." Ben spun around. "Where are your bags? You've got to pack."

Daniel grabbed the young man's arm. "Slow down. Tell me what's happened. Does it have something to do with the Magistrate?"

"It's on orders from Abraham Woodhull."

"Abe?"

"Did you realize his father is the Magistrate in Setauket? Richard Woodhull. The man you met last night?"

Daniel put his hands up to his head. "God damnit. I knew I couldn't pull it off. Setauket, I can barely pronounce it, let alone convince anyone I'm from there."

"Listen, Daniel. It's too late for self-recriminations. What's done is done. General Howe is on a rant. He's hunting down everyone he thinks is a spy for the Continental Army. Abe is trying to stay a step ahead of him. That's why I'm here. Take what you can carry and get the hell out."

Daniel collapsed on the edge of the bed, dazed.

"Damn it, man. Get yerself straight and listen to me. Howe has already killed one of us."

"What? What do you mean?"

"Nathan. They hung him. Caught him with papers on him, and--." Ben stopped abruptly. "Can't even bury him." His voice hitched.

Daniel squeezed his eyes shut. Nathan Hale dead? "My God. He was just a boy."

"Nate knew what the risks were. So do you." Ben clenched his jaw and his eyes turned cold.

Daniel suddenly saw the confident, winsome Ben Tallmadge turn into a hardened soldier who'd been touched by death.

"You've got to go, Daniel. André knows, now with this Setauket foul-up, make no mistake. He knows and he will be angry. For God's sake, the man's been duped, his position is on the line."

Ben was right. He had been foolish to ever consider André a friend.

"Did ye hear me, Daniel? If ye don't get moving, I will have to carry you."

Ben went to the wardrobe and opened it. "Where's yer bag? Start packing. I'm not gonna lose another friend."

"Yeh, I hear you." Still, he couldn't find the strength to move. It was like he was still in a dream and his limbs were too weak to obey his brain.

Ben went to the window and peered out. "What time do you open the bar?"

"Not til' late afternoon."

"And, when does André usually make an appearance?"

"Could be any time."

"Then, this is it, man. Get your bag." Ben almost shouted. "Think of your wife, man, your family."

The dream mist suddenly lifted. Those words spurred Daniel to action. He kneeled on the floor and pulled a rucksack out from under the bed. He began throwing his belongings in it. He moved to the desk and pulled open a drawer, began tossing things about.

"What are you looking for?"

"This." Daniel lifted out a pistol, A Duval flintlock that he'd carefully maintained.

"Good working order?"

"Perfect." Daniel stuffed it in the bag. He added a pouch of gunpowder and one of cloth-wrapped lead balls. Then he began rummaging through his belongings in the room.

"Go before word gets out and André comes looking for ye," Ben said. "There's no one on the roads. With the fire, the whole town is in confusion and all hands are at the scene. You won't be missed at the tavern for hours and then, well, you'll be gone."

"Aye." Daniel straightened and looked directly at Ben. "Now, you, my friend, must leave . . . and quick. You canna be caught with the likes of me."

Both men stood and grasped each other's hands.

"Good luck, Benjamin Tallmadge."

"Good luck, Daniel Ainsley." And Ben was out the door.

Daniel struggled to collect his thoughts before leaving. His horse was at the livery down the street, in good stead. The bar was locked up tight and not scheduled to open for many hours. André would be sleeping off a drunk a while longer. God will it so.

He picked up the rucksack, slung it over his shoulder and headed out the door. The sun was making its way high in the sky. His lame leg kept him from moving as fast as he needed. He passed the greengrocers but unlike his dream, it was locked up tight. No one about. He made good time to the livery. There, he saddled his horse, loaded it with his belongings. He would have to get supplies along the way, somehow.

A sudden thought occurred to him. He had to go back to his apartment.

He poked his head from the barn door. If André showed up, he was a dead man. He mounted his horse and rode back, tied it in front of the Tavern and hustled upstairs. In his apartment, he rummaged through his wardrobe, under the bed, nightstand, and finally, his desk. Was there anything that could lead André to Brattleborough, or even the direction he would be headed? Nothing. He could find nothing. He prayed he had not inadvertently said anything about his home in their conversations. Nothing for it now. He turned to the door again. Stopped.

He ran back and grabbed a small leather pouch, tucked in the far corner of the wardrobe. It contained the sketches that André had made. With a final look around, Daniel left the rooms above the Black Horse Tavern for the last time.

Chapter 36

Helen

Brattleboro, Vermont, January 2019

Christmas came and went with no resolution to the Daniel Ainsley mystery. The holidays were festive, although only a little snow had fallen. Helen threw a small party for friends visiting from New York, and for Julianne, Bella, and Marie. Dave couldn't make it since he was on duty. Probably a good thing, since all the guests were women.

The house became an Inn once more and her city friends adored the rooms she had prepared for them.

The first evening after dinner and over eggnog and brandy, the company was treated to a presentation by Helen about a *concept* for her next mystery. Everyone had settled around the huge fireplace in the living room, and Julianne kept it blazing with a nearby stack of firewood.

"Let's hear this idea, Helen," Sandra Marr, her editor said.

"Yes, don't keep us in suspense." An old college friend, Beth Stein, agreed.

Helen shot pointed looks at Marie and Juli before she began. Honey dropped down beside her chair with a delicious sigh.

"All right," Helen began. "Picture a beautiful old maple tree in front of handsome rural farmhouse in the Green Mountains of Vermont. On the tree are carved four sets of initials, each dating back to a different time period that the tree has lived through." Helen took a sip of eggnog. Her audience sat riveted.

"Now, this is not an ordinary tree. Oh no. It's a three-hundred-year-old *enchanted* tree and the initials carved on it . . . once they are observed by the owner of the farmhouse, would disappear for a time. Until the identities of the initials were uncovered, and the mystery of their lives was resolved."

"That is brilliant, Helen," Carla Rodrigues, another dear friend said. "Wouldn't it be spectacular if it were true." The others nodded.

Helen caught Marie wink at Julianne.

"I wouldn't mind an enchanted tree in my yard," Jill Harriman, Helen's long time agent, offered. "Maybe it could be rubbed like the Genie's lamp to bring me anything my heart desired."

"And what would that be?" Beth asked.

"Let's just say he would be tall, handsome and--."

"Let Helen finish, Jill. I want to hear the story," Carla said but smiled at Jill.

"Well," Helen said, "So far, three mysteries have been solved, with a fourth still a cold case . . . in the story, that is."

"I would read it in a heartbeat," Sandra said.

"And so you shall. As soon as I write it."

Laughter all around.

"It will appeal to readers who enjoy historical mysteries, to history buffs, to crime solvers, and to those who delight in fantasies," Julianne said. "After all, what better way to meander through history and mystery than being guided by a wise old maple tree that dates back three centuries?"

Bella added, "And, we book sellers would know what sells."

Helen grinned but said nothing.

"Wait a minute," Jill said. "Isn't there an old maple tree right out front? Is that the tree you mean? Are there initials on it?"

A ripple of excitement went through the group.

"Yes, and yes," Helen said. "The roots for my story."

"Of course," Carla said. "It's not really an enchanted tree, ladies. For heaven's sake."

"Tell us more," Beth said.

"And risk giving away the whole plot? Not on your lives."

The conversation drifted to other topics and Helen was relieved that she could hide the truth from her friends without feeling guilty.

The women left two days later after delighting in fine wine, excellent food, smart conversation and even a bit of hiking. They promised to get together again when Helen visited New York City in a month for her annual cancer check.

True to her pledge, early in February, Helen drove down to the city. Part of her looked forward to seeing her friends again; part of her felt jittery about her medical appointment. Funny, even though she knew in her heart the cancer was gone, she worried the doctors wouldn't agree.

She forced her mind to switch gears. A month had gone by and she still had not started her book. She felt at a loss. She could never begin a book until she first knew how it would end. Once that piece fell into place, she'd fly through, developing characters on the way.

Writer friends were baffled by her writing method. "Don't you use outlines, character sketches, plot themes?" they'd ask.

Yes, and no were her answers. The plot would be worked out in advance once she knew the ending. Characters would start in an outline but would constantly morph into new people, each fighting for their own identity, so that by the end of the book they did not fit her original concept of them. She maintained that she only needed the outline to ensure that a redhead in one chapter did not become a brunette in another.

In this latest book, she had no ending. Helen planned to use her foray into the city to research Daniel Ainsley. She knew his name appeared in one New York City Gazette in 1776. Why not others? Or other newspapers? Plus, she could also scout out the Black Horse Tavern, which, shockingly, was still in the same location on William and John Streets. Her only clues, written in Daniel's own hand: a "General" and "the venerable one."

Now, as she unlocked the door to her high rise apartment in The Buchanan on East 48th Street, she felt a twinge of angst. Helen loved the building, modern and sleek above, Edwardian elegance in the lower entry and lobby areas. Management had been taking care of it while she was gone. She walked in, dropped her bags in the hallway, and headed straight for the tall windows that overlooked 48th. A peculiar sensation washed over her. This was not home. Not any longer. New York was merely a rest stop. Home was Brattleboro.

Her cell rang. Dave. She smiled as she answered. He always made her smile.

"Hey," he said.

"Hey yourself."

"How was the trip?"

"Not bad. I even remembered the way."

"That's encouraging. What're the plans for today? Or is it too late to start work?"

"Today, I will meet with book people and give them a preliminary concept. Then, I will jot down all the things I need to do tomorrow."

"Research, you mean?"

"Yup."

"When do you go to Sinai?"

"Tomorrow afternoon."

"Nervous?"

"Always."

"I wish you had let me go with you."

"You'd be bored during all the research. I only have to be at the hospital for twenty minutes. Not worth the trip for you." She paused. "But thanks. I really appreciate the offer."

"All right then. Uh oh. Sounds like there's some police activity going on. Dispatcher is waving."

"I'll let you go."

"Take care, Helen. Call me tomorrow?"

"I will. Bye." She disconnected. Looking out the window again at the busyness on the street below, Helen felt a similar disconnection. She missed Marie. She missed Julianne. She missed Honey. And she missed Dave. Damn.

She did what she always did when she was at a loss. She opened her laptop and began writing.

What better time to visit a tavern than night? She hadn't planned on it, but it made sense. On the same day she arrived, Helen stepped out of the taxi and stood outside the Black Horse Tavern in lower Manhattan. She'd done her homework and learned that the bar was a popular night spot for the thirties and forties crowd. Hopefully, someone early fifties could pass. She smiled to herself. When was the last time she'd been to a bar by herself?

The building was in the middle of the block on John Street. Holiday decorations were still up, a wreath on the giant wooden door, lights blinking in the windows. She grabbed the wrought iron handle and pulled the heavy door open.

Inside she could hear live music from a small stage at the far end. A trio was performing a soft folk-rock song. Helen didn't recognize it but liked it. She headed to the bar, which was lightly occupied, and found a seat at one corner. She looked around. Most tables were taken and several booths in the corner accommodated larger groups. It was a Tuesday night, so she expected it would not be crowded.

How would it have looked back in 1776? Darker, with no electricity, smellier when many didn't bathe, furniture rough-hewn from early tools, sawdust on the floor to sop up the spills.

The bartender approached. She started. For a brief second, she saw Daniel Ainsley . . . her memory of him from John André's sketch.

"Sorry, did I scare you?

"No, I thought for a moment I knew you."

"Oh yeah?" He smiled. "And who'd I remind you of? Famous star?"

"Actually my ancestor, from many generations ago."

He squinted at her. "What can I get you?"

"Whatever's on draft."

"That'll do, then." He walked off.

Odd, she mused. Why was he bothered by my mentioning my ancestor?

He set a beer down in front of her. He smiled now. "So what's this about your ancestor?"

She smiled back. "He used to run this place. Many years ago."

"Yeah? How many?"

"Let's see. Two hundred forty three, to be exact. 1776."

"Nah, you're joking."

"I'm not. His name was Daniel Ainsley and he was the barkeep here during the American Revolution. Frankly, I was really surprised to learn this tavern is still in existence."

"Holy Christ." He grinned. "I mean that's a long time back."

She nodded.

"I knew the place was here back then but never gave it much thought, you know? My family has owned it for generations."

"Oh? How many generations?" Helen sat up straighter on the barstool.

He turned to some photos behind the bar and pulled one down. "This one's the oldest one I have. 1880s. Great, great, great, I don't know how many greats, grandfather. But they go back earlier than that. Thing is photography doesn't go back much before the Civil War."

"Your family owned The Black Horse all the way back to the Civil War?"

"Yup. Can you believe?" He left to serve a customer.

Helen stared down at the photograph in the dim light. A dark-haired man with a handlebar mustache stood behind the bar she now sat at. He wore an apron and held a bar rag in his hand.

She swallowed hard. He returned. "What's your name, if I may ask?"

"Patrick. Patrick Moore." He stared at her. "You look familiar."

"Yeah? My name is Ainsley. Helen."

"Shit, the mystery writer. Damn. I've read your books. Well, some, anyways. They're great."

She beamed. "That's always nice to hear." He ran off to serve another customer and returned. "So, you trying to track down this ancestor?"

"How'd you guess?"

"You're a mystery writer. Sure you would be."

"I am, actually, Patrick."

"Pat."

"Pat." She weighed her words. "Would there be any possibility you or your family would have anything left over from the early days of the Tavern? Anything at all . . . I don't know what that would be even. Some documents, papers, artifacts--?"

"Ha. Artifacts, right. Now you sound like an archaeologist."

She laughed. "I am in a way. Scratching through the dirt to find old mysteries."

He ran the bar towel over the bar for the fifth time. "Nothing I can think of that goes back that far."

"Yeah." Helen shrugged. "Just a thought."

"But I can ask my grandfather. He's still around and his brain is sharper than mine."

Helen's eyes lit up. "That would be awesome, Pat. Can I give you my cell?"

They exchanged numbers and Helen left a twenty on the bar as she left.

Waiting for a cab, her brain spun in circles. Could Patrick's grandfather possibly have found . . . and saved something from the early days of the Tavern?

Chapter 37

Winter had turned out to be soft and gentle, light on snow and easy on cold. Helen had made considerable progress on her book but only because she broke her own rule. She began writing before she knew the ending.

Since her trip to New York she had not found out much more about Daniel Ainsley. Patrick Moore, the current owner of the Black Horse Tavern had nothing for her. Foolish to think he might after two and a half centuries.

From newspapers she learned that Daniel ran the Tavern. Check. He lived in the apartment upstairs. Check. He hobnobbed with John André and his loyalist followers. Check. Was Daniel a Tory? Was he a spy? Did he go home before the revolution ended? Had he been injured? Did something happen to his family in Brattleboro? No answers. Checkmate.

A whole, long season had passed. The weather had warmed up the last few days and Helen looked forward to gardening. Honey came bounding into the kitchen where she and Marie were having breakfast.

"I think someone needs to go for a serious walk," Helen said. Honey barked her assent.

"You go ahead. I'll take care of the dishes."

Helen kissed her grandmother on the cheek, grabbed a sweater and left. Outside, she stopped at her maple and examined it for the initials DNA. They had not returned. How could she find the last pieces of the puzzle? The place where Daniel secreted the key to the mystery.

She took off with Honey down the trail by the brook. Honey ran up ahead and then back to check on her.

Helen hadn't taken her phone since cell service was spotty in the meadows and woods behind them. She would just enjoy the day with Honey. When she returned, Marie was waiting on the porch.

"Anything wrong?" Helen asked.

"You had a phone call, dear. From New York."

Helen's heart ratcheted to high. "Not the doctor?"

"Oh no, no." Marie stood and put a hand on her shoulder. "You know the doctor said the cancer is gone. Remember? Months ago."

Helen sighed. "Of course. It's just--."

"I understand. Cancer is not something you can forget or dismiss." Marie pulled Helen into an embrace. "You are just fine, my sweet girl. Just fine."

Helen blinked back tears. "It really takes over your life, doesn't it?" She coughed, put her fingers on her lips to compose herself. "Now, who did call?"

"Someone by the name of Patrick Moore. He left his number."

"Oh. Yes? Wonderful. What did he say?"

"That he had a tidbit of information."

Helen raced inside to get her cell and began dialing.

He picked up on the second ring. "Helen, how are you?"

"Great, Pat, just great. Thanks for calling."

"Well, it's not much, but grandpa remembered something. Just a bit of gossip that had been passed down over the years, and all the way back to the Revolution."

"What?"

"One of the guests that visited the Tavern always created a stir. He didn't come often, and only at certain times when the British were off gallivanting somewhere else."

"Who was it?"

"George Washington. The General himself."

Helen caught her breath. "Did you say *the General himself?*"

"Course. He was the man, *the* General."

"Pat, if someone spoke about the General back then, could they have meant anyone else?"

"With an emphasis on *the*, no, there was no one else. I mean there were lots of generals, Clinton, Howe, erm, Burgoyne, maybe. On the patriot side, Greene, Knox, even Benedict Arnold, but he doesn't count as you probably recall. Ha. Anyway, those generals come to mind. But when they say *the* General, they meant Washington. No doubt."

"And he was at the Black Horse Tavern?"

"No doubt about that either. So, does it help? Do I get an acknowledgment in your new book?"

"You absolutely do. Thank you so much."

Helen clicked off and danced back out to the porch to tell Marie.

"That is something, isn't it," Marie said. "Our Daniel knew George Washington. Maybe they were friends, or--."

"Or maybe they were enemies."

"Helen, you don't believe that."

"No, but there's still one clue to go. That's where the answer will be."

Vermont captured every season with gusto. Spring was no different, if and when it arrived. Too often these last years, winter leaped right into summer. But this year spring sprang into all its glory with tulips, crocuses, daffodils, and hyacinths, blossoming in glorious colors. It seemed like the winter didn't even exist. Helen felt like a spring flower herself, opening its petals to the sun.

She gazed in the mirror and was pleased with what she saw. Her hair had completely grown back and she liked her new style. She had put on some weight and didn't look as gaunt. And she had energy. Gobs of it. Just like the old days.

Dave seemed to appreciate her too, she believed. It brought a smile to her lips.

Honey barked and she looked out the window. Dave drove up and stepped out of the police SUV.

Helen greeted him at the front door. "You're early."

"I wanted to see you."

She leaned into his kiss. "Sit down a few minutes and tell me more about what this event is."

"Yeah. I didn't want to get your hopes up. It may be a bust."

"Hopes up? About what?"

"Well, the last clue in your Daniel Ainsley mystery. We were trying to figure out what the *venerable one* meant. I heard it being used the other day by one of the local Native Americans."

"He used the word venerable?"

"Yes, in the sense of ancient and revered."

"So this lecture that we're going to is about that?"

"Not exactly, but it will give us a chance to ask him what he thinks about Daniel's note."

"Ahh, of course. Who is he?"

"His name is Jeremy Littlebrook, and he's a member of the local *Abanaki* tribe."

During the talk, Helen found her interest piqued in the historical roots of the small band of Native Americans in southern Vermont. As is often the case with Native Americans, the *Elnu Abanaki* were pretty much written out of the history of a region, as if they didn't exist before the white man established residence. This always made her sad.

Following the program, Dave introduced her to Jeremy and he was happy to help her with her quest. She explained Daniel's note, explicitly his reference to the *venerable one*.

"So," he said. "You think he hid something in or near this *venerable one*?"

"I do. What did he mean? Any idea?"

"Yes. My people often hid things there for future generations."

Helen stared at him as Jeremy broke into a grin. "It's really no mystery."

She smiled at his choice of words.

"A venerable one, in this case, is a tree. A very special tree, mind, often very old, beautiful, like a queen. Yes, she is the queen of trees. With many graceful branches reaching out to the sky and dozens of twisted and dark hiding places between them and in her body, her trunk." He stopped. "Do you know of a tree like that?"

Helen turned to Dave, who said. "We know of one."

They drove back to the house in silence. Marie met them at the door.

"So," Marie said after they told her what they'd learned. "The answers were always right here."

They stood gawking at the tree.

"Do you want to do the honors?" Dave said.

Helen nodded.

He helped her step onto the bench that circled the great maple, handed her gloves and a flashlight. She began by probing the nearest branches. Then she moved around searching other branches within reach.

"Nothing?" Marie said, hands wringing in front of her.

"The branches are pretty solid, no niches or holes, really, in which to hide something."

"You may have to get up higher to look down into the trunk," Dave said.

"How about a boost?" Helen said. "I can sit right up in this rest between two branches and look down into the heart of the trunk."

"Is there much space inside? It's not solid?" Dave said.

"No. Looks like it's been eaten away or it's just old and is withering within."

"Be careful, dear," Marie said.

Dave helped her get up into place and remained below to catch her if she slipped.

"Okay, here goes." Helen shined the light into the deep recesses of the venerable one. "I don't . . . see . . . anything." She kept moving the torch light to cover the entire interior. "I see some sort of nest, maybe squirrel?"

"Okay," Dave said.

"Wait, there's something . . . kind of grayish or whitish color. Don't know if I can reach." Helen leaned in as far as she could. Dave held onto her legs. "There's something here." Her voice echoed strangely through the trunk. "Got it, got it." She pushed herself up from the trunk and held onto a branch.

"What is it?" Dave asked.

261

"Looks like an animal skin." Helen gasped. "Goatskin, of course. That's what Daniel said he used to protect it. Oh my God, oh my God."

"Take it easy," Dave said as he helped her down.

"Look at this. It was here all along."

"Let's take it inside so we can see it better," Marie said.

The three hurried into the house and directly to the kitchen.

Helen spread the treasure out on the table.

"You do the honors," Dave said.

She gently unwrapped one layer, then another and still one more of the beautiful goatskin protector. Inside was a folded up piece of that same cloth-like paper that was in the pouch. Helen unfolded it and flattened it as gently as she could.

"This is the affidavit that Daniel described. Verifying that he worked for the Continental Army--."

"I knew it, I knew it." Marie clapped.

"And it's signed by General George Washington."

"Holy crow," Dave whispered.

They all stared down at history.

"What's that with the document?" Dave asked.

Helen picked up a piece of fabric, purplish in color, in the shape of a heart. It was embroidered with sprigs of leaves around the edges and inscribed in thread across the face was the word *Merit*.

"Helen," Dave said. "This is a badge of Merit, given to soldiers during the Revolution to thank them for above and beyond service to their country."

"Like a purple heart," Helen said, tears welling.

"This is considered to be America's first military decoration," Dave said, shaking his head.

"Daniel won a purple heart," Marie said. "Ain't that somethin'."

The three gazed down at the heart for several long minutes.

Suddenly Honey howled outside. Then she set up a frenzied barking. They all rushed outside to see her racing around the tree.

Helen sprinted to the venerable one, her beautiful maple tree. Just as she had hoped, the initials of her ancestor had reappeared.

DNA.

There to stay.

The End

Afterword

The Tree of Lost Secrets is a work of fiction. The story takes you back to four time periods in history and many of the people, places, and events during those time periods are based on historical fact.

The action takes place for the most part in Brattleboro, Vermont. Situated where the Connecticut and West Rivers meet, the town had originally been settled by Abenaki tribes. To the east, is New Hampshire. To the South is Massachusetts. It was named for Colonel William Brattle of Boston (who, incidentally, never set foot in his namesake town.) The name is unique to Vermont, and you will find no other Brattleboro in the country. The original spelling was *Brattleborough* and you will see it spelled that way until 1888 when it was changed to its modern spelling.

The Ainsley Hill Inn and Tavern is fictional and modeled on the Old Constitution House in Windsor, Vermont, built in 1777. It is located, in my imagination, in West Brattleboro, not far from Abbott Road. The Inn was built in 1766 and had all the quirks of old, historic homes. There are not many of that vintage in Brattleboro today. Helen confirms the date of the Inn when she finds a colonial copper coin embedded in the hearth. Coins were placed in hearths to identify the date of construction and this coin, a 1766 Pitt Token, is an authentic one.

The Arms Inn and Tavern that Daniel visited was, indeed, a real Inn in Brattleboro built around 1762. It no longer exists but today would be located near the Retreat Farm.

In the first back story, I have set my characters in World War II, Italy. The incident of the massacre at Sant'Anna di Stazzema was, sadly, real. In August of 1944, the Nazis punished the whole town of 600, including women and children, for their partisan activities. They burned the church with the residents in it.

One role of partisan activities, like the one Salvatore took part in, was to obstruct roadways and railways and set up confusion for the Nazis. The idea for the scene in the book came from my research into the famous Art Train, that was derailed to prevent a huge cargo of art from leaving France and winding up in Germany.

Moving back in time, the next story takes you to World War I and Halifax, Nova Scotia. There was much fear that Germany would invade the Halifax Harbor and filter into Canada and the United States. In fact, Halifax Harbor was a hub for ships sending supplies to Allies in France and Great Britain.

In an effort to foil attempts of U-boats entering the Harbor, wire mesh nets were installed and pinned to the harbor floor by concrete weights. Tillie, could, indeed, see the large round floats at the surface that kept the nets upright.

For those readers who caught the small mention of a cemetery in Halifax where many dead from the Titanic disaster rested, this is a little known fact. Five years earlier, the city served as the center for recovery operations when the Titanic went down in the North Atlantic. Tillie and Kurt could well have visited Fairview Cemetery where over one hundred bodies had been buried after being rescued and identified by Haligonians in 1912.

On December 6, 1917, a series of events occurred in Halifax that led to the worst disaster in the history of the world at that time. A munitions ship in the harbor and a large cargo freighter crossed paths. Because of poor communications and stubbornness on the part of the captains, the result was a catastrophic explosion that equaled the atom bomb at Hiroshima years later.

It was so close to the shore that it ripped through the whole town of Halifax, razing virtually every building in sight, and sending debris and broken glass flying, rendering many blind. Two thousand died instantly and a total of ten thousand were injured, homeless, and in shock. The town of Boston was one of the first to send responders in the form of doctors, nurses, supplies, food, and water.

More than a hundred years later, Halifax continues to thank the city of Boston for their help by trucking a huge tree to the Boston Commons every Christmas.

Brattleboro was a small stop on the underground railroad. Station agents in town provided help and lodging for slaves escaping from the south. Many kept moving north but it is conceivable that some stayed to make their homes here. There were many sad, desperate stories that came out of this terrible time in United States history. I felt compelled to write a new, fictional one, with Abby and Elias.

There are at least two known underground railroad stops in Brattleboro. One is the Jeremiah Beale House in West Brattleboro, a red brick building across Western Avenue from the Baptist Church. Supposedly a tunnel exists between the two buildings and was used for escaped slaves.

The other safe house was owned by Charles Frost on Flat Street. There was a room in his house where slaves could find a bed, food, and directions to the next stop on their journey: Bellow Falls, Vermont.

In the last story, I set the Ainsley Hill Inn as far back in history as possible. The reader will no doubt recognize some of the characters: John Stark, from New Hampshire, who gave that state its motto: *Live Free or Die*; a mention of his wife Molly, who, amusingly, has her name on myriad trails here but never actually stepped foot in Vermont. Benjamin Tallmadge and Nathan Hale, fellow Yale friends who became spies for George Washington and the Continental Army. Nathan Hale was, indeed, hanged for a spy on September 22, 1776.

Daniel Ainsley is a product of my imagination. Brattleboro at that time was a hotbed of loyalist sentiment, so Daniel, a passionate patriot, was a rare individual.

He agrees to spy for Washington in the guise of a barkeep in New York City. The Black Horse Tavern was a real tavern on John and William Streets in downtown Manhattan but is no longer in existence today, as I claim.

The great fire of New York City did tragically happen on the night of September 21, 1776, and close to 500 houses were destroyed. It was deemed to be an accident and not the result of sabotage.

The British officer that befriends Daniel was authentic. John André was a smart, erudite, and talented young major who was liked by many. He was a poet and does have a statue in Westminster Abbey dedicated to him, and, if you ask Helen, for some surprisingly inane poetry. He was also an artist and the sketch he did of himself (in the story) was real. In fact, it was a self-portrait done on the night before he was hung as a spy by none other than General George Washington.

Finally, Daniel Ainsley hid an affidavit, signed by Washington, acknowledging his valor in the Continental Army. He also received a Merit Badge for his service. While Daniel is fictional, the affidavit and Merit Badge of service are real and were awarded during the American Revolution for extraordinary courage. In fact, the badge was made of a purple cloth and embroidered with the word *Merit*. The first Purple Heart.

After living in California for many years, returning home to Vermont has been nothing less than a magical experience for me . . . a return to nature and the Green Mountains. The enchanted maple tree and prescient golden retriever added that *fantastical* element I desired. Writing in an exhaustive year of a deadly pandemic, political chaos, and economic upheaval . . . well, I presumed we all needed a little magic in our lives.

Lynne Kennedy, Brattleboro, Vermont,
July 2021

Acknowledgments

Writing is an isolating occupation particularly over a cold, snowy Vermont winter. Researching is a more social one. I would like to thank the many people who helped me make this book as authentic as possible and got me through those secluded days.

First, the volunteers at the Brattleboro Historical Society for providing the historical context within which to begin each back story. Maps were invaluable in setting the geographical locations for where the stories "might" have unfolded. Actual historical events gave me a scaffold upon which to build the narratives.

Next, thanks to Detective Lieutenant Jeremy Evans at the Brattleboro Police Department for helping me understand the procedures for uncovering and removing remains buried for many years, ie: which agencies would be involved, and how and where forensics would be done. Small towns have different methods from large cities for solving crime.

In searching for a proper, venerable tree to be the keeper of long-hidden secrets, I would like to thank my friend Diane Spiak for providing local maps and guides of ancient trees in Brattleboro and surrounding areas.

As always, I owe a great deal to my husband, John, whose historical wisdom and guidance made it possible to keep going when I stumbled along the way. He believed in the book from the very start.

Now, so do I.